An Unrivaled Faith

Book Two of The Romalo Legacy Series

Emily Hamsher

WestBow Press®
A Division of Thomas Nelson & Zondervan

This is a work of fiction. All of the characters, names, incidents, organizations, and dialogue in this novel are either the products of the author's imagination or are used fictitiously.

WestBow Press books may be ordered through booksellers or by contacting:

WestBow Press
A Division of Thomas Nelson & Zondervan
1663 Liberty Drive
Bloomington, IN 47403
www.westbowpress.com
1 (866) 928-1240

Because of the dynamic nature of the Internet, any web addresses or links contained in this book may have changed since publication and may no longer be valid. The views expressed in this work are solely those of the author and do not necessarily reflect the views of the publisher, and the publisher hereby disclaims any responsibility for them.

Scripture taken from the King James Version of the Bible.

ISBN: 978-1-9736-7075-9 (sc)
ISBN: 978-1-9736-7077-3 (hc)
ISBN: 978-1-9736-7076-6 (e)

Library of Congress Control Number: 2019910645

Print information available on the last page.

WestBow Press rev. date: 08/09/2019

"To my dear sister, a true leading lady, whose bold strength and quiet nature grace her with an unmatched serenity. Thank you for being the one I can count on and look up to. Thank you for being my sister."

In Honor of Ruth Sarah Hamsher, 1916-2000.

Prologue

"Seven of my most elite scouts have returned from the borderlands. The rumors are true."

Gabriel slowly drew his eyes up from the paper in front of him, his entire being stiffening as he moved.

"What are you saying, *Regele meu*?"

"Our kingdom is on the brink of war, and our greatest chance of keeping the throne is to dispute their claim by solidifying our own. You must wed."

Gabriel knew exactly what his father, the king of Brasov, was saying. He needed heirs. He needed a queen, and he needed one now. His father continued to recount the findings of his men, but the words felt far away. A tangible weight had begun to settle onto his shoulders, each grievance was another stone added to his burden until he thought he would be crippled by the crushing force of it all.

It had now been several months since the initial breach on their sovereign nation. Gabriel had been wont to take immediate action, striking against this unknown rival who had taken up arms against them with a great show of force, but the king had instead gone to his counsel in an effort to send forth scouts to dispute the claim; seeking peace above war.

“What about the daughter of Count Aguillon? I believe your mother is acquainted to her cousin.”

Gabriel returned his attention to the inevitable task of finding a wife, preferably one whose family would make a formidable ally against their mysterious enemy. His father began listing off possible brides, each one connected to wealth, position, or power. The prince found himself only half-listening as they made their way down the list. *If it hadn’t been for Lucian, I wouldn’t be in this predicament.*

The reality of his thoughts chafed him, and yet he knew he no longer placed any blame on his younger brother’s shoulders. Though it had taken him months to forgive the younger man for stealing away his betrothed and capturing her heart in the process, if Gabriel was completely honest with himself, he was somewhat relieved to not have had married. At the time he hadn’t been ready for the life-long sentence to a near stranger, in fact he wasn’t sure if even now he was agreeable in finding a helpmate suitable enough to run the kingdom alongside him, for that is what she would have to be. He certainly would not settle for anything less, most especially some of the emptyheaded, vainly proud misses his father had been listing off.

“Gabriel? Are you listening to me?”

Shaking his head to keep from further distraction, he straightened his shoulders, and returned his gaze to the stacks of paper before them. “Pardon me father, I seem to be overwhelmed by this whole process.”

“Well,” his father grumbled, his voice deep and cultured, alerting any listener to the regal heritage of the speaker, “perhaps we should take a break from all this. I know it has not been so long since you were last engaged, maybe it is too soon.”

“*Nu*, Your Majesty, I assure you I was not trying to shirk my duty.” Leaning towards the king, Gabriel composed his features, wanting his father to be certain of his willingness to comply. "Ah yes, the daughter of Herr Burkhart Nuremberg. Her name is Katya, correct?"

He thought back to the last time he had seen the Germanic lord's daughter, since her family had often spent their summers in Brasov when they were children. It was just before the girl's mother had passed away, for he recalled how sickly the woman had looked. All in the castle had pitied the small child whose world was about to be turned upside down, but not a single tear had he seen pass from her large eyes. Instead he remembered distinctly the blue flames sparking from their depths and the way her chin had lifted itself into the air as if to ward off the unwelcome sympathy of others. Even as a young boy, he had admired her courage.

"Her father is a man of prestigious gains. Though his title was only inherited from the passing of his elder brother, he has done well for himself." His father grimaced. "Still they are ranked below many of the others on our list."

"Besides she is much too young for me," Gabriel added as he pictured again the gangly little girl from his youth. "Who else is there to consider?"

"There is always Lady Serbana." His father's tone was hesitant at first- as if he expected his son's immediate rejection- but then the timbre gained ground and grew confident. "You two have known each other since birth. Everyone imagined she would be your pick; even your mother and I were surprised when you came to us instead."

Gabriel thought on that for a moment. He was in a desperate situation, and she *was* the most obvious candidate, but that was just it. Everyone always assumed they would make a good match, that they would fall in love, and for a time Gabriel had believed it himself, but even though she was a lovely girl there was something missing. He wanted more than just a fair face, and regal demeanor. In the last six months he had realized something in seeing his brother and his betrothed together; he wanted love. He hesitated to say as much to his father, so instead he threw out his normal excuses.

"I find her conversation dull and her attachments clingy. She ought to make any man a suitable bride, but a queen? I think not." He hated to sound so severe, but truly he would choose almost anyone over Lady Serbana.

"I see." The king's ruffled brows belied his consternation. "If you are not agreeable to making a decision in such haste, then we will have to take further action. Perhaps we can invite some of these ladies to join us here at the castle. Our harvest festival is drawing nigh, is it not?"

"But that is only a fortnight away!" Gabriel cringed at his own hesitancy.

"The sooner the better, my son. As future king you must prepare yourself to serve your people above your own desires. The kingdom comes first."

It always does, Gabriel thought grimly. But he said nothing.

"It is decided then, in little over two weeks' time Brasov will have what she needs to hold her ground. Either that, or we go to war."

CHAPTER 1

The carriage rumbled and raged against the rocky terrain, jostling Katya about. Her teeth rattled within her head, producing a dull ache at her temples. She squeezed her eyes shut and sank deeper into the furs that covered her from the coming winter's chill hoping not to get sick. Again. Though this journey was one she had often made with her parents as a young child, it had been many years since she had traveled from the heartland of Germany.

"I should 'ave left you home!" her father barked, his mood growing darker with each passing mile. She wondered at his disagreeable manner. It had been his idea to return to Brasov after all this time.

"*Enchuldige mich*, Vater. May we not take a short rest for a time? I am sure to be recovered quite soon."

Rather than answer, he thrust his fist to the roof of the carriage, slamming it again and again until the coachman pulled them to a halt. Katya pushed open the door, and very nearly threw herself from the wooden encasement; her lungs snatching in crisp air with each staggered breath. She knew it was more than the motion of the carriage that sent her into such fits, her father's unpredictable nature did more to turn her stomach than anything else. With caution, she took several steps forward sure to not move too far from sight lest her father cut short their reprieve.

"Oh Mutter, how I wish thou were with us." Blinking back the tears of grief that had long past stained her soul she tossed her face to the sky hoping that the sweet breath of the north wind would steal away her sadness.

The last time her eyes had touched these hills her mother had been with them. Each summer they had visited the native lands that had fostered her when she was a child. Having grown up with her Romanian father, Katya's mother knew nothing of Germany until she was forced to live with her grandmother after a severe plague had killed her parents. That was when she had met Katya's father. Burkhart Nuremburg always said that Katya looked just like her mother did when she was younger, sweet and innocent, with eyes the color of a crystal spring. *Or at least he used to say things like that*, Katya thought pensively.

"Katya! *Komen Sie*!" Hearing her father's biting command she drew in two more deep breaths and then hastened back into the frosty interior.

"With all these stops, we'll not make it in twice our expected time."

"I'm sorry, Vater. I will try to be less burdensome."

"Nevermind that. Driver!" He glanced at her from the corner of his eyes. "It's been so long since I've set foot in Romania. I suppose 'tis trepidation that has me so melancholy."

"I too am nervous, Vater." Her words offered him a smile, before he turned back to his own window.

Once again the carriage lurched them into motion, carrying them interminable miles to a faraway place that held only bittersweet memories for her. The one solace that Katya knew she could cling to was seeing Elisabeta again- the daughter of King Romalo was her closest friend- again. Every summer, they had played together among the palace gardens and citadel streets, and even though they hadn't seen one another in almost seven years' time they often wrote to each other leaving nothing unsaid.

"Why are we going to Brasov? Does it fair better in the winter than Germana?" she asked.

"*Nein*, at least not so very much. I have business in the Romanian country- things that need be attended to. Besides, it will be good for you to be among your mother's people. Do you not wish to see your family, or at least the few who remain?"

"Oh yes, Vater, very much so!"

"And of course I should like to visit Frau Schüller, should she be in residence."

Katya took a moment to search her father's passive face, to see if she could catch the tail of whatever thoughts were running through his mind. *Perhaps the rumors are true then.* She had overheard their housekeeper, Mrs. Keens, whispering about Herr Nuremburg and his search for a new wife, but hadn't given it any credit until now. The thought of having another lady in the house sent a small pang through her heart. Still, she couldn't renege upon the hope that it might bring back the spark in his stony brown eyes.

He looked older, her father did. With his well-weathered face and graying temples she almost didn't believe he was only four and fifty years. The once proud shoulders that had carried her around were now stooped, and the enigmatic smile that had treasured her childish fancies, was now securely hidden away behind an unchanging grimace. It would seem that something in him had shriveled up and died, much like the beautiful form of her mother, Katerina Nuremburg. *What took her from us? A disease perhaps?* She wished she knew, but her father never said. He didn't speak to her of such things. In fact, he hardly spoke to her at all when they were at home. Unless she sought him out specifically, it was as if he wasn't even there.

"Is Aunté Rina expecting us, then?"

"*Ja*, I sent word ahead of us."

"*Das ist gut*, then we will be staying with her and Herr Ranald?"

"As my business pertains to King Andrei, he has offered us a place within his citadel. But there will be plenty of time for you to go and visit with them, I am certain."

Katya was relieved to hear they were staying inside the castle. It would give her more time to spend with Elisabeta. Satisfied with what he had shared, she turned herself back towards the open portal and resumed admiring the rolling hills dusted with snow. The pit in her stomach was finally beginning to dissipate.

When at last they reached the outskirts of Brasov some three days later, she couldn't help but relish the sound of cobblestone paths beneath carriage wheels. To her, it was the sound of her childhood, the gentle clip clop of horses' hooves, like the joy of rediscovering an old toy.

"It hardly looks like it's changed. Don't you think so, Vater?"

The older man unfurled his arms and stretched back across his side of the carriage, shifting his head towards the window. "A wretched place as it ever were. I'll be glad when it's miserable face is behind us."

"'Tis been a long journey for us both. With some rest, tomorrow will bring you more cheer. I am sure of it."

"I hardly think so. If it weren't for the summons of the King, I would not have made this journey. This city stole *meine* Katerina from me, and I'll not forgive it!"

Rather than add fuel to the fire of his outburst, she simply tightened her lips and moved her eyes to rest on her hands, which were now clenched in her lap. No matter what her father thought, she knew Brasov to be a beautiful city. The way it fit each stone house or shop next to the other, like pieces of a puzzle snuggled edge to edge, mesmerized her. It was much different from the spacious *marktplatz* back home, with the half-timbered houses and the generous stalls of the vendors selling their wares. Looking around, she knew she could no more blame this foreign land for her mother's untimely demise than she could God. He had the power over life and death, and He had seen fit to take her mother home. Who was she to question it? If her mother had taught her anything while she was with them, it was to put her trust in God alone, no matter how her faith was tested.

The carriage slowed in front of a large iron gate; the castle shone with a soft amber glow, beckoning them *wilkomen.* As it was nearly dusk they were shown directly to their rooms, a light repast soon ushered in by the maid. Though she still didn't have much of an appetite, she finished off the warm bread and cheese slices before removing her travel clothes.

Hanging her dark woolen kirtle over the chaise, Katya imagined herself to be somewhere in the southwest tower. She mentally drew a picture of the hallway that led to the main staircase. Next, she removed her linen coif brushing out her wavy tresses as she continued her tour of the house, her mind's eye taking her in to the Great Hall and the illustrious throne room where the king and queen met daily with people from the village. *Ah, how I have missed this place*, she thought, feeling almost at home within the massive stone walls that held her. Once finished with her nightly ministrations Katya fell into bed, eager to be well rested before she would venture out in hopes of finding her beloved Elisa on the morrow.

Another two months had passed, and still he had yet to secure a potential bride. The harvest festival had come and gone. He had been introduced to a number of maidens, all of whom seemed chiefly eager to be his next *prinţesă*, and yet none of them had moved him. Not even a little. He remembered one in particular, a lovely chit from the kingdom to the north. The Russian duke's eldest daughter had been one of the first presented to him, before any of the festivities had begun.

At the start he had thought her to be pleasant company, her wide lips curved in a generous smile that brought attention to her rounded face and golden-brown eyes, but she had hardly said a word to him. In fact, he wondered if she even spoke any of his language at all, for she had simply nodded her head to whatever he said. Before long, he was exhausted by his own conversation, and had begged leave of her with the excuse of making other introductions.

Another young woman, Lady Camille, as she was called, had been seated next to him for the lunch portion of the festival. At that point he had been hoping for a respite, but it seemed that his parents had schemed to bring before him a whole string of women. All the more variety from which he could choose his bride. This one's conversation had been enjoyable, her interest in the Brasov countryside genuine, and he could tell from the way she carried herself that she was well endowed -in more ways than one, if her expensive gown and plunging neckline were any indication. But as the meal had progressed, he detected a certain odor emanating from her person. Though the meal they shared largely contained vegetables and fish, the woman smelled heavily of meat. Like that of pork loin if he were to be specific. The scent had turned his stomach upside down, and he couldn't wait to be free from her putrid presence.

He imagined having had chosen *her* for a bride. *Prince Gabriel and his pungent princess.* He shuddered involuntarily at the thought. Perhaps he was being too picky, but if he was going to be spending the rest of his life with this lady, *and* he was expected to run a kingdom with her at his side, then he needed to be sure. Indeed, he needed someone like his mother. He wanted someone like Adelina. *Nu, I'll not let myself dwell on a thing that will never be.*

Having risen well before the sun, Gabriel crossed over to his balcony window looking down to the cross bridge just in time to see a band of dignitaries arriving from the country neighboring them to the north. His father was growing anxious enough to send for help. In fact, he was hosting a council of foreign noblemen later in the week, the members of which had already begun to congregate within their borders. His eyes moved beyond the inner bailey, to the Carpathian Mountains in the distance, whose snow kissed peaks drew his gaze and alerted him to the winter that was now approaching. *How quickly time has passed*, he thought to himself. *Why, it is almost Christmas!* The prospect boded well for him, as the harsh weather would stay the queries of war, but only for a short while. Indeed, not long enough.

From behind him, he heard the approach of his valet. A slight smile tucked itself into the corner of his cheek. He still hadn't an inkling as to how Rogen always seemed to sense his moods, and knew him to be up before the sun. The other man was only three years his senior and was close to him in height and build, but where Gabriel's hair was dark and his face thin, Rogen's head was tousled with light strands and he boasted a round face that made him look boyish, but still firm enough that plenty of misses sought his attention. They had known each other since they were children, a fact that had given him great unease when his father suggested the man be his valet. Thankfully Rogen had always performed his tasks with an austere countenance, saving Gabriel the trouble of having to remark upon their estranged stations.

"Ah, Rogen," he said as he turned, "punctual as always I see."

"Tis my pleasure to serve, Your Highness."

Lifting his arms, he allowed his shirttail to be pulled over his head. "The cream doublet and blue surcoat will suit me for today."

"Yes, Your Highness."

Standing before the mirror, he watched as Rogen finished layering him with black breeches and a darker blue jerkin, upon which he now adjusted a plated neck piece with engraved markings and small jewels. Being royalty, Gabriel was always sure to dress the part, most especially when they hosted foreigners. He was soon to be king after all, and he wouldn't have anyone looking down on him.

"That will be all, Rogen." The other man bent at the waist in a perfunctory sign of respect, gathered up the discarded clothing, and ushered himself out the door.

Before he could stop himself, Gabriel wondered what things would have been like if the two friends had remained just that. A true sign of weakness, when he could no more alter his heritage than he could stop the coming war with an extended winter. Checking the reflecting glass once more, he headed for the stairs most determined to reach the breakfast room before the others had a chance to awaken.

He didn't even make it to the Great Hall and he was hit with the welcoming fragrance of buttered biscuits, cured sausage, and if he had to guess, a rousing dish of caramelized figs, one of his mother's favorites. Sauntering through the large arched doors, held open to him by servants, Prince Gabriel looked about the empty chamber. The first one after all.

"*Buna dimineata*, Your Highness." The cook called to him from across the large oak table, where she had just removed the last silver lid from the last silver bowl. Caramelized figs peeked out at him.

"A very good morning indeed." He smiled to himself before dismissing her back to the kitchen.

Unlike his mother, he wasn't overly fond of socializing with the servants. In his mind, there ought to be maintained a degree of separation between themselves and peoples of the lower class. He soon finished his meal with little fuss, his mind already skipping ahead to the next task. By the time his body had joined him in the library, Gabriel was perusing through the scrolls of the upper shelves. Silently, he begged his ancestors to shed some light on who their furtive enemy was. Surely, such information would be contained amidst these primeval texts. Why, the man had made claims to his throne! Claims that could only be supported by lineage and birthright.

The sooty parchment held between his long fingers told him nothing. It offered no hope, no quick sign of avoiding war, nothing but delimited insight into crop rotation and a personal ledger entry from his great-aunt. Both of which held no assistance to his present quandary.

"Have even these failed me?" His whisper echoed against the blessed bindings of his closest companions. In all his years of training to become king, he had never felt as helpless as he did now when even the shelves of his father's library seemed to have abandoned him. He wondered if he even had what it took to lead a nation, to navigate the waters of war, to make his father proud. Stifling the urge to grow morose, Gabriel re-bound the scroll and kept searching. *I will find answers, and when I do, God help the man who stands against me.*

As tall as he was, he had no need for a short ladder. Instead he lifted himself up to his forefeet and slid his hand along the back half of the top shelf. Something small and folded had tucked itself along the wall, having half slipped behind the wooden encasement. Gabriel felt for its edge, gripping it firmly and pulling it down.

Moving to the armed chair nearest the window, he sat and inspected the unassuming scrap. When he had brushed aside the years' worth of dust, he opened it and found himself staring into the face of a wolf. The symbol was boldly printed upon the paper, and Gabriel wondered if he had seen it's like before. It certainly wasn't the crest of the Romalo family, nor the Brasov nation, so where did it come from? Below the image was written a language he knew naught of. *What does it mean?*

He lifted his head to the sound of church bells from the castelle's cathedral. Their dainty chime noted the hour for morning vigils. He easily imagined the willowy silhouette of his mother making her way amongst the small flock that drifted toward the ever-imposing sanctuary. Thankful that he was only required to attend one of the many invocations offered by the church, Prince Gabriel slid the small slip into his shirt pocket.

The continual din of the bells reminded him of the meeting he need soon be attending. Surely his father would have knowledge of what he now possessed. After returning the remaining scrolls to their proper place, he made quick work of showing himself to the King's Apartments, where he knew his father would be waiting for him.

The servant heralded his entrance. "Prince Gabriel, Your Majesty."

"Thank you, Travan. You may leave us."

He watched as the man bowed out of the room, his head turning back to his father. "*Sa traiesti mult*, Father."

"And to you also, my son. Come, we have much to discuss."

Without word, Gabriel followed his father to the long narrow table that was centered in the larger portion of the room. The interior of the castle seemed to maintain a drafty chill, requiring rooms like this one to host two fireplaces. One posted at each end making the shape of the room to be narrow at its front and back and wide in the middle.

"I have been going over this in my head the last few days, but it will be good to get a second opinion. It seems as though our strongest boundaries are here, and here..."

The rounded edge of a meter stick traced the southern and western edge of their territory.

"...with the north being our least protected access point, as we share that land with our Germana brothers. If we were to be attacked along the western edge, where the most troops have been spotted, I deem it necessary to withdraw at least three of our larger regiments to assist us from the eastern gate."

As he scanned the large maps of their nation, the curves of which he knew well, he listened to his father's monologue. The paper in his pocket soon began burning a hole in the vest. Gabriel rubbed at the spot, as if it were a real flame against his shoulder. He couldn't help the curiosity that was exploding inside of him. Waiting for a distinct pause in his father's speech, he boldly inserted himself.

"To know our own weaknesses and strengths will be of great benefit, I believe. It would seem fitting to have the council of our allies, should we require their aid, and I will devote more of my time to understand our military options, but there is another matter that I would care to talk over with you."

Gauging for his father's reaction, Gabriel cautiously withdrew the leathery parchment from his vest. He hoped above all hope that the symbol would mean something, rather than turn out to be a childish fancy, like he now feared was so.

"In the library, I found *this*. Do you recognize the symbol? Or perhaps the inscription on it?"

At first, his father seemed pensive, almost irritated, at having been interrupted, but then Gabriel watched as the other man caught sight of the image. Recognition flashed in his eyes before he blinked it away. The color faded from his cheeks, leaving his face a chalky white. The image of the wolf stared back at them.

"From the library you say?"

His voice was suddenly detached, as if Gabriel's answer held no importance whatsoever, but they both knew better.

"Yes, it had fallen behind some of the scrolls."

"Well I couldn't say. I can't imagine how it would have ended up there. Certainly by mistake."

"So, you do recognize it?"

His father glanced at him. A look of, *was it fear,* touched his irises.

"No. I must be going now. Something has…come up. If you will excuse me."

The king then pivoted on his heel, sweeping around the table top before exiting through the large oak doors. It was a long while before Gabriel dared to move. *Father clearly knows something.* Something he didn't want to share with him, perhaps even something he couldn't share with him. *But what?* Surely if the king knew information about the claim this Dark Lord had to the throne he would use it in order to stop them from war. *Wouldn't he?* Following in his father's footsteps, Gabriel left the study. So busy was he with his musings that he nearly ran smack into a lady as he rounded the next corner.

"My pardon."

"Dear Gabriel, how many times have I had to warn you about walking with your head down? Surely this isn't how you are to welcome all of your guests?"

Gabriel's eyes moved to his sister, who stood with her hands on her hips, a playful grin splitting her angelic face. The little minx sought to embarrass him in front of her friend, but he would not be fooled. Turning back to the lady before him, he stretched out his most charming smile.

"Guest, you say? Surely this dear lady has been here before. Why, her beauty precedes her."

Elisabeta blinked. *Ha!* He thought to himself, *take that, dear sister.*

"So, you do recognize her? You see, Katya, I knew you'd not been forgotten."

Katya? Gabriel paused sluggishly. It seemed his sister had indeed gotten the best of him. His mind worked to put two and two together. Just as he began to recall who the lady was, he noticed her lips were moving, though her voice was much too soft. *What was the girl saying?*

"I'm pleased to see you again, Prince Gabriel."

If the red tint on her cheeks was any indication, she had taken his words to heart. He thought for a moment, racking his brain again as to where he might have met this woman. Taking a chance to appraise her more deeply, he saw that he had embellished her beauty. Compared to the dozens of dames who had passed through the castle halls, and the countless countesses that had graced his courts, she was nothing spectacular. From what he could see beneath her wimple, the lady's hair was a rather lifeless color of wheat, her face plain. Even her eyes, though a rare shade of blue, held no draw.

"The pleasure is mine." He listed out in all politeness, scrambling for a clue. "You're here for the winter, I presume?"

"Yes, Your Highness. My father and I are staying within the castle. He intends to meet with the king along with the other dignitaries. I myself will take the time to be among friends, and possibly visit what 'tis left of my family here."

He didn't know why she rambled so, but it mattered not. The added evidence put more of the pieces together. *Ah yes, Katya*

Nuremburg. Daughter of the notorious Herr Nuremburg. She has indeed grown up. He couldn't help but notice that she had lost her plumpness to soft curves, and now boasted a round face no longer holding any sign of childishness. She had certainly become a woman.

"Yes, she even has agreed to take me with her to the *limba germana*. Won't that be a treat?"

The girl's face lit up with a beatific smile. "Only if you promise to behave yourself, of course."

To her credit, she had a certain aurora about her as though she beamed with a genuine delight. He could see why his sister was so captivated by this woman, even he had a sudden wish to stay in her enveloping presence.

"Indeed? What a spoil sport you have turned out to be! Do you not remember the mischief we oft' got into as children?"

"Our parents had to give us such sound scoldings. I felt worse for them than I did for own sorry selves."

"That is your ever-compassionate heart speaking. It's one of the many reasons I've missed you so."

"You have been equally missed; mischief and all."

Gabriel watched the interchange with little bemusement. Seeing their close friendship, even after all this time away, irked him. It was a needless reminder that he had nothing of the sort. Rogen's face flashed through his mind. His one would-be friend. *What need have I for such folly? A tag along would only become a nuisance. Indeed, who could possibly understand what it is to be king? Besides, most of the noblemen my age would just be a bore.*

"Let us not detain you any longer, Gabriel. I'm quite certain you have more important things to fill your time with than reliving our childish memories."

His sister, ever the observant one, gave him a wide berth of escape. One he gratefully took.

"If you will excuse me. *Prințesă*, Frauline Nuremburg." He courteously bowed to both, and made his getaway.

From the first moment that their eyes met, she knew she belonged to him. His swirling gaze was full of depth and mystery, very unlike the cold steel of her father. Prince Gabriel's irises were a soft brown, like that of a bear cub, and somehow when he looked at her, she felt the warmth of their embrace.

"Though a little taller, and perhaps a little wiser, he's still the same old Gabriel." Elisabeta remarked, as they watched him continue his elegant stride down the hallway. "What think you, Katya?"

She wanted nothing more than to call him back, but her tongue had stuck itself to the roof of her mouth. Loosening its unwitting pull, she glanced at her friend.

"*Natürlich*, it has been some time since I have seen him, but he hasn't changed all that much. And yet, he seems different from how I had pictured him."

"Yes, it is as if he wears the crown already."

Her friend's tone held a slight sarcastic note, as if she wished for the younger version of her brother, the one they had both been fond of as children.

"Well never mind that, we have much too much to catch up on, and I refuse to waste a moment of our time together!"

Katya felt herself being pulled along. Her gaze had returned to the empty hallway, and she wondered when she would see him again. Before she could think more, Elisabeta escorted her out the main doors and into the inner bailey. The two of them walked arm in arm, the perfect picture of childhood friends.

"Oh, how I have missed this!" Her lungs took their fill of the crisp autumn air. Being farther south than Germania, this land slowly awakened itself to the cooing of it's winter mistress. "Isn't it lovely?"

"I am a summer lover myself, but...the slow decay of all that is bright in the world does have a sort of...appeal."

Katya laughed at Elisabeta's enigmatic expression, and how she then nestled herself further into her fur coat, one that, Katya thought, fit more for the peak of winter.

Elisabeta was an unusual sort of girl. She was akin to a forest sprite whose moods changed quickly, but whose zest for life brought great glee to all in her company.

"You are a balm to my wounds, dear Elisabeta."

"Does it pain you then, to be back here where she is buried?"

It didn't surprise her at all that she knew exactly what was on Katya's thoughts. Though they hadn't seen one another in years, and had kept in touch only through the few missives that were passed between them, it was as if they had been knit together from birth. No distance could separate their kindred hearts.

"More than I can say."

The path took them beyond the western gate, and into the royal gardens that stretched out before the castle mount. Katya searched her mind for the words to speak. Finally, she had a friend in which she could confide. Someone who would understand her plight, and ease her deepest fears.

"I have been wont to return to my mother's land for years, but father was never in good spirits. When he had announced our visit only a few short months ago, I was hopeful. Perhaps we would come and find healing. Perhaps things would return to how they were before...before she died. But now, I...I do not know."

"How is your father?"

"Everything changed when we left here. Some days I see pieces of the man from my childhood, and others I am scared for him. There are rumors that we are here for more than just business with the King."

"What kind of rumors?"

"Ones of Frau Schüller. Have you heard of her?"

Elisabeta paused for a moment, her motion stopping them both beneath the arched walkway covered with pergola vines. They were the kind that wove through the wooden lattice above, their wide winsome leaves offering a filtered shade. It's gentle fragrance tickled her nose, and she noticed that she wasn't the only one drawn in by their aroma. Tiny blue butterflies flitted about, resting on the cream petals.

"She also is in residence this winter. My mother has had her at court before, and from what I've seen she carries herself in a graceful manner. Though looks are often deceiving."

"I should like to meet her myself. If indeed Father has set his sights on marrying again, I pray that he chooses a woman of gentle nature, much like my mother was."

"He loved her deeply, I know, and if you are to have a *steifmutter*, as you would say, then we must both make sure she is worthy of the position."

The sound of the German brogue on Elisabeta's dainty lips seemed almost comical. *Stepmother indeed.* Katya disliked even the thought of someone trying to take her mother's place. The two of them resumed their walk around the pavilion, talking on several topics.

"You must certainly take me with you when you make your plans to visit your aunt. I haven't journeyed into the German sector in so long that I've nearly forgotten how much fun it can be. Nearly."

Katya smiled. Though it wasn't her real aunt, she had always considered her as such. "I'm sure she would be delighted to host you. Aunté Rina, always said you were her favorite royal, besides the queen of course."

"Of course." Elisabeta gave her a sly grin, as she turned them down the path that led to the fountain.

"So, tell me, *lieber freund*, what has kept your adventurous mind at play all this time? Surely you have at least a few tales to tell?"

The younger girl needed no further encouragement, as she plunged exuberantly into her latest scheme. Katya listened raptly, a small sigh of contentment escaping her lips. *Oh, how good it is to be among friends.*

CHAPTER 2

It wasn't until dinner the next night that she saw him again. It seemed the king was hosting a large gathering of nobleman from a great many countries. Seated as she was, nearer the head of the endless banquet table, Katya was able to see the many faces that filled the hall, her eyes rested upon one face in particular. Prince Gabriel looked mighty fetching in his suit of deep violet, with the slit sleeves of gold to match his chest piece. She wondered at his thoughts, for he too seemed to be searching the crowd surrounding them. When his eyes met hers for the briefest of moments, a heated blush splashed over her cheeks. She quickly moved her gaze elsewhere, not wanting to be caught staring. Thankfully, Elisabeta soon sat down beside her and struck up a conversation.

"To think these are all nobleman and their families, so many of them having traveled many miles to be here."

"Few more miles than we have traveled, but have they all come for a similar purpose?"

Elisabeta leaned in closer, her voice dropping to a deliciously conspiratorial tone. "I haven't had the chance to tell you, nor am I supposing you have heard it on your own. Our country is soon to be at war."

"At war? But with whom?" She couldn't help the rise of exclamation in her voice.

"Shh! It has yet to be determined, since Father is stern upon finding a more peaceful solution."

"Did he tell you that?"

"Goodness no, he would be in a right fit to have learnt that I know anything at all."

"How do you know then? *Nein*, let me guess. You just so happened to be walking past as he and your brother were discussing such details. Hmm?"

"Can I help that I have the ears of a fox?" Her grin was more cheeky than repentant.

Katya's mind exploded with the idea of it all. *Who would seek to harm this small Christian nation? What would it gain them?*

"So, then why gather all these diplomats?"

"Because if war *is* inevitable, as many have conjectured, then Brasov will need strong alliances. Look around you, my dear. These families are of closest connection, and greatest support to our kingdom. When the time comes, God willing it never does, these will be the men whose armies stand alongside our own."

The picture her friend painted sent shivers down Katya's back. Did her own father know that this was why he had been summoned? Did he plan to align himself and his money to the throne of Brasov, to the people of his late wife? She hoped it was so.

Their conversation was halted by the entry of the first course. So gallant was the occasion that even the servers were dressed in their finest. It seemed the king was indeed seeking to win his guests' favor. Looking across the table at her father, she wondered what sort of humor he was in this evening. His disposition seemed cheery enough, but she knew better. Only this afternoon he had hidden himself away in his room. Not even her offer to join him on a ride was enough to cajole him out of the hollow pit he often retreated to.

She prayed that no one else saw how very ill he was. To her, the signs were all startlingly clear. The circles that darkened his cheeks from the nightmares that tormented him, the eerie glow behind his eyes, as though he were succumbing to a constant fever, and the ever-changing moods that were as unpredictable as the summer rains upon the highlands back home. Her mind seemed to take her to a dark place where she felt trapped and alone. *I must be strong. Father will get better, you'll see.* She coaxed herself softly. *Perhaps after his meeting tomorrow with the king, he will have found some greater purpose. Never forget, there is always tomorrow.* Her mother used to say that to her, whenever she was feeling downcast, and now she quietly said it to herself.

In an effort to not give away the peculiar shift in her own mood, she quickly engaged the young gentleman seated on her left. He said that his family was from Romania, and lived just outside of Brasov. As the boy talked on, she allowed herself to be lulled by the rise and fall of his words. Where her language was all harsh tones and throaty accent, the tongue of the Romanians had an almost musical quality to it.

"You are from Germania, *da*?"

"Yes. My mother was born here, but my father, Herr Nuremburg and I have lived there since her passing."

"*Scuzele mele.*"

"Thank you."

The final course of poached duck with roasted legumes and plum pudding interrupted them, but Katya didn't mind. She had had enough socializing for one night, and was glad when they finally called for the minstrels to come and play for them. She watched with excitement as the side doors were opened unto the ballroom, and a throng of people slowly gravitated towards the amber glowing gallery.

"Come Katya, you must dance with me!"

"If you insist." With little opposition she followed Elisabeta out onto the floor, fitting herself in with the lords and ladies who were lined up. The first dins of the violin set her heart to soaring.

"How long has it been since you've attended a banquet?"

"I can't recall truly."

"Well tonight, you will dance to your heart's content."

And dance she did. Until her feet felt good and sore, and her side ached. She couldn't remember the last time she had had so much fun, or had laughed so hard. When she finally came up for breath, she realized just how exhausted she was.

"You mustn't leave me yet!" Elisabeta cried, pulling at her arm.

"Never fear, there are plenty of young men to keep you company." Shooing her friend back to the dancers, Katya went in search of some refreshment.

The tables to the rear of the room were filled with large punch bowls and delicate glasses. She filled herself a cup of the pink liquid, hoping it was chilled, and then found herself a bench to sit upon. From her place in the room she could neatly take in several groups of people. Apart from those dancing, there were also small clusters of people who stayed close to the fireplaces at either end. Nearest to her she noticed a group of men who seemed to be surrounding the prince, though he didn't look too keen on being crowded for attention.

Without drawing notice, she slowly scooted herself closer, eager to catch the smallest bit of happenings. She needn't scoot too close, for the voice of the man speaking was greatly impassioned, his booming words reaching her ears with little interference.

"Your highness, surely you do not suggest that we face this stranger on the battlefield? I am sure he is not called the Dark Lord in jest!"

"I suggest nothing. I only advise that we remain open to better understanding our enemy. Perhaps he will not be reasoned with."

"That does not forfeit us from trying! King Andrei is a man of peace, as was his father before him. Are we to assume you will take another stance?"

Katya felt her breath catch. Was this man seeking to challenge his future sovereign? Watching the prince closely, she took note of the twitch in his jaw, the flash in his eyes, and the subtle rise of his shoulders. She could see that the comment had hit its mark, and he had poised himself for battle. He then drew up to his full height, cutting an impressive figure, and neatly tucked his arms behind him. Many would assume this to be a haughty pose, but what they couldn't see was the way his hands were clenched at his back, a motion she knew to be an act of will, a force to keep the true Gabriel hidden. She didn't know how she knew it, but she did.

"If you will excuse me, Count, I have other matters that need attending."

"Humph!" The odious man clamped his mouth shut, and glared after the prince.

It wasn't until their eyes turned towards her that she better understood the prince's intention.

"Excuse me Lady Nuremburg, would you do me the honor?"

His hand lay unfolded before her, his voice beckoning her eyes towards his. Laying aside the now empty glass in her hand, she quickly hid her startled expression beneath a gentle smile.

"You may indeed, Your Highness."

"It seems I have been neglecting my role as host this eve, a habit I intend to forgo. Besides, your company far surpasses the unseemly lot that has kept my attention this last hour."

His voice was raised for others to share in their dialogue, and directed with just enough finesse so as to give the other man the cut, while at the same time encouraging the giggles of a nearby group of misses.

"Well played, my lord." She said evenly, as soon as they were far enough away.

"Truly madam, you have saved me from a dreary end. I feared I wouldn't ever get away from their pestering."

"Pestering, Your Highness?" She did her best to feign innocence, pretending that he hadn't just caught her eavesdropping on his private conversation. With the grace of a royal, he offered her a small smile that acknowledged her faux paus. Thankfully he didn't comment on it.

"Yes, it would seem that not all are welcoming of change."

He led them to the center of the floor, relinquishing her hand only to take his place at her side. The music started up, and the two of them moved in unison, forward three steps and then to the left. With one hand he gently gripped her waist, and with the other he held hers outstretched. She felt all of a sudden light headed, and thought perhaps she should excuse herself. It seemed she was still overtaxed, but he dissuaded her.

"Tell me, my lady, are you pleased to be back in Brasov?"

"Very much so. If it had been up to me, we never would have left, but my father…"

"Yes?"

She wondered just how much she should share with him. "When my mother passed, he didn't take it well. In fact, I'm not certain he has ever fully recovered from his grief."

"And how is Herr Nuremburg faring now?"

"It would seem coming here has done him some good. He seems to be finding peace." *Please let it be so*, she prayed silently.

"We all hope for peace. I know Elisabeta is herself most improved by your company. Why, she hasn't seemed to leave your side all night. In fact, I am even now surprised the two of you have been separated." They turned about face as he said this, his words reaching to her over his shoulder.

Weaving in and out of the other couples, she kept her eyes on him. He was so handsome, and she so very simple. When they came back together, standing face to face, she looked up into his eyes. For a moment she wished she could lose herself there, but all too soon the song came to its end, and with it the fanciful thoughts playing about in her head.

"I thank you, my lady." He bowed over her hand, and then took his leave.

She made her own exit, eager to put distance between them. *Really Katya, what were you thinking? It isn't as if he's taken a great liking to you, he was only being kind. And you just so happened to be an easy escape.* No matter how sternly she chided herself, she couldn't seem to be free of him. Even after the banquet was over, and she had tucked herself into her bed, still her thoughts drifted to him. Did he really think the country would be forced to go to war? And who was this Dark Lord they had been speaking of?

Another early morning put Gabriel up and about before the rest, making him most anxious to begin the assembly. To his consternation, the other noblemen proved less willing, their sluggish forms slowly slipping into their seats, each one struggling against the effects of little slumber.

"Gentlemen, let's take our seats."

King Andrei, leader of the sovereign nation, addressed them. "Firstly, I take this moment to thank each of you for accepting my invitation. I wish only that I had called you together under better circumstances, but alas, it seems even the most peaceful of kingdoms can come under attack, and we are indeed under attack."

Gabriel scanned the faces of the men around him, each one perking up at the severity of his father's tone. All had traded their light jackets for thicker ones, some even wearing a traditional woolen *cojoc*. He looked intently, searching for which ones would stand with them if it came to conflict, and which would turn their backs.

"A great enemy has positioned itself at our western most border. The threat is insurmountable, but it is in this nation's greatest advantage to avoid war at all costs." The king paused, his eyes carefully glancing from one to the next, encompassing them all in what he was about to suggest.

It was what impressed Gabriel most about his father, the way the older man pulled people together. He had a knack for creating assembly amongst men, men who would fight for him, die for him. *May it not come to that,* he pleaded to whatever unseen forces cared to observe.

"Each of you are comrades, neighbors. Friends. I have called this gathering to seek your counsel. Brasov is a nation that is favorably connected with its surrounding allies, near and far. To put it plainly, if we suffer, you suffer."

A cacophony of murmurings rang about the table. Gabriel agreed with the sentiment. It was why he was so eager to hear from these men who represented such a wide span of families, and nations.

"Our enemy calls himself the Dark Lord, and is leader of a numerous army. What do you know of him?"

One gentleman from the far side of the table spoke up. "*C'est dit* he is of Romanian blood, *mais* no one knows from whence he has come, nor who his people are." Monsieur Jeromè, was an old friend of his grandfather's, the late King Marius. His family was from France, and were of the nobility there.

"Preposterous!" Domn Frazier shouted, his voice louder than it need be. He was one of the oldest men in all of Brasov, and generally hard of hearing. "Having Romanian blood does not entitle you to the throne. Else, I'd be the next in line!"

The men around him laughed, but Gabriel did not join in. He thought the man was half mad, while others seemed to hang on his every word, as if having lived for so long had given the man incredible powers of acuity.

Herr Gustavo, a man from Germana whose family were wealthy landowners, and was one of their strongest allies, added in. "I have heard tales that he is not a man to be trifled with Your Majesty. He has caused quite a stir in our lands as well. His men have pilfered weapons, food stores, and much more to amass his army. And those who have stood against him, did not live long enough to gain retribution."

The King nodded, "Whoever this man is, we will seek to negotiate terms of peace."

"Any negotiation with this Dark Lord is certainly contingent upon whether or not his tie to the royal blood lines are able to be verified. This must be our first priority."

The men of the council looked at Gabriel skeptically. *Would he ever find his place among these?* One pair of eyes stood out in particular, and Gabriel wondered what thoughts lie behind the calculating gaze of Herr Nuremburg. Knowing him to be Katya's father, he hoped the man was not hunting for a young gentleman to marry his only child off to. Rumors abounded about the man's own upcoming nuptials with the Lady Schüller, and Gabriel had seen for himself the attachment they had shared at the ball.

"You make a good point my son. Either way we will have till winter's end for a decision to be made. By then we ought to know our opponent better."

The men then began talking amongst themselves, the cadence of their chatter rising slightly. Each debating what should take place, and how they need to proceed. All at once their attention was drawn to the back of the room where the side doors had opened, allowing entrance to a small band of men, whose leader was not unknown to them.

"Prince Lucian!" The name was carried upon the waves of the men's whispers, reaching Gabriel long before his brother actually did.

"Prince Lucian, you have returned to us at last."

"*Iartă-mă*, Father. I know my timing is of the worst sort, but it would be to my great chagrin to miss this gathering."

"You are welcome among us. Come, be seated here." Their father motioned to the chair at his left, directly across from where Gabriel was. "How was your time in Carpaé, I take it Radu is in good health?"

Lucian and Gabriel shared a knowing look, communicating that the two would need to meet in private to discuss the real reason he had taken a leave from the castle. His brother then turned in response to the king, "He is, as is his family. *Domn* Vasile sends his warmest regards."

"It is good to have you back," King Andrei's voice pointed to the rest of them as he said, "Now let us return to the discussion at hand."

As they jumped head first back into the frigid depths of warfare, Gabriel became keenly aware of more than one set of eyes watching him as if having his brother in the room suddenly brought on a comparison between them, the king's two sons, and only heirs to the throne. *Unless of course this Dark Lord has a genuine claim, but how could he?*

With little conscious thought, Gabriel drew his shoulders back, shaping his facial features into a perfect mask, so that none would be the wiser to the niggling doubts that crept along the edges of his mind. It wasn't long before the dialogue grew heated, those against conflict became as outspoken as its counterpart.

"You speak tales of amity and concession, but will it be accepted? I say enough of your talks, let us prepare for war!" Lucian's impassioned speech stilled the air in the room, and he immediately lowered his voice. "Many pardon's father…"

"Speak freely, my son."

Lucian nodded before he continued. The tense pause, like bated breath, made Gabriel's skin crawl.

"It is no lie that I have been both attacker and defender in a great many battles. The gravest folly made by any is to assume peace can be made when there is a call for war. Wait too long, and there won't be a city left to defend, a nation left to surrender."

"Your words quicken a fear in our heart's brother, but your wisdom cannot be dismissed. I wonder only at the cost that comes with war, as do we all." Gabriel asserted a level-headed austerity to balance his brother's heightened claims. He saw a door open to discern the men's true loyalty. One that he stepped in to cautiously, not wanting to overplay his hand. "These men have been brought here for a summit of passivity. We ask only for counsel in the midst of our trials, no more."

"You needn't ask. If it comes to it, we will stand with you." Monsieur Jeromè spoke first. His sure tone paving the way for others to follow suit.

"So will we," added Domn Frazier.

"I haven't ever drawn back from a fight, and I certainly don't plan to now." Herr Gustavo looked to his brother as he said this. They both shared a nod of agreement, before turning to the king and offering him their sign of allegiance, a fist to the heart.

Gabriel breathed deeper. *It is done.* If war should be their only option, at least they wouldn't fight it alone.

Having concluded the day's session, the men filtered out through the double doors, some lingering to expound upon the events of the morning. Making sure he wasn't sidelined into unwanted conversation, Gabriel took the back way out, escaping into the private corridor as he waited for his brother to join him.

"Eager to hear what I've found out, brother?"

"More than you know. Let us make haste, I too have news."

The single hallway led them unto a small sitting room well hidden from the main passage. The space was one of many among the citadel's secrets. When they were children, hiding here had seemed like no more than a game, now it almost alarmed him that they need use its confinement to keep away from speculative foes.

"Shall I go first then?" Lucian smiled his roguish grin. The affect was lost on Gabriel. He still felt uneasy about the way their father had so quickly dismissed his findings.

"This is more serious than I thought. What is it that has you acting so?" As if the walls themselves had ears to steal away their confidences, "Gabriel?" He held up his hand to quiet his brother until he felt them truly secure. Then he spoke, but only just above a whisper.

"There is more to this than we know. Father has not told all."

"What say you?"

Gabriel quickly caught his brother up to speed, sharing about their father's abnormal response. He then pulled the small faded parchment from where he had it kept.

"What do you make of it?" He watched his brother closely. The other man quickly perused the piece, flipping it over and back before returning it.

"I know naught, Gabriel. It looks like a wad of gibberish to my eyes. But it may indeed lead us to the truth about the Dark Lord."

"What did you learn about him?"

They both knew Lucian's trip was far more than a pleasantry visit to see an old friend. In fact, his time spent with Radu was a guise to gather information about the foreboding intruder.

"My past may not be what I would have wished, but it certainly comes in handy to have such reach. In all my travels, in all my conquests, never have I seen such stealth, or crossed paths with one who is veritably a ghost."

His brother's words pounded him forcibly, and he had to shift his weight in order to stand against the disappointment surging within him. "You learned nothing then?"

"Not all was lost. My man from the east reported back insight, but they are rumors at best. Tales of entire villages consumed, as if none had ever lived in their hollow dwellings. The only survivor an old cripple who said the Dark Lord is no more than an evil wraith come to steal away the souls of any who cross his path."

If it weren't for the edge of fear slicing Lucian's words, Gabriel would have thrown it all out as hearsay, but he knew Lucian to be a man of great sense, a hard-wrought soldier who feared little.

"There is something else." The hesitation in his voice made Gabriel's ears perk up.

"Speak man."

"It seems there is a man in connection with this Dark Lord who would have motive to hate us. To hate *me*, rather."

"Of whom do you speak?"

"A Count Denla Quóis. The man to whom I…er…sold Adelina. Of course, I stole her back before any serious harm was done."

Taking in his brother's discomfited expression, he couldn't help but be slightly amused at the red hue tinging the other man's jaw just beneath his winter beard.

"And I assume he didn't take too well to your sudden change of heart."

"No indeed. Nor was he tickled by our… exit scheme… shall I say. We left him strapped to a chair in his nether garments, his men equally bound and exposed before his castle."

"Surely you jest!" Gabriel couldn't believe his ears. How could his brother have been so senseless as to mock a prestigious man, especially one with noble French heritage?

"I am not proud of the man I was, nor would I blame you should you be cross with me over the results of my previous actions. I could not have assumed he was connected with someone as devious as the Dark Lord."

"This is grave insight indeed." Gabriel let his head fall forward, feeling defeated already.

"Surely God is with us in this, brother. We may not have always seen eye to eye, but I will stand beside you now."

His brother's confidence gave him a fleeting sense of hope. Their history was anything but standard, yet still, they were brothers and as such, would see this kingdom well defended.

"If only we can unearth the grounds for the claim he has made. Then perhaps we can refute it, and be done with such allegations."

Lucian's voice had returned to its normal timbre. "Having an army as large as the one we face, as well access to fighting resources, will most definitely give us the advantage."

"Yes indeed. I thank you for your aid in this brother. As second in command to our defensive militia, your role in this is superlative."

"It is I who is thankful to be given a role I can serve my family in, at last."

They moved their conversation out to the open corridor, having made sure none were around when they stepped from the hidden enclosure. Traversing down the main staircase they were met by Lucian's wife. The very same woman who had at one time been betrothed to Gabriel.

"Adelina, my love! I had it in mind to seek you out, and yet here you are."

The young couple embraced each other, and Gabriel could see the sincere and deep affection that was held between them.

"My father, along with several others have adjourned to the stables for a hunt, but my darling husband was not among them, much to my dismay. I wondered at what had kept you from your Kip, and now I know. *Salut*, Prince Gabriel."

Her curtsy was as elegant as her dictation. Everything about her screamed that she would have been an excellent queen of Brasov.

"*Prințesă* Adelina, it is indeed my fault for having kept him away from you."

"No trouble done. Rather, I am glad to have caught up with you both. As you know, the Queen's birth celebration is soon coming, and I had hoped to assist in your plans for her."

Gabriel turned briefly to his brother, whose face was a reflection of his own, with a slight twitch to the brow.

"Plans, my lady?"

"Yes. You see I would be delighted to aide in putting something together for her. A small soiree perhaps?"

Her green eyes twinkled up at him, and he couldn't stop his gaze from traveling to her full pink lips. Her beauty was breathtaking. He pulled his gaze away, reminding himself that she was no longer an eligible maiden, and was certainly not his. *But she could have been.* The tiny insinuation stole across his thoughts before he could contain it.

"I think naught, madam. Much is underfoot this winter, and I'm afraid we haven't the time for more parties."

Rather than put up a fuss like most of the woman he knew, she only lifted her chin and pressed him further. "I must disagree, Your Highness. Indeed, this kingdom would be bolstered by a sense of normalcy. Why, talk of war is already filtering through the streets, the stench of conflict clinging to the air. Would not a celebration of the beloved queen be a healing balm to quiet the fears of your people?"

He looked again toward Lucian, who only stood admiring his wife in all her tenacious charm. How did his brother do it? Steal away this woman. What great trait did his brother possess that he did not?

"Your words, though honeyed, ring true. If you are able to take care of the arrangements, and see to it that your plans will in no way interfere with the agenda of the council, then you have my blessing. Perhaps you can even induce our sister to assist you. A noble feat, I'm sure."

"It would be a pleasure. Thank you, Gabriel!"

He watched her move toward Lucian in her excitement. When the couple shared an embrace, Gabriel turned his face away. Though the majority of his resentment had worn off, it still disappointed him to see them together. Not that he didn't agree with the rest of the kingdom, for they certainly made an envious match. Rather, it was only the reminder of his own loss that spurred his next words.

"I'll leave you two to your homecoming; much is left for me to do this day. It is good to have you both home." He bowed in earnest, and then made up his mind to avoid the lovebirds in the future, at least until he had full reign over his own emotions.

CHAPTER 3

"Haven't you decided yet? I'm most certain Aunté will be pleased to see you, no matter what dress you're sporting."

Elisabeta came around the dressing curtain just in time for Katya to catch the roll of her eyes.

"Katya, my dear pet, a lady of your aunt's taste will have taken in every last detail of my attire before I have even fully stepped from the carriage."

She chuckled slightly as the girl returned to her seclusion to try on yet another gown. This one being her fourth. The first was too blue, the second too plain, and the third…well she didn't quite remember what was wrong with it, but it too had joined its counterparts among the heap on the floor.

"I do see your point."

It was true after all. Aunté Rina had spent two summers in Paris, and one in Rome. Her travels abroad made her acutely refined to the latest trends in fashion, as well as a source for royal gossip, both of which were Elisabeta's singular passion.

"How does this one look?"

Oh, it's lovely! Yes, this one suits you best. Give it a twirl."

The dress splayed out as she turned in a full circle, like deep green waves on a moonlit lake. The scooped neck was lined with black lace, looking ever so soft against her creamy skin, but it was the sleeves that did it the most justice. They were flared at the ends where the black lace was used again, stretching almost to the floor.

"I have not seen anything like it. Where did you come across such designs?"

"Your aunt isn't the only one who has connections to the French court." Elisabeta's smile bespoke of her secret, one Katya was sure she would share when necessary, or whenever it suited her best. "I believe we are ready at last." She sighed as she looked at herself one last time in the large ivory encased looking piece, centered neatly on the far wall of her boudoir.

"I only hope Aunté Rina doesn't believe us to be kidnapped by hoodlums, or lost to the sea of workers that often crowd the streets at this hour."

"What works! She'll think nothing of the sort. Nevertheless, we best hurry, or we'll miss your visit with her altogether."

Though the dress she wore must have weighed a ton with all its flounces and skirts, Elisabeta was a bird in flight, forcing a much clumsier Katya to chase after her. When at last they were lifted into their carriage and driven out the castle gates, Katya's stomach loosed a million little butterflies.

"I haven't been to see them in so long, I quite fear they won't recognize me."

"Of course they will!"

"Do you think they are cross at us for having stayed away so long? I almost wish father had deigned to join me, but he was called away to another meeting."

"How could anyone be cross with you, when you were but a child at the time? Only wait and see, all will be put right soon."

Elisabeta patted her hand gently as their carriage butted and bumped its way down the narrow streets. The streets that slowly changed shape and form, moving them deeper into the *Hermannstadt Provinz*. Leaving the outskirts of Brasov, they were transported into another world altogether, one filled with speckled cottages and thatched roofs.

The Germana people had begun to settle in this land many generations before, having come in aid against the foreign invaders known as the *Cumans*. Many had traveled from the western Holy Roman Empire to call this place home, and though the wars were long past, they had been reluctant to leave. As Katya herself well knew, this place had a way of stealing your heart.

"Oh, look Katya, the *marktplatz*! It's even grander than the trading centers we have."

"*Ja*, *dat* is the *deutsche* way." The corners of her lips turned effortlessly upward as she took in the vast town square, spilling over with shops and their keepers. Having come midday, they were able to see it at its peak of business.

"It seems as if everyone in the world is out this day. I only hope this doesn't deter us further."

Though Elisabeta seemed put off by the additional traffic, Katya relished in the added time it gave them. Slowly, as if this moment would pass too quickly, she drank in the sights around her.

"Do you smell that, Elisabeta? It's coming from that shop with the red drapes. It is the one that sells fresh *kekse*. My mother's favorite."

The scent made her reminisce about all the times she and her mother had walked these very streets.

"Mmm, I can almost taste it. Do you remember all this then?"

"Bits and pieces. Mostly, I just remember her."

"What was she like?"

"She was gentle and soft spoken, but her eyes would always light up when she was telling a story. Vater used to laugh over the tales she created. She was…She was beautiful. I wish I had more of her looks to keep with me, but I favor my Vater. At least I have her eyes and my *muttermal*."

She slid her sleeve up a fraction and pointed to the half-moon marking below her right wrist, one identical to the very one that had been on her mother's wrist.

"She had always said that we were two halves of the same sky, two beats of the same heart." The words slipped out before her throat closed upon itself. Turning back to the crowd of people she pushed pass the choking grief. Instead, she counted shop colors until she had calmed herself.

The congestion soon dispersed, allowing them to resume their drive to the mouth of a large villa. Standing at the entrance was a petite woman waving to them with golden ringlets bouncing beside smiling cheeks.

"Aunté Rina!" Waiting only for the carriage attendant to hand her down, Katya ran up the stone steps and rushed into her aunt's arms.

"Oh my *liebling*! *Wie ich dich vermisst habe!*" She went off into a fit of German whilst she kissed Katya's face and cheeks a dozen times.

"I miss you too dearest aunt." Reluctant to ever leave an embrace that was as warm as this woman's, Katya entwined her hands and squeezed tighter.

"Heavens child, you'll have me tied up in knots if you don't loosen up. Now come, let me look at you."

Obediently she stepped back, presenting herself fully. She too had been careful in choosing her gown, though not nearly as picky as her friend. From her wardrobe, she had taken a formal day dress of robin's egg blue. It not only accented the light hair that peaked out from beneath her circlet, but also pulled more color into her cheeks and gave a sort of vibrancy to her eyes.

“My, what an elegant lady you have grown to be. One just as *schöne* as your mother.”

Katya beamed at the praise, perhaps this time with Rina would be all that she had hoped. She would ask her about her mother, and even seek advice on her father’s worrisome decline.

“And who might we have here? Katya, did you bring me a surprise?”

Elisabeta, ever graceful, glided toward them. Climbing the steps, she came to a standstill and offered them a partial curtsy.

“Aunté Rina, you remember my dearest friend and daughter of King Andrei, Elisabeta Romalo.”

“You are exquisite, *Prinzessin*. Indeed, you both are a wonderful gift this day!”

After showing them around her grand estate, one that she shared with her husband Herr Ranald and her two children, Rina then led them onto the back terrace where tea was being served.

“Sit, my darlings, I want to know all about the happenings at the castle. Is it true that Prince Gabriel is looking for a bride?”

Elisabeta needed no more encouragement. She unraveled the whole tale of how Gabriel had once been betrothed to Adelina, the lady who was now married to his younger brother Lucian, and about the alliance the King had sought to foster between Gabriel and a daughter of a French ambassador shortly after that. Though the *Hermannstadt Provinz* wasn’t more than thrice miles from the *castellele*, the secluded sector often didn’t receive news of the nation until much later.

Katya herself absorbed every word, much of it being unknown to her. Especially the bit about Gabriel’s betrothal. Was the king really pressing him to marry? Perhaps that would explain why so many of the dignitaries had brought their daughters. She wondered which of the fine ladies would capture the prince’s heart. *Surely one has caught his eye already.*

"All of this in little more than a summer past! How exciting." Rina's words were whispered in a thrilling rush that instantly reminded Katya of Elisabeta. The two seemed to share more than a few similarities.

"Mutter?" A voice called to them from within. The person to which it belonged was a young girl who peeked out at them through the open doors.

"*Komen her*, Britta."

Britta approached shyly. She wore a white dress with puffed sleeves, and a green ribbon holding back wisps of hair just as curly as her mother's.

"Ladies, this is my Britta. Britta this is *Prinzessin* Elisabeta." The younger girl, who couldn't have been more than eight, curtsied politely. "And this is your cousin. You may not remember her, but her mother was one of my closest friends. The sister I never had."

"It is wonderful to see you again Britta." Katya smiled at the girl encouragingly.

"*Sie est* Katerina's *tochter*?"

"*Ja*, Britta."

Though the girl had spoken to her mother, her eyes had never left Elisabeta. It seemed her friend had yet another admirer.

"You are very beautiful, Your Highness." Her quiet words were made even more elusive as she blushed and tucked her chin.

"You are most kind to say so Britta, but it is your dress that is most elegant. You must share with me who accomplished the stitch work for the flowers on your hem?"

The girl beamed somewhat, stepping slightly out from behind her mother. "I did, my lady. Mutter thinks it well for me to pursue my creative interests."

"Your mother is very wise indeed. I must say you have peaked my curiosity. Would you care to take a turn with me about the garden?"

Britta's heart was captured. She looked to her mother for permission, and then went skipping toward the worn path between hedges, Elisabeta's tinkling laughter flowing close behind.

"Britta is very demur around most people, but she has taken a liking to your friend."

"It is hard not to. Elisabeta is like a spirited puppy. One does not go very long before they are filled with delight."

"And you, my dear? What are you like?"

Katya thought for a moment, unsure how to answer. She was more like a scrappy mutt when compared to someone like Elisabeta.

"Perhaps I am more akin to one of father's hunting dogs. Sensible and obedient."

"*Nein*. I think not. There is more to you than that."

"Father doesn't seem to think so."

Rina paused, as if taking in the meaning of Katya's hastily spoken words.

"Your father is a very hard man, and though you may resemble him in looks, it is your mother's tender spirit that shines so brightly through you."

Leaning in, Katya replaced her cup of tea to its saucer and looked intently toward her aunt.

"I was hoping you could tell me more about her."

"What would you like to know?"

A world of possibilities opened before her, and she had to sift through the grains of questions her father had left unanswered. One rose to the surface, while the rest fell away like chaff.

"Why did she die so young?"

"*Welche*? You mean you don't know?"

Katya shook her head, wondering at the surprise on her aunt's face.

"Oh child, your *vater* has done wrong by you in this." Setting down her own cup, Aunté Rina adjusted her mauve skirt. "You see dear Katya, your mother was exposed to the same illness as her parents. When they knew it was too late for them, they sought to spare their only child from the wasting disease. It was how we met."

Katya watched as Rina's face softened, and her gaze grew distant in remembrance.

"We lived close by, and our father's both served in the militia together. I remember the night she came to live with us. A fever burned bright in her eyes and her clothes hung about her frame with neglect, but I thought she was the loveliest creature I had ever met. She fought the illness for two long weeks and overcame it. Still, she was never as strong as she was before. When she left for Germana, I thought my heart would break into pieces, but when I heard of her marriage to your father, I felt sure that she would return to us. And she did, every summer."

The words soaked into Katya's heart, each one filling a space the same way tart pooled into the pockets of strussel when one made *linzer auge*.

"One summer your mother told me she was with child. She always knew you would be a girl." Rina reached out and gently patted Katya's cheek in a motherly gesture. "All our hearts were filled with joy, but soon Katrina grew sickly, and was confined to her bed. The doctor thought for sure you would be lost to us, but your mother didn't give up hope. After you were born, your mother herself didn't recover for several weeks, and they said she wouldn't be able to bear any more children. Then, about *seiben* years ago, she grew round once more. This time, it was as the doctors had said it would be. Her body wasn't able to keep either of them alive very long."

Taking in all that her aunt was telling her, Katya felt heat rise into her cheeks, and tears burn behind her eyes. *Why hadn't father told me?*

"And the babe? I don't remember her being with child."

"She was not far enough along for anyone to suspect, and your father was so consumed by his grief that he shut himself away for the rest of the summer."

"Was that why I had to stay with you and Herr Ranald? I thought perhaps they didn't want me to become poorly like Mutter."

Aunté Rina nodded somberly, glistening tears clinging to her lashes. Katya's heart felt cold in her chest at how her father had kept her in the dark, and she wondered how she would forgive him. When she said as much, her aunt gasped and clasped Katya's hand with a surprisingly firm grip.

"*Nein*, Katya. You must not hold on to your offense. It is not how your mother would want you to go on. She would want you to pray for him, and remain strong in your faith, child."

Soft voices grew louder, alerting them to the return of the other ladies. Aunté Rina, seeing that Katya needed a moment further, drew herself up and swished over to meet them.

She would want you to pray for him. The words repeated themselves in her mind, pulling her into a clouded memory she had forgotten was there at all. Katya saw herself at her mother's bedside, the still form only a shell of the woman she had known. With labored breath, her mother had reached for her hand. Katya had looked up to see her father's weeping face, and the anguish in his eyes had frightened her.

"Mutter?"

Her mother pulled her closer, her voice broken up by the fever. "Katya, remember that you belong to the Lord now, *da*?"

Katya had nodded her small head, remembering how she had given her heart to the Lord with her mother and Friar Wilhelm their priest.

"Very good, my beautiful girl. Now you must promise that you will stay close to Him. Even when I'm gone, you must always know that He is with you. Will you do that for me, *dragă mea*?"

"Yes Mutter, only do not go!"

Her mother had only kissed her head, and patted her cheek. Then she had said the same to her father, making him promise to not turn his back on the Lord in anger, but to serve him faithfully. Her father begged Katrina not to give up, not to leave them. But she had only smiled and said, "The Lord is faithful, Burkhart," before she slipped away into the early dawn.

Drawing her mind back to the present, Katya knew it was her faith that had gotten her through all these years. When her father had stopped making an effort to play with her, she had felt the Lord's tender love. When he grew distant and stopped going with her to the chapel for prayer, she felt His gentle hand guide her. Even now when she struggled to move past the anger swelling up in her chest, she felt the firm nudging of His Spirit to honor her mother's request and give grace.

Heavenly Father, may my faith in Thee be as pure as my mother's. I forgive my father for his unkindness. May Your love be balm to his wounded heart, and may we both do right in bringing glory to Thy Name. Amen.

Katya wondered if her father remembered his promise to Katerina, the way she did. He didn't seem to. *But I don't know that for certain, for man sees the outward appearance, but it is the Lord that judgeth the heart. Perhaps Vater did think of it, and was trying to get back to the path of righteousness.*

"Katya, won't you come see who is here?"

Leaving all thoughts of her father at the small table, she followed her aunt's voice in to the pristine house, where she was met by her cousin and uncle.

"Herr Ranald! Georg! How good it is to see you again."

Together the family spent the hours of the day reminiscing over Katya's childhood, sharing stories of gatherings and mischief, until even Elisabeta was overtaken by fits of laughter. When the time had come for them to depart, Katya stood and made her farewells.

"I will come again, Aunté. Vater believes we will be here until spring."

"Of course you will; perhaps you might even come for a few days to stay with us. That way you won't have to fuss over the trip back and forth."

"Be sure Burkhart knows he too is welcome to our abode." Herr Ranald added briskly, his smile assuring her that the invitation was in earnest.

"I will. Thank you for this wonderful time. May the Lord be with you until we meet again!"

"And also with you, my dear. *Prinzessin* Elisabeta, your company was most enjoyable."

"*Mulțumesc*, Herr Ranald. It is I who am honored to have come."

Stepping back into their carriage the two girls waved their goodbyes, and rode off into the evening. When they returned to the keep just before the supper hour, Katya headed straight to her room to change. She still hadn't adjusted to the delayed meal times that were observed here in the castelle, where dinner wasn't served until the eighth hour of the day in accordance with the evening prayers.

Though she and Elisabeta were on the same floor, the hallways stretched between the east wing and the west, leaving Katya to cross paths with more than a few persons. The one person she did not expect to pass was her father, but it seemed as if his presence in the hallway that led to her room was not merely chance.

"Guten nacht, Vater."

"From where have you come, Katya?" His words were slightly stammered, causing Katya to slow her steps with caution, but perhaps he was only tired after his day's meeting.

"I have only just returned from a visit with Herr Ranald and Aunté Rina. You should have seen Georg and Britta, Vater. They have grown so big."

"Humph…you should have been here, like the other ladies."

"I told you I would be away, but you said you didna' wish to go."

He moved forward and staggered, and would have fallen had she not reached out to catch him. Shrugging her hand away he found his balance. It would seem he had been using the wall as a prop to keep himself upright. Seeing that something was amiss, she kept talking, but his eyes had already begun to glaze over. *Oh, nein! Not another one of his fits.* Though she wasn't around him often enough to know how long this had been going on, she had seen him get like this once or twice before.

"Herr Ranald sends his regards. They both hope you will come and visit them. Aunté Rina even shared a little about Mutter, about what she was like as a young girl."

She looked around to see if there were any spectators, but thankfully she was the only one who had to witness his wretched state. He began to talk again, his words jumbled. All she could make out were fragments here and there.

"Katerina?" His eyes seemed hollow as he looked at Katya. It was a site that did not bode well with her.

"No, Vater, it is Katya." She moved closer, hoping to steer him back to his bedchamber. *Perhaps there is a doctor here who can aide him*. The physician back home always prescribed laudanum, though it only ever worked to send her father into further oblivion.

"I must go find her. Where have you gone, Katerina?....do not leave me..."

"You aren't well, perhaps we should go back to your room. Then you can have a lie down before dinner this eve. Would you care for me to walk you there?"

He shook his head like a petulant child, and his brows furrowed together in anger. That was when his words began to slur.

"I ssshhould never have let it happen. How can I make it better...my...my love, I am not strong enough."

"Please Vater, it's Katya, your *tochter*. Just let me help you."

His cold eyes, sharpened on her, and his face twisted up. "This is all *your* fault! What have you done with my Katerina? Where have you taken her?"

Seeing that she was getting nowhere in her reasoning, she stepped toward him. Before she could gage his next move, he shoved against her and sent her reeling. Even in his incoherent state of mind, he still had the strength of an ox, so she fell hard. It would not have been so bad, had there not been a small wooden table directly behind her. When she fell she hit her head on its edge, and could feel a small trickle of blood above her right temple. The gasp that sounded round the hall was strange even to her ears, until she realized that it had not come from her own lips.

Gabriel had been on his way to find his father, since the man had been avoiding him ever since their previous discussion, when he had stumbled upon the scene before him. He had only been there long enough to see the girl fall backwards into a table. Her head smarting against the solid surface with an audible crack. By the time he reached them, Herr Nuremburg had crumpled to a heap on the ground, where his daughter had reached out to catch him.

"I forgive you father. I forgive you."

She repeated the phrase softly, but it wasn't she who was crying. It was the lord. When he laid a hand on her shoulder, she stopped in her rocking, but refused to look up at him. From what he could see of her profile, he knew why. Shame covered her face like a widow's veil, and his heart clenched painfully.

"He isn't himself, Your Highness."

"Katya, isn't it?"

"Yes, my lord."

"Come, we will get him back to his chamber."

She nodded and bent to speak softly to her father. Though the words were unclear, whatever she said seemed to do the trick, for the man stood of his own accord.

Looking into the face of the perpetrator, an uneasiness settled in Gabriel's chest. The man looked out of his mind. His face was drooped, his mouth hanging open, and his glassy eyes were fixed instead on a distant spot somewhere behind them. It was as if they were not there at all. Turning to Katya, he noticed a red stain on her shoulder.

"You're bleeding!"

She too looked down, and then felt for the cut behind her ear where blood trickled from. With little thought, he removed his cravat, and handed it to her.

"Thank you, Your Highness."

Herr Nuremburg had continued to stumble toward them, incomprehensible phrases tumbling from his lips. Gabriel kept himself positioned between them, uncertain of whether the man would strike out in violence again. When he made a move to apprehend him, she reached out to stop him.

"*Bitte*, Your Highness. My father is not well. He knows naught what he has done."

Gabriel was struck by the intelligence in her ice blue gaze. The compassion in them pleading for him to show restraint.

He kept his voice gentle as he spoke. "How long has he been like this?"

This time she did not avoid his gaze, the resignation in her voice turning it to a whisper.

"Not long after my mother passed, his moods began to change. I did not know he had gotten so bad, but now...I fear the worst."

"Still, his behavior is inexcusable. I cannot allow him to wander the halls of the castle like this."

He turned back to shout for the guards he knew to be posted at the far side of the hall, but before he could beckon them hence, she came and stood before him.

"If we only get him to his bed, he will be much restored after some rest."

Gabriel watched as she went to her father, speaking softly to him in her native tongue, to which the man nodded calmly, much changed from the one who had acted out only minutes before. He knew that to involve the guards, and make a spectacle, would do more harm to her own reputation, so against his better judgment he capitulated.

"I will help you see him to his room, but guards will be posted outside his door this eve, and if I hear of but one more incident, he will have to be removed from here."

"Thank you, my lord."

Together they half walked, half carried the man to his quarters where they laid him across his bed. Katya then tucked a quilt over him after she removed his boots. Gabriel barely noticed her actions, nor did he engage her further as he escorted her to her own room, bowing shortly before moving on. His mind was already mulling over what he would do next. Surely, he couldn't allow this to go on.

His opportunity didn't come until the next evening, when she was present again at dinner. All day he had fought with himself over his present course of action. He was in no way impulsive like his brother, nor ambitious like his sister. After endless hours of internal debate, he knew what he would do, and if he played it out just right, the result would be to their mutual benefit. With little direction, his eyes sought her out among the row of faces seated across from him. She often sat toward the lower end of the table, but tonight without her father at her side she was positioned near his sister. Thus, finding her form was an easy conquest.

With the honeyed glow of the candlelit hall, he took in her round face. Her hair was piled atop her hair in a pinned array of blonde waves, and her dress opened up around her neck, the deep gray fabric contrasting her bare skin. He saw none of these things though, only an end to his search. A queen for his throne.

He glanced to the hollow of her throat. No sign of blood remained, nor did he expect any, as she had cleaned up the wound, no doubt applying cosmetic to cover the bruising, but he could still see it. He could still see the look of terror in her eyes when she fell back, could still feel the squeeze in his own chest when a desire to protect her had flooded through him. Next time he would...*There need not be a next time,* he reminded himself. *Tonight, I will see to that.*

She soon squirmed under his narrowed gaze, and he quickly looked elsewhere hoping he hadn't given anything away. The dinner hour passed swiftly enough, and he waited only until the chocolate *chec* was served before he stood and made his move. Counting his paces to her seat, he carried out his carefully calculated contrivance.

"Lords and ladies of the court, those Brasov born and those from afar, I welcome you to this joyous occasion. This night I have put a cease to my father's endless propositions of betrothal. I'm certain he thought me a hopeless case."

Many of them laughed, others gasped at his clearly unexpected declaration.

"The joining of our two families will not only boost our countries' alliance, but will send a clear message to our enemy. The future of this nation is assured, the throne indisputable."

He paused, patiently allowing their minds to conjure up wistful tales, and then positioned himself directly before Katya. His hand reached out to draw her up beside him. She looked positively pale, and he almost begged her not to faint. He sought to comfort her with a smile, but his lips only stretched into their usual business-like grimace. Instead he lightly squeezed her hand, hoping he could crush some of his assurance into her palm.

"Fräulein Katya Herman Nuremburg, I would be honored if you would grant me your hand in matrimony."

Hushed whispers spread among their audience. In the agonizing moments it took for her to form a response, Gabriel rehearsed the reasons for his proposal. By wedding her, he would be securing her father's aid in the coming war. She herself would be free from the destructive attentions of her father's unstable nature. The kingdom would have a secure future for the throne. Indeed, his claim would be well established.

'Tis no falsehood, he told himself weakly. *I shall marry her for no other reason. Certainly not because of her sorrowful eyes that were two pools of swirling blue depths, an ocean he could easily drown in, nor for the way she so readily stood up to him, her pert little nose barely reaching his chest, making an adorable picture that warmed him. And most assuredly not because of the way she had looked at*

him as if he alone could rescue her, as if he alone would be the hero of her tale.

"Your Highness…I..," the briefest indecision made itself known in the darkening of her irises, and he watched as it flickered like a dwindling flame before being snuffed out by the strength of her willpower, "Your Majesty, it is I who would be honored to serve the kingdom of Brasov and it's people at your side."

Her skirts crinkled as she bowed low before him. He felt pleased with himself. It was true that he had given her little choice but to accept him, still he was glad to have it done. He leaned over her hand, pressing a kiss to her white glove. When they rose, they were carried away upon the cheers of the well-wishers who quickly surrounded them.

CHAPTER 4

Brasov awakened itself the next morn from a deep slumber, it's cool breath bringing a frost upon the land. All was bathed in a winter coat of white. Only the sky remained an untouched color of cerulean blue. Gabriel withdrew from the window of his father's study, moving nearer the fireplace. His father was pacing in front of him, his muttered words just out of reach. Gabriel suspected he would soon share his displeasure over the events of last evening. Unfortunately, he could not wait for the other man's unhurried deliberation, for he had words of his own that need be shared.

"Father, I have asked that Lady Katya and Herr Nuremburg join us this morning. They will be with us shortly. I only thought to prepare you that my words with the man will be short and few. This is no normal match made between us. Though I am certain of our marriage being to the best advantage of our kingdom, in light of our present circumstances, I have chosen Lady Katya for her sake as well."

King Andrei opened his mouth to speak to Gabriel's hasty assertions, but was cut off by the activity of the guard who opened the door and presented their guests.

"Your Majesty, Your Highness."

Gabriel acknowledged Katya with a tip of his head, but when he turned to her father, he offered no pleasantries.

"Sir, I have asked your daughter to become my bride, to which she has accepted."

Herr Nuremburg's disgruntled face passed from him to his daughter, and Gabriel noticed how she conveniently avoided his gaze. It would seem this was the first he was hearing of the arrangement. *All the better.*

"I have naught sought your permission, but I believe this arrangement to be in both our best interests, and as an ally of our country I know you will see it that way as well."

"Well, I never…"

Gabriel continued right over top of the sputtering lord.

"Your approval of this match in both word and deed is much desired, but unneeded," Gabriel then took a step toward him, his eyes locking upon the man who stood both taller and wider than he, "I trust you wish the very best for your daughter, do you not, sir?"

The threat of his words lingered in the air between them. The man was clearly affronted, as is he had no clue as to why Gabriel would speak to him in such a way. And perhaps he did not, but the look of disbelief on the elder man's face was enraging. When he had finished, they stood glaring at each other. It wasn't until a small voice reached between them, its gentle resonance a sign of peace that Gabriel pulled himself back. He didn't quite catch all of what she said, for she spoke in low tones and his German was rusty, but whatever it was it had a similar effect on her father.

The man's demeanor shifted entirely. He cleared his throat, and Gabriel could see the evidence of tears in his eyes. He then turned toward his daughter, clutching her shoulders while pressing a kiss to her forehead and then drawing her into a hug. The way Katya held herself stiffly in the man's embrace, made Gabriel wonder if this were a rare occurrence, but after piecing together all that she had said about her father's detachment, he knew it was so.

"Forgive me, *Mein tochter*."

"All is forgiven, Vater."

The man then turned back to him. "My blessing is yours, Prince Gabriel. Katya does indeed deserve the very best. More than I have been able to give her. I ask only that you be sure that she is loved above your throne and your crown."

Gabriel chafed against the man's words. *Love? What did love have to do with their arrangement? Surely he does not think I have chosen his daughter based on mere affection.* In truth, he wasn't even entirely certain he held a keen attraction for her.

"Your Majesty, in regards to an alliance, I will see that my daughter's dowry is an ample supply for the coming war, and I will see to it that the other *deutsche Herren* are prepared to stand with you."

At last Gabriel's father had his turn to speak. Though he concealed his emotions behind a regal bravado, his son knew well that he didn't enjoy being left out of the particulars, nor did he like to be caught off guard.

"In times like these, we have need of every available ally. It is my hope that though this alliance has been hastily made, it will grow into a prosperous match between our children, our families, and our nations."

"Let it be as you say, Your Majesty."

The door to the study opened once again, and the posted guard heralded their guest.

"The Queen come for Lady Katya, Your Majesty."

"Thank you, Costa." Gabriel shared a look with his father, before moving forward to kiss his mother's cheek.

"*Buna dimineata*, Mamă."

"And to you my son."

Turning to Katya, he quickly added, “My mother will escort you to the solar, where I will join you shortly.”

“Yes, Your Highness.”

The attendants then escorted all of them out, leaving Gabriel with a less than pleased companion.

“It would seem you have thought of everything, have you not?” His father’s voice was gruff, and Gabriel noted the not so subtle hint of disappointment.

“I had no intention of springing this on you, father. Though I would think you would be pleased at me having chosen a wife.”

Rather than answer him directly, King Andrei resumed his pacing, this time with a much heavier step. When it seemed as though he would not speak at all, he turned finally, his hand rubbing his black beard streamed with gray.

“You have thought this match through then?”

“Indeed, I have. Her family is well connected, she has Romania blood from her mother’s side, and her character is becoming of a future queen.”

“So, there is no affection between you?”

“I didn’t find that to be pertinent. I hardly know her. The throne is my objective, and I have found a bride as you suggested.”

“You are right to think of our people, but even if we should be faced with war, it will not last forever. This lady you have chosen will remain even after the fighting has ceased.”

The caution in his father’s tone was lost on him. The threat of conflict, and the ever-looming Dark Lord was too pressing. It consumed his so that his only thoughts were of defending his nation, and protecting his future. When he said as much to his father, the older man nodded slowly and blinked away the remainder of his argument, saying only, “Do not forget the Lord in this, Gabriel. It is He who will make a way for us.”

Nu, Father. Gabriel shrugged away his words. *It is I who will fight for us, not the Lord.* Seeing himself dismissed, he made his way to the solar where his future bride sat waiting for him.

Katya listened demurely as the queen chatted on about the ladies she had at court, and the upcoming winter festivities. As much as she tried to pay attention, she couldn't help but sneak glances at the door, as if he would somehow sense her impatience and reveal himself. *What is taking him so long?* She thought. *Hadn't he said he would be joining us shortly?* She had woken this morning with uneasiness about the arrangement made between her and the prince, but seeing him defend her like that, even against her own father, had warmed her to the toes.

Fearful of her father's grave disapproval she had made an effort to speak her peace. In the moment she hadn't meant to bring up her mother, but the words had poured forth from her wounded heart with unexpected force. Now she was glad she hadn't held them back.

"I'm sure whatever is keeping him must be urgent, my dear."

Katya blushed at having been found out, her eyes slinking back and away from the closed portal.

"Of course, *Eure Majestät.*"

She didn't know why she was having such a fit of nerves. Just the other night she had prayed for the Lord to aid her in her plight with her father; surely He must have a hand in this.

"From the look on your face I can see that this is as much a surprise to you as it is for everyone else, *nu*?"

"Ja, we haven't had much time to know one another. Then last night, with my father he…well it would seem he has chosen to aide me, but with little mind to how this would all play out."

Katya wasn't sure how her candid reply would be received, but the queen looked at her unfettered. Instead her face grew soft with a gentle kindness that helped her to relax.

"Gabriel never acts impulsively, it's out of his character. He is too much the makings of a future king to do so. If he has asked for your hand, then it is with great thought to both you and the future of his kingdom. Ah, here he is now."

Turning to watch him enter the room, Katya nearly forgot how to breathe. In his proposal last evening he hadn't mentioned love, or even the slightest affection, only a need to see the throne protected from their enemy, yet still she had accepted him. It was more than a desire to be safe from the uncertainty of her father, or even the fear of having to return to Germana and be parted from this place, rather she had accepted because she knew him somehow, and though it couldn't quite be described as love, she was falling for him. Falling for the soon to be king of her mother's homeland.

"Mother, thank you for keeping Lady Katya entertained. Might I have some moments alone with her?"

"Why, of course Gabriel. You two *are* betrothed."

The queen produced a beatific grin for them both. A smile that said she was privy to something neither of them yet knew. The couple stared after her, neither one quite ready to be alone with their thoughts. Katya turned towards him first. She felt more than saw the tension gather in the muscles at his shoulders and neck. When he finally looked her way, she noticed that his hands had once again resumed their post as an anchor behind his back.

"We must wed soon. With hints of war on the horizon, it would not be good to wait. You are certain of your role in this?"

She didn't hesitate this time. Her mind was made up. For whatever reason they were brought together, she felt strongly about being the one to stand at his side.

"Yes, Your Highness."

"Of course, you may call me Gabriel. The marriage will be in name only, until we have had the time to become better acquainted." The prince struggled over those last words, before rushing on. "Once the ceremony has been conducted, your things will be moved into the apartment joining my own quarters. You will need to begin regular visits with my mother, where she will be able to instruct you on all the duties and responsibilities that will become yours once I've had my coronation in a year's time."

That made her still. What was she signing herself up for? To be partnered to a man with whom she will one day soon lead a nation, and only bear his name. She blushed slightly. *He did say it wasn't permanent. Besides he is right to point out you hardly know one another. Perhaps it is for the best.*

"Have you any questions?"

She had plenty, but none she was willing to voice in the moment, especially with him looming over her as he was, all formal and matter of fact. So instead, she shook her already aching head, and folded her hands neatly across her skirts.

"Very good. I am most pleased to see that you are taking things so well. If you have need of anything at all, you must not hesitate to seek me out."

"Thank you, Prince Gabriel."

He gave her a polite smile, all very neat and tucked together, the very one he had given her when they had danced together a couple weeks ago. In it she saw that his charm lay only on the surface, attached to no real warmth, but only a friendly regard. With great effort she returned his smile, her heart breaking a little. His brown eyes narrowed the tiniest bit, as if he could sense the change in her, but he said nothing. He then turned to go, pausing suddenly before he reached the door.

"Oh, I nearly forgot." He crossed the floor in three long strides, seating himself in the chair beside hers, the one the queen had recently vacated. From his pocket he withdrew a small wooden box that once opened, revealed a ring.

"It belonged to my great-grandmother. My father had kept it for me until I was old enough to keep it myself."

"It's absolutely stunning, Your Highness."

"Gabriel, please."

"Gabriel then. How do you call this?" She pointed to the large oval cut rock with deep violet hues encased within the golden band.

"It's called *ametist.* I would be honored if you would wear it, indeed 'tis yours."

"I will cherish it, *danke.*"

She held still as he delicately lifted her left hand, sliding the ring onto her third finger. The band felt cold against her bare skin, and she shivered. Pressing a feather light kiss to her hand, he relinquished it to her lap. And just like that her whole world was turned upside down in the course of a single day's span.

When she got back to her room it was to find Elisabeta waiting for her. The girl had stuck herself into the little alcove of the window seat, a place that gave her direct vision to the doorway. Katya smiled, knowing her friend must be anxious to see her since they hadn't even a moment to themselves after last night.

She saw the moment Elisabeta had caught eye of the jewel now resting upon her hand, for she pushed off the wall like a slingshot, propelling herself forward with a gasp.

"*Vai*, Katya! What is this?"

"Your brother gave it to me."

"Well of course he did, who else? Come, let me see."

Katya smiled and stretched her hand out obligingly. She allowed herself a fraction of giddiness. *I am soon to be wed, and to a man I would gladly love.* That single thought sent her heart racing.

"'Tis all so sudden. I hardly expected Gabriel to ask so soon, though I had my suspicions. Has it been a whirlwind romance? I imagine the two of you couldn't help but fall for each other."

Katya couldn't seem to get a word in edge wise, but neither was she wanting to diminish her friend's day dreams. *So what if we aren't marrying for love, cannot the Lord bless our union in His timing?* Wistfully she willed it to be so.

"Good heavens! That means we are to be sisters!"

Elisabeta then grabbed Katya by both of her hands and started jumping about, her infectious laughter filling the room.

"I had always wanted a sister." For a moment she thought of the unborn babe her mother had carried. *Would it have been a girl?*

"It is the same for I, and now I will have two of the most wonderful of sisters. One I also call friend. Come, we must go share the news with Adelina. I'm sure she is eager to know you like I do."

Katya brought them to a standstill. "I'm certain she was present last evening, and knows all. Besides, won't that be a bit strange for her? Meeting the woman who will become queen instead of her?"

"Not at all. Adelina has very much relinquished any desire to be queen. She says the Lord has given her a heart for Lucian alone. Isn't that romantic?"

"Yes. I'm glad to know she shares our faith so diligently."

Elisabeta gave her a sly smile. "You know not the half of it my dear, but she will have to be the one to tell all about how she came to be Lucian's bride. Did Gabriel say how soon you are to be wed?"

"In two weeks' time. He was certain the wedding should take place immediately."

“Two weeks! Well then, we best be going. We haven’t a moment to spare!”

When they reached the southern garden, a place claimed to be Adelina’s favorite, Katya had to brush her hands against her skirts to keep them from getting clammy. Her nerves were frizzled over the uncertainty of her reception, and a bit of timidity at meeting Gabriel’s previous betrothed. *Come Katya, where is your strength? The girl is only a few years your senior, surely she will not be so fierce.*

“Elisabeta, come and sit with me? This day is just lovely. Truly the Lord has blessed us!”

“As lovely as you are, dear sister. We have come to share joyous news with you!”

The other lady was seated upon a stone bench, one that was positioned in front of a large fountain. Though Katya had caught a few glances of the woman, she was surprised to see her beauty was even more genuine up close. As willowy as the drooping tree that sat across the yard, the Lady Adelina was a sight to behold. It was no wonder Gabriel had wished her to be his queen. She was not only elegant in every way, but her features were nearly flawless, a plain fact that made Katya want to shrink further into her kirtle.

“And you must be Lady Katya? How wonderful it is to finally meet you!”

She nodded her head shyly, just before Adelina pulled her into a tight embrace.

“I hope we are not disturbing you?”

“Not at all. In fact, I was just praying for some company. With Lucian being so busy with the council, I find I miss my family so much more. But now I may thank the Lord for sending me you.”

Katya was a bit perturbed by the woman’s openness about the Lord, for it reminded her of her mother, who often spoke in a similar manner.

"I believe congratulations are in order, Lady Katya. I am delighted to know Brasov will be graced with one of strength as I sense you carry."

Staring into Adelina's eyes, to be certain if the lady was simply playing a role in front of Elisabeta, Katya was contented to find that her green gaze held only kindness, and perhaps even some well-guarded hesitancy. *Mayhap she is also uncertain of how I will receive her.* This made Katya feel much more relieved.

"I thank you, Lady Adelina. It is my hope to serve Gabriel and his people in any way that I can. I look forward to becoming part of his family, and also perhaps part of yours."

Though it wasn't posed as a question, Katya looked intently at the woman before her, hoping that her thoughts were displayed openly on her face.

"I would be delighted to call you such. I think you and I will be great friends." Adelina smiled broadly, her whole face lighting up.

"Friends, sisters, confidants. I'm just glad to see that you won't be leaving me again. Oh my! Just think what Aunté Rina will say once she's heard!"

Elisabeta was right, Brasov would now be her home. She wouldn't have to be parted from what little family she knew, instead, she would gain more family than she had ever imagined.

"I hadn't thought about that. Of course she will want to fuss over every little detail of the wedding. She has always been like a mother to me."

"You deserve to be fussed over. It isn't everyday a girl gets married and becomes queen!"

Elisabeta rolled her eyes as she said this, but Adelina placed a gentle hand on Katya's arm.

"'Tis alright if you are nervous. I certainly was, both to become a princess and a bride."

The woman seemed to see right past her false bravado.

"Yes, it is all a bit sudden. In truth, I am not even sure of what it takes to be a queen, or if I am worthy of the task. I have never even been to court, except for when I was a child."

Before speaking any further, Adelina grabbed her by the hand and pulled her toward the bench, where she sat her between herself and Elisabeta.

"In ourselves, we will never find all that we need to be a great leader. Rather it is in the Lord that we find the strength to face uncertainty, the grace to love our people, and the wisdom to lead a nation. Do you believe the Lord has called you to this?"

The love that poured from Adelina's eyes was otherworldly, and Katya couldn't help but feel a peaceful presence in their midst. She quickly searched her own heart to find an answer.

"Yes. Yes, I do feel the Lord's hand in this."

"Then nothing shall be impossible for you. You need only believe."

Only believe. It was what her mother had begged her to do with her dying breath. *Lord help me to believe, and forgive my unbelief.* She knew it to be a quick prayer, but she offered it up with her whole heart. To have a faith like her mother's, like this woman's, was what she really wanted. More than a kingdom, more than a throne, she felt a growing desire to be a model of faith for the people she would one day serve.

Andrei could not believe it was already the day his son would be wed. The older he got, the more quickly time seemed to pass, slipping through his fingers like water that could not be caught. He had been king a long time, but never had the crown weighed so heavy upon his head. Even at his coronation when his own father had set the golden diadem upon his dark tresses, and he had been humbled beneath the prominence of his position, he had not felt the crippling pressure that he did now. And to think he was soon to pass this on to his son. He shuddered.

"Is anything amiss, Your Majesty?"

"Nu, Irgo. Thank you, that will be all for now."

He waited only until the man had carried out the remainder of his night wear, before dropping onto the small bench nearest him. His head slunk down into his hands, and even though he felt the crinkling of the freshly pressed collar that he had been dressed in, he didn't move from his defeated stance.

"Oh Gabriel, have I truly prepared you?"

He knew without doubt that he had done all in his power to equip and train his son to be a great warrior, and a mighty king. He had made sure Gabriel would be a man of honor and integrity, but would he also be a man of faith? When they had spoken weeks ago, Andrei had sensed a stiffness in his son that if left unchecked would soon become a coldness in his heart.

"Andrei, are you in here?"

He quickly straightened himself, wanting to keep his beloved wife from worry. "Yes, my love. I was only collecting up my thoughts ere we adjourned to the hall."

"And what heavy thoughts they must be. Your neck tie is skewed."

She moved closer to adjust his shirt. Even after all these years, her nearness still affected him. Without thought he moved his hands to grip her waist, pulling her against his chest before he buried his head in her neck.

"Now you will have us both a mess." She chuckled, wrapping her own arms around his neck.

"I love you most dearly, lady wife."

"And I you, husband. Now, tell me what has you distraught? Is it something about Gabriel? He has been so very determined these last few weeks; it's as if the trouble abroad is consuming him."

"I feel as though I am to blame."

She moved back to see him more clearly.

"What mean you by this?"

He remembered back to when Gabriel was just a boy, his brown hair had grown long enough to curl around his eyes, and his cheeks were always marked with red hue from his playful exertions. The day after he turned six, Andrei had gone to seek him out for his first lessons, but he was nowhere to be found. He recalled having searched the castle for nearly an hour, his patience growing thin, as he had his own work to be done. When he finally found his son sitting within the bailey of the chapel, playing cross sticks with the priest, he had been very abrupt.

"I told him kings didn't have time to waste among the chapel courts; that it was a priest's job to seek the Lord, but a king's job to lead his people." He squeezed his eyes shut in an attempt to rid himself of the distasteful memory, "I was so blind back then."

"But Andrei, that was years ago."

"Still, I wonder how much of my own foolish pride has been passed down to our son."

It wasn't until his youngest had returned home to them that he had begun to see his own mistakes. For years he had thought himself invincible in his reign as king, that he could do no wrong. Now he knew better. He only hoped that Gabriel didn't have to suffer the cost of his own stubbornness.

"Come, let us pray. Only God is mighty enough to change a man."

Together they bowed their heads, enfolding their hands into one another's. They beseeched God to carry out His will in each of their children, thanking Him for the way He had brought them all together again, and for the promises He had in store for their kingdom. When they finished, King Andrei felt much relieved, he only wished the lingering heaviness upon his heart would lift.

Having made it down to the Great Hall where the ceremony would soon be observed, King Andrei took his place upon the raised dais. Next to him stood Father Griere, lead priest at the chapel positioned near the south most end of the castle. Having taken in the large mass of lords and ladies elegantly dressed and standing ready for the processional to begin, he glanced back towards the men standing across from him.

Gabriel was dressed in the traditional white vest, the silver crown of Brasov upon his head. Andrei could see that his face had also been cleanly shaven by the best man as a symbol of his new life. He wondered if the two brothers were getting along, for he knew the road had been bumpy for them both.

When the orchestra began to strum the opening lines of the age old *fericire de nunta*, he fixed his gaze forward. The first to walk towards them was his own daughter, Elisabeta. Her smile seemed to light up his whole world, so much joy did he feel in seeing her. In her hands were scented petals, tossed upon the threshes as a sign of blessing for the bride's path toward her new husband. He felt a squeeze to his right hand.

"She's breathtaking, isn't she? I do so hope Gabriel will cherish her."

Though Melita's voice was indiscernible to others, he knew exactly what she had said, and he replied by returning the pressure to her hand. He continued watching as his future daughter-in-law navigated the field of foreign faces that dipped like flowers in the wind, bowing in honor of who she would soon become. Beside her was Herr Nuremburg. Andrei furrowed his brow at how pale the man was, and wondered if they might yet have another scene on their hands. But then he imagined how he would feel if it was him heading towards an altar, about to give away his only daughter.

The Lady Katya was friendly of face, and soft in form. Though she was dressed in a traditional Romania *fotă* with long cream sleeves, she had chosen to wear a Germanic veil, making her a picture of two worlds meeting as one. The king was pleased to see that a peaceful look rested upon her. She would need whatever quiet strength she possessed to stand beside his son in the coming days. Indeed, if they knew all that was involved in the intruder's charge, would they posess the fortitude to continue on? To protect the truth of what lay within their kingdom?

I think naught, 'tis best they remain in the dark, he reminded himself. *At least for now.* Once he and Gabriel had seen them through the drudgery of war, then he would share with his son the legacy of their people, and the burden that had grown heavier with every passing year.

As the young woman took to the stairs to stand beside Gabriel, Father Griere led them in the ritual of marriage, speaking blessings in the ancient form of their mother tongue. Only few knew what was being said, but the message resounded clear to all. Man and wife, two becoming one before God Almighty. It was a great mystery that he himself had had the privilege of discovering for the last three and thirty years. As the ceremony concluded, they applauded as Gabriel gave a chaste kiss to his new bride, and then were ushered into the banquet hall for the planned wedding feast.

"It seems they will need time to grow fond of one another."

"You noticed that also? I can't help but think of how we were: mere strangers."

He too remembered their arranged marriage, and how nervous he was the entire day of their wedding. Drawing his queen into a nearby alcove, he quickly pressed a kiss to her lips, loving the way she still responded to his touch.

"But not anymore."

"Nay, and neither will they be estranged for long. The Lord has brought them together, and He will help their love grow, just as He was faithful in growing ours."

She didn't know what she had thought marriage would be like, especially marriage to a prince, but certainly not like this. It had been a week since the haste of their marriage ceremony, and Gabriel had been true to his word in giving her space for their "in name only" relationship. Yet the space he gave her made Katya feel more alone than she ever had within the empty halls of her father's dwelling. Though here at the castle she was constantly surrounded by maid servants, guards, and people of the court, she felt adrift among them.

Moving into the princess' quarters hadn't proved too difficult, in fact the entire transition into her new role was fitting her like a glove. It seemed to be the one thing keeping her from going mad; that and the ever-present company of Elisabeta, who proved to be an anchor in the needless waves of monotony.

"Now, you must pay attention to this bit, for this will be your sole responsibility at my mother's party. As acting hostess of the castle, you will welcome each guest addressing them by their proper title and rank. For the evening, all eyes will be on you I'm afraid. That is, when they aren't on the Queen herself. It is your first event as *prințesă*, you know.

"*Ja*, I am aware. 'Tis my hope to remember my own name, let alone all others."

"You will do splendidly. Never you fear, we will run through the guest list half a dozen times if need be." Adelina's enthusiasm was spoken with exactly the right amount of confidence to make Katya feel more sure of herself.

"What day is this to be?"

"Mamă's birthday is not until the next *Duminică*, but lest she suspect us, we are planning to surprise her the eve of this week's end."

"It is good we are not in Germania then. Many believe celebrating early brings bad luck to a person."

"You don't think Herr Ranald will be offended, do you?"

"Nein, he was never one to be superstitious."

Still, that gave her only four days to learn all one hundred of the guests that would be in attendance, and find a suitable dress for her position as hostess. She wondered whether Gabriel would assist her in her duties. Surely he wouldn't keep his distance from her forever. *'Tis not as if he has been avoiding you. Why, you see him every evening at dinner, and oft times at the midday meal as well. During which you choose to stare at your food, as if it is the most wonderful thing on God's green earth.* Anything to avoid the unenviable silence that shared a seat between them.

Elisabeta did not seem aware of her inner turmoil, for she continued on with her instruction. "Once all have been seated, the traditional toasts will be given by both the King and Prince Gabriel. Then dinner will be served, a special seven course meal with my mother's favorite dishes, and then dancing! During which your sole task will be to flit about, seeing that each guest is well taken care of."

"This, I can do. I remember Mutter doing the very same during the parties she hosted."

She watched as the younger lady then looked over the list in her hand, a piece that stretched on for forever, telling them of the work still left unfinished.

"Now that we have that covered, we must look to garlands and vitals. Adelina dear, will you see to the décor? Then I will check with cook since I know all of Mamă's favorites."

"Certainly. With all the talk of war, I must say I'm surprised we are still able to plan a celebration."

Katya was beginning to dread that word. *War.* It was all anyone ever talked about around here. Knowing it to be a real threat she wisely held her tongue, still she couldn't imagine her whole life being consumed on something that may or may not be inevitable. *Surely if they had a choice they would do anything but, wouldn't they?* What was worse was the coming season, supposed to be held upright with cheer and communal festivity, was now dampened by woe. Only this morning she was standing at the window, taking in the streets that lay outside the palace walls. From her place upon the second floor, the world below looked gloomy, as if a palpable fog hung over the land, a foreshadowed stench of blood, and death, and the loss of countless countrymen.

"Naught will put off this event. I say we party on! The people must see us as beyond the common pale."

"Indeed Elisabeta, we should keep up the morale, lest we all succumb to the depth of pessimism."

"I couldn't agree more. You are both right. Besides the Queen deserves her birthday to be unhindered."

"Oh, I can't wait to see her surprise! It has been years since we were able to pull something off like this. Too often she is on our case and the whole thing comes unraveled."

Katya had to admit she too was looking forward to the party. Though being a hostess would require her absolute attention, she hoped it would give her time to get to know the people better.

The three of them finished their morning tea and excused themselves to complete their small jobs. Katya had planned to be of assistance to Elisabeta and the cook, but she was called away to the sun room for some visitors. When she came into the room, she was pleased to see it was her Aunté Rina and Britta.

"*Mein leibling*! How marriage suits you, why you are absolutely stunning this day."

"Danke, Aunté." Katya blushed even more beneath the weight of the compliment, not because it rang true, but because she didn't want her aunt to know just how inaccurate she was.

"I see you have brought Britta with you. *Guten tag*, cousin."

"Guten tag."

Though she had seen the whole family at the wedding and the customary three days celebration that followed, her aunt was so overjoyed to know that Katya would not be going back to Germany that she had promised to visit often.

"Come, and sit with me here."

She showed them to the lavish sitting area that reclined before the grand glass doors, opening to the south gardens. The room was a soft yellow, giving the space a warm glow with the morning sun shining through behind them. Both doors were left shut to keep out the chill, and fire places on either side of the room offered comfort from the small blaze in their hearths.

"Would you care for some tea?"

"Nein, we have only come for a short visit. We have been in town shopping for gifts. Christmas is soon in coming, you know."

"Yes, it does seem to sneak up on you, and this one most of all. I wonder what it will be like to celebrate here in the castle, with a new family."

Katya looked to the window, her mind juggling the sudden changes that had come with this act of faith, as she was now referring to it.

"Oh, Christmas in the Burg is *wunderbar*! Vater took me and Georg to see the candle lighting ceremony. You should have seen the boughs of red blossoms, and the stringed garland that smelled just like cinnamon."

Britta was positively radiant with excitement as she described to them all the things she had seen.

"My, but that does sound lovely. Mayhap you can come again this year, and enjoy it with me."

The girl looked to her mother for permission, which was given with a simple nod.

"Yes, thank you. I would enjoy that very much. Do you think I can invite my friend Rose? She has never been inside the castle."

"But of course, I would be delighted to meet your friend."

"And how is your father doing, Katya?"

Katya looked into the face of her aunt, sitting closest to her, and saw a look of genuine concern. "In truth, I do not know. He has moved from the castle, and is said to be staying with Herr Wilhelm, another of the dignitaries from Germany. Though he had seemed more at rest during the wedding, and perhaps even a little more relaxed around me, I wonder now if it wasn't just relief he was feeling."

"What do you mean?"

"Well, he had made it seem as though his intentions of coming were for far more than the King. That maybe he was looking to remarry. With me out of the picture, that end will be much easier met."

"Oh, you must not think him so cold, my dear. Have you spoken with him?"

"Nein. I don't know what I would say."

"Surely Gabriel would go with you?"

She shook her head gently. "I am not so sure. He is so busy here and all."

"Then you must pray. God will have an answer."

"Ja, He always does."

Her aunt was right. She needed to take it all to the Lord. In fact, she wondered why she had not sought out the castle's chaplain. Making a mental note to do just that, Katya was almost startled to see her husband glide through the open doors in front of them. How had he known she was here? Was he looking for her, or had someone told him of her guests?

The three ladies stood as he approached, but he quickly put them at ease. "Please, do not rise on my account, I am only sorry to have just come. I was held up by the keeper of the grounds, who had much on his mind for me to hear. Business as usual."

She watched as he offered them an endearing smile, his head leaning in as if to say he would have much rather spent his time with them. *He is certainly charming*, she thought, wondering at the difference in him. Over the course of the next half hour she watched her husband perform, as if he were an actor on the stage.

His company was stimulating, his conversation amusing. He even moved to stand behind her at one point, his hand resting gently on her shoulder as if they were to all the world a couple newly wed. She couldn't help the way her heart began to beat faster in her chest, nor could she restrain the hope that rose within her breast at his attentive nature. Tuning in to what was being said, she noticed that her aunt had just invited them both to dinner.

"I am only too pleased to know that Katya has such good family, and it would be my absolute delight to accompany her to your home in the coming weeks. As is our home open to you and Herr Ranald. Katya's family is, of course, my family now."

She felt his gaze on her head, and looked up to catch his eyes. She wanted to see for herself what he was about. His smile crinkled his lips, their upturned corners pointing like arrows to the depths of his eyes. In his irises, she could see golden streaks woven through fields of brown. It was as if he was giving her a taste of what could be between them, making her heart long to know him better. He returned his gaze to her aunt, and she felt a squeeze at her shoulder.

"Thank you, Your Highness. It is I who am pleased to see Katya here with you. She has always been dear to me, like my very own daughter." Aunté Rina put her arm around Britta, but it was Katya she embraced with her kind eyes.

"I am not want to cut this short, but we must needs be getting home. We wouldn't want our packages to freeze in this weather."

"Not my new gloves! Mutter, come, we must get back." Britta had already jumped up and was tugging at her mother to hurry. Katya smiled at the girl's naiveté, and moved to give them both hugs, before Gabriel assisted them into their coats.

"Come again soon, I love your visits."

"Ja, we will. Guten tag, my dear."

"Guten tag."

She watched them depart, thanking the Lord for the blessing she had found in her aunt. She didn't know why, but she felt she would soon need the other woman's steadfast strength.

"Katya." The sound of her name on his lips drew her to a halt. She had been about to return to her earlier task, unmindful that Gabriel still lingered behind her. Turning, she met his stoic form, and immediately missed the playfulness that had ensued from him just moments ago.

"Ja?"

"In the future, I would like to be notified when you are entertaining guests. Had I not stumbled upon you this morn, your company would have come and gone."

Her brow crinkled in response, for she was uncertain of what he was getting at, though she only had to wait seconds before he revealed all.

"There are certain appearances that need be kept. Though it is no one's concern but our own, I would not have people thinking there is anything amiss between us. You understand?"

"Yes, my lord."

He shifted his stance, making Katya aware of his discomfort, but then he merely nodded his head, as though nothing more need be said.

"Very well, I will see you this eve. May you find enjoyment through the rest of your day."

"The same to you."

He then bowed to her, and left the room, but it was several minutes before she even moved from where she stood. It would seem his charade was not as genuine as it had felt. *He was only keeping appearances. It would have been better if he had not, for now I hope for what I cannot have from him.* Where she wanted companionship, instead it was his pride that kept her company. In truth, she couldn't even say they were friends. Indeed, they were nothing more than perfect strangers.

CHAPTER 5

The first snow fall came to them mid *decembrie.* It swept in silently borne upon clouds of gray that darkened the sky and hid the sun from the earth. Many were overjoyed to see the white flakes fall from the heavens, but not Gabriel. He had merely turned up his coat against the day's chill, and kept on moving. He had been married for a whole month now, but little had changed in his life. His days were clouded with various engagements; his agenda stacked with training, preparation, and the ever-growing number of war council lords who vied for his attention.

This day had kept him more occupied than the rest. It was now well past the midnight hour and he still had yet to see his bed. Rubbing his neck, he trudged down the dimly lit hallway. Though much had been accomplished in the last weeks, their decision was still yet to be decided. *Tomorrow*, he reminded himself, *tomorrow we will have our answer at last.* At least, that is what he hoped for. Turning down the last corridor that would lead him to his bedchamber, he pulled up short, startled to see another form before him. *What is this?*

"Who goes there?"

Surely this intruder knows this to be a private floor? A small shriek met his ears and Gabriel watched as the figure turned toward him, revealing the shocked face of his wife.

He told himself it was the stress of the day that had blinded him from seeing it was her, but a trickle of embarrassment slid down his back all the same. *How does a man not know the form of his own wife? How indeed…* He finished making his way to his own door, passing it only a few steps to stand beside where she was.

"My pardon. What are you doing out this late?

He hadn't meant to sound so abrupt, for he knew he was more cross with himself than with her.

"I was just…that is I could not sleep, Your Highness."

It irked that she continued to call him by his title, but what did he expect from her? *She hardly knows you, and then you nearly frightened her to death, when all she wanted was a repast from the kitchen.* The glass in her hand told him what she was about. Now that his mind had settled, he took her in. She was dressed in her night gown, a pale blue robe pulled tight about her shoulders. She must have come straight from her bed, for her hair was left abandoned to the elements. The wisps around her face seemed to go every which way, and he felt his hand itch to smooth them back from her forehead.

"I'm sorry to have frightened you. I will leave you to your midnight snack. Good eve."

He turned away, but was called back to her side with a gentle, "Gabriel?"

When his eyes met hers, he was surprised by the humor that twinkled there. He supposed this all was rather humorous, and he was pleased that she found it to be so.

"I pray you sleep well this night."

"Thank you, Katya. *Noapte buna.*"

Watching her disappear into her room, the very one that was connected to his own, he wondered again why he did not follow her. In the moment it seemed like second nature to want to join his wife in a blissful sleep, to be comforted by her nearness afore he would go to face the enemy. But instead, he commanded his feet to find their own bed. Returning to his room, he tried to ready himself for the day to come, but all he could think about was the woman who slept only a room away.

In the morning, Gabriel was awakened from his sleep by the sound of Rogen coming to dress him. His eyes were like starch, and he had to fight against the weariness that threatened to pull him back under. For the short while he had slept, he was haunted by dreams of an angel, an angel with a halo of blonde waves, blue eyes, and sweet lips. He had chased after her again and again, but every time he came within reach of her she always seemed to evade him.

"Are you well, Your Highness?"

"Yes, quite."

He lifted himself from beneath the coverlet and the furs, and stood to stretch. His muscles pulled tight against the tension welling up in them. Today he would meet the Dark Lord.

"Shall I fetch your blue or black tunic, my lord?"

"Black, and also my arming doublet. I intend to cut an imposing figure this day, even if it means donning my plate mail."

Though he would be dressed in layers for the weather's sake, he would cover it all with his battle garb.

"Yes, my lord."

By the time he met his brother in the stables, he knew he had chosen well, for Lucian was similarly dressed, his armor reflecting the morning sun, and a full sized blade fastened to his hip.

"Has father yet arrived?"

"Only just. Come let us mount up."

Handing off his helmet to the stable lad who stood near, he leapt atop his horse. Once his helmet was in place he followed Lucian out of the barn. Before them stood a small detachment of armed and well-trained soldiers who would be accompanying them to the field. The King was among them.

Whereas his sons had chosen short waisted cloaks, King Andrei was sheathed in a long damask linen with white fur that stretched behind him like a hero's cape, covering both he and his horse. Across its tail was the Romalo coat of arms, a clear sign of Brasov's sovereignty.

"Let us ride!"

As one they rode passed the northern gate house and beyond the outer wall post. Their herd thundered along the road that would lead them directly toward Tala Hal. A vast and exposed turf where they had sent word for the Dark Lord and his attaché to meet them. Though he often enjoyed a brisk ride, the break neck pace set for them held no thrill this day. Even with the support of the nobles, as well as the proposition of peace that was scrolled neatly within his saddle bag, Gabriel still felt a disquiet within the pit of his stomach.

He wondered at the outcome of what would occur. Would the Dark Lord hear them out? Would he be able to discern the true reasons behind the invasion of their kingdom? Soon the clearing came into his line of vision, and he slowed his mount to match the others around him. Looking about, his eyes searched for signs of their opposition.

"Look there, it is the Count." His brother had sidled up alongside of him and spoke in low tones, drawing Gabriel's attention to the small troop that drew nearer.

"He is the man with the hat?"

"*Da*, I have never known him to be without one. Though he wears them in all shapes and colors. Which do you suppose is our infamous Dark Lord?"

Sharing his sense of incredulity, Gabriel disentangled his eyes from the garish man and took in the others. The men who come with the count looked like no more than ruffians, a scourge of black coats against a backdrop of white. Instantly he was reminded of the men who were once led by his own brother. Their scarred faces certainly held malice, but he could not detect the sort of cunning that he knew would be in the eyes of their leader.

"I see none who fit his description."

"You think he will not come?"

"It would seem that way. I suppose we are left to negotiate with his *marionetă*."

"A shame. I would know the face of the man who causes our land such strife."

He nodded his head in agreement. Though Gabriel kept his emotions in check, internally he was raging. *Blast the infernal man, that he would not show his face this day! A thousand curses upon his head!*

"Laissez-nous procéder."

They were now close enough to hear the projected voice of Count Denla Quóis, though their horses were still ten yard lengths apart. He sought to unclench his fisted hands when he felt the nervous energy of the beast beneath him. His mount's hooves danced a pattern in the icy slush. The animal was trained for combat and would easily charge if Gabriel gave but the smallest signal.

A blazing hatred for the men who would ravage his land stole its way up his chest, but he forced it back down with a learned sense of self control. He then saw the King move to meet the Count at the halfway point, their two animals sloshing through the thickened snow until they came muzzle to muzzle. Waiting only until his father motioned him forward, Gabriel spurred his own steed on. With a twisted grin, the count addressed them in a heavily accented speech.

"You have come to beg mercy of us, *oui*?"

The king did not rise to the bait, stating only, "We know naught from whence you hail, nor why you have come here."

"The Dark Lord needs no reason to conquer." Though the words were said with an even tone, the count's gaze moved beyond them to where Gabriel knew he had sought out Lucian, his eyes full of revenge.

"That matters not. We seek only peace for our land, and protection for our people. Here are our terms."

Gabriel drew the parchment from his bag and extended his hand to the other man. The count swiped the document from him, unrolled it long enough to glance over the words written there, and then let it furl back up.

"I will take such terms to the Dark Lord, *Monsieur*, but know this, the price you will pay for peace will cost you much more than what it will take for you to surrender."

Again, Gabriel watched as his father held his tongue, making him wonder at the older man's thoughts. Count Denla Quóis' eyes narrowed with the rebuff, having clearly expected some sort of response. It seemed his father had been wise in not giving the man any sort of excuse to carry out a fight right then and there.

"We will expect your reply by winter's end." The king paused, his tone taking on a dark note that made even Gabriel tense. "If none is given hence, the first bleat of a christened lamb, the first melting of a frozen stream, and our armies will return to this field, where your men will taste death at the tips of our sharpened blades."

And with that they turned their horses and left. Though all seemed to go well, Gabriel still had the nagging feeling that they weren't out of the woods yet. Even if their enemy agreed to their terms, what would he enact in return?

The dark figure returned to his tent, where he did not have to hide his licentiousness. Moving to the short table in the center of the room, he withdrew the ash bag from within the folds of his black coverings, and began to spread them out in the shape of the hex. Once the circle took its form, he placed the scroll given him by the count in its middle. Striking a match against the wooden surface, the man set flame to the papery texture. He hadn't bothered to read its contents. The article shriveled up before him, until it was nothing but charred remains, its message eaten away by a thick smoke. He breathed in the fumes, and barked a laugh before closing his eyes.

Wordless chants drew forth from his lips, as he called down curses upon his enemies. Feeling the heavy presence of the spirits, he opened his mind and let them come in to him.

The Count is soft. He must not be trusted. The voices mingled and mixed with his own thoughts. *Kill the Count.*

"No, I have need of him yet."

Though the count was a senseless jester, a mere puppet in his plot against the kingdom of Brasov, he could prove a useful tool. He felt himself be pulled back into the darkness, his body shuddering against the force of it. *He only wants revenge.* We *want total destruction.*

"If it weren't for the woman he kept..."

Take her for yourself. Use her for your own advantage, then kill them both.

"She *is* rather attractive."

The Dark Lord, or Helel, as his mother had named him, toyed with the idea set before him. He envisioned the count's woman, her dark red hair and brown eyes. She was slender, and full bodied. On her he would be able to breed a son. An heir to the land he had conquered, to the wealth he had stored up. But a son would need his mother, and to bring her in would be to trust another human. Something he could never bring himself to do.

"No, I will let her be, let them both be for now."

Withdrawing from the table, he opened up his coat and untied the strings from the woolen brace. Once they were made loose, he hastened to a nearby stool, his breath hissing through his teeth. Pain immediately choked him. With the aching flooding him like a rushing river, he could no longer hold back the dam, and so came the surge of memories.

He remembered his own mother. Her garish face, and soulless eyes. Though she had always been a weak sort of woman, hunched over as she was, she had been the only thing good in his life. The two of them were outcasts because of her crippled state. Everywhere they went people shunned them, spit on them, as if they were no better than dogs. *It's all* his *fault. He is to blame for having left us so destitute.* But the Dark Lord had taken care of that.

He still recalled the feel of the other man's life draining away from his body, beneath the strangle of his fingers clenching his neck; the look of shock on his face in seeing his only son again. Helel had only been ten and four at the time, and yet it hadn't been hard to find the worthless coward. His notorious drunkenness making his trail easy to follow. *Good riddance*, he thought, feeling a sort of powerful pleasure at the reminiscence.

It wasn't until mother had learned the way of the dark arts that people's rejection soon turned to fear. And with fear came respect, and respect, reverence. Since then they had been able to travel far and wide, healing people's sickness with homemade potions. Those who did not bring gifts to her, she had cast curses upon, only lifting them when they finally capitulated to her wishes.

His mother had been the only daughter of a nobleman who had died when she was a child. Before she had become sickly. She had brought Helel to this land once, when he was very young. She had Romanian in her blood and sought to be reunited with her own people, but even they had cast them out. In every new town they set up shop, she had reminded him of her people's rejection;

swearing to him that one day she would take her vengeance. As fate would have it, his mother had died before she ever got that chance.

Now he was left to carry out her wishes. It sickened him to hear of the Romanian people's good fortune. From every town he had subdued in the last few years, he had been met by the tales of the nation of Brasov. It was said that their king was of good nature, the nation having giving itself over to the Christian faith a few generations passed. Where he covered the land in darkness, they exuded light.

"How I would kill to snuff out every last flicker of life from their bright little souls."

The Dark Lord rubbed at the sores that spread across his neck. It would seem his mother's hatred wasn't the only thing she had left for him. Only years after she had passed had he begun to notice the signs of her sickness flowing through his own veins. Soon he too would be completely hunched over, and before he was ready, death would claim his ravished body. Having remembered the ingredients his mother had used, he had been making his own form of the elixirs for some time, but even they aided him only so much. He needed something more powerful.

Let us help you. The voices beckoned to him. He knew that to accept their healing would cost him greatly, but at this point he felt he had no other choice. He needed to see the kingdom of Brasov at its knees before him. To know that his mother's vengeance had been fully carried out. *We can give you what you want. We can see them pay for what your mother suffered.* When they called to him this time, he gave himself over completely.

The day of his mother's celebration of birth had come at last, and at no better time. Having heard no response from the count,

Gabriel felt bowed beneath the weight of his own anxiety. Only a week had passed, but still Gabriel wondered if their offered treaty had yet reached the Dark Lord. *Perhaps this party will do us all some good*, he thought wistfully.

Though winter often lasted well into the month of *Martie*, he knew that his father would not wait so long. If confirmation was not given before then, he feared the coming year would be tainted with the march of their troops upon the frozen field. Speaking of troops, he knew he was expected at the training grounds before the midday meal, so he hurried his steps to find his sister. It seemed she was of a similar mind.

"There you are Gabriel! I have been looking for you all over."

He hadn't even made it to the central staircase, and she was there waiting for him with an impudent grin that endeared her to them all.

"Forgive me dear sister, I was caught up. How can I be of assistance?"

"Well, for starters you can assure me that you will keep mother otherwise engaged until we have all the guests in the banquet hall?"

"That will not take much effort, as you are not the only one who has been remiss of my company, I'm sure there is much we have to catch up on, and she will be delighted to have me all to herself for the afternoon. There is something else, yes?"

"*Da*…there is one other thing. 'Tis only that she seems so nervous, though I'm sure she is very much up to the task. Perhaps if you were to check on her…"

"Speak sister! Only do not prattle on so, you need only ask."

"Right, then do check in on your lady wife this day, Gabriel. She is wanting of your affirmation. What is it grandmother always said? 'A kind word is a raven's company?' Whatever that means."

She laughed and patted his shoulder as she moved ahead of him and down the stairs.

"Katya is hosting this eve, then?"

"But of course. She will one day be the lady of this castle. Is that not why you wed her?"

The look she threw him was more befitting of a scolding mother. It would seem that not all were fooled by his charade of an adoring husband. He should have known Elisabeta would have found him out. His sister had a way of seeing into the hearts of people. She was not merely beautiful, she was cunning, and that set her apart from all the rest.

"I will see to it immediately. You have my word, I will put her fears to rest."

At least in this he could be truly useful.

"Oh, I am so glad! Thank you, Gabriel."

Mayhap he was an abject leader, and a pitiful husband, but when he saw her young face light up with joy, he knew that somehow he had not failed altogether.

"For you, sister dear, anything."

He stopped at the steps' bottom to press a quick kiss to her head, before moving off to fulfill her wish. Though it had seemed an easy enough task, he found himself somewhat nervous when he went in search of his wife. Having been detained so often, he had easily allowed the full schedule of his days to keep him from making any effort at getting to know Katya. Indeed, they were no closer than they had been on the day of their wedding- though it was now several weeks behind them.

"Indeed, what comfort have I to offer?" He said the words to no one at all. His feet unsure of where to turn, now that he had made it to the first floor solar.

"Talking to yourself, my lord? Or perhaps you were offering up a prayer. If so, I shall not disturb."

Had he not felt the tingle of awareness at his back, he would have jumped at her voice directly behind him.

"Not at all. In fact, I was looking for you."

"You were?"

Her words held an edge of surprise, and though he couldn't blame her, the small bit of yearning that colored her face made him stammer with his well-formed reply.

"Um, yes. That is, tonight is sure to be a grand occasion, with many guests in attendance."

"Oh, I see. You needn't worry, Your Highness, I have been formally educated as to all my duties. I know what is expected of me, and I will perform each task as if it were for my own mother."

With this she looked away from him, raising her chin and clasping her hands in front of her bodice. It would seem his lady wife had a bit of fire to her. He liked that, and he knew it would be a necessary trait when faced with countless people of the realm.

"I am confident of this very thing. I am sure you will do splendidly."

"Oh?"

Her shoulders relaxed the tiniest bit, as her eyes peeked back at him.

"Katya, I have come to offer my assistance to you this eve. I wanted only to wish you well, and though you are certainly capable of all the duties you will perform, should you have need of me, I will be close to your side."

The vote of assurance seemed to do the trick, for he watched as she softened completely before him. *What a wonder this woman is! All at once soft and yet firm. Strong and yet sweet.* He couldn't help the genuine smile that tugged at his lips.

"Thank you, Gabriel. I admit I have been fretting, if only for your mother's sake. She is deserving of the very best."

"Indeed, but as you will come to find, she is very easy to please."

"And you? Are you easy to please Gabriel?"

He felt a discernable shift in the conversation, one that he was not yet willing to indulge.

"Unfortunately, no. Well, I am sure you have much to make ready. I myself am headed to the courtyard. I bid you good day."

Evading her further, he adjusted his route to take him the long way round; lest they cross paths again on his way back through the inner bailey. Once he caught sight of Lucian and the ten score of men with him, he removed his outer vest, draping it over a nearby post.

"Come to join us at last?"

"Only to give you a well met match, brother. Surely you tire of these men? Some of them are still wet behind the ears!"

A company of outraged cries surrounded them. Gabriel laughed sharply, filling his lungs with the bitter cold air. It felt good to be outdoors, undeterred by entrapping meetings. The walls of the castle had confined him for far too long. Out here he was just a man, not a prince, not even a leader. He was just flesh and bone like the rest of them. Here in this circle of dirt there were no dignitaries to appease, no war strategies to memorize, and no image to uphold. There was only the feel of the sword in his hand. The lure of victory over his opponent.

"Let us begin."

The two of them sparred for over an hour, until they dripped with sweat and their arms became heavy. Finally, Lucian pulled back, flinging his sword toward the ground where it stuck straight into the frozen soil.

"Have you had enough then?"

"You are a worthy opponent Gabriel, and you fight with a ferocity. But there are other things I must attend to. Another time perhaps?"

"You may regret your offer when I have bested you more than just once."

Laying down his own weapon, he moved to scoop up his leather vest. The temperature had dropped immensely as the afternoon sun warned him of the late hour.

"It seems I too have places to be. You have trained these men well, brother."

"I thank you."

"Do not delay overly long here, our sister's temper cuts just as quick as these blades, and methinks she will not hesitate to flay you should you be late to the gathering this evening."

Lucian raised both his hands in surrender, his face splitting into a large grin. "I have not forgotten so easily, and I will well heed your words."

After returning to his quarters to wash and dress for the evening, Gabriel followed through with his plans to commandeer his mother's afternoon. Just as he had suspected she was more than pleased to receive a visit from him, and easily accepted his excuses of his day's meetings being cut short. When it came time for their evening to begin, Gabriel followed his parents to the reception hall, and watched as his mother's face lit with surprise at the unexpected additions to their dinner.

"Why Andrei, what is this?"

"*La multi ani*, my dear."

"But my birthday isn't until next week."

The king pressed a soft kiss to the queen's cheek, as her three children stepped forward to embrace her.

"Are you very surprised, Mamă?" Elisabeta fairly bursted with triumph.

"Oh yes, I couldn't have imagined anything more wonderful!"

Gabriel offered his mother a kiss of his own before going to stand beside his wife. Katya stood regally at the entrance, greeting each guest as they entered. Dressed as she was in a deep topaz gown against skin as white as snow, he had to admit she looked the part of a future queen.

He leaned in to tell her she looked beautiful, but the words were stiff on his tongue, so instead he settled for a pleasantry. "How are you faring, dear Katya?"

"Well, Your Highness. It would seem I have been able to remember each of the dignitaries present and their families."

Her smile wasn't the least bit smug, only content. It seemed to please her to have done well, not for her own sake, but for the sake of those she was aiding, and though he knew it was not expected of him, he lingered at her side. Somehow her gentle presence stretched wide enough to envelop him, and he too felt at peace being near her.

The evening passed rather effortlessly. All the guests were handpicked, and among them were the queen's closest friends and family. Even Adelina's parents were in attendance, as Gabriel remembered that Adelina's mother was a childhood friend of the queen. Towards the end of the night the crowd slowly dispersed, many of the families making their way outdoors to the central garden, where they would bless the Queen with good wishes. It was said that should they see a shooting star, the recipient of the wishes would be blessed with many years of good fortune.

Gabriel's favorite tradition was yet to be carried out, but he knew it was soon in coming. Looking into the faces of those who surrounded him, and seeing their joy, he was glad he hadn't canceled the party. Even in the midst of turmoil the castle was meant to be a beacon of hope, just as it was this evening, as the nation gathered to celebrate their loving Queen.

Though not all were invited, Gabriel knew that many more filled the streets this night to sing out their good tidings. The palace garden was so well lit by candles and lanterns that it didn't take him long at all to see the gypsy children who were standing by the south gate. His heart leapt in excitement. This was what he had been waiting for. He nodded to the guard who was posted there, and stepped back to let in the flood of small feet. Turning to follow their progress, he caught sight of Katya, and wondered at her expression. Her eyes were wide, and her brow was knit as if in disdain. Was she displeased?

He looked again at the scruffy children who now approached the queen, their young voices singing out the traditional Romanian tune. Many of them were poor, the poorest of the land, but Gabriel had always had a soft spot for the *Romani* people. It would seem Katya did not. Immediately his thoughts became shrewd. *She is just like all the others, haughty and vain. Perhaps she is even repulsed to have to host them as well.*

In other nations the *Romani* lived as slaves, but here they were free. Free to live out their faith unhindered. When their beautiful song concluded they reached out their hands for the customary treat, but there was no *savarina* to be offered.

"Lady Katya?"

Her face was a frozen mask. Immediately he was filled with anger. *Does she dare shun at them?*

"Come children, I'm sure cook has prepared you something sweet in the kitchen. Shall we go and see?"

Fuming, Gabriel watched as his mother stepped in and escorted the small group of child performers indoors. Already the crowd was shrinking as people headed home for their beds. He knew the hour was late, and he himself was ready for slumber, but it nagged him that she had been so dismissive.

"Tell me, why did you not have any *savarina* for them?"

"I didn't know."

He searched her face while she spoke.

"That is, Elisabeta, she didn't tell me…I'm sorry Gabriel. Please, I must go and make amends with the Queen."

Ei mea! Her strained voice was proof enough. *How could I be such a fool? I judged her as arrogant, when instead she was simply ignorant of our people's customs.*

"Go then."

He waved her away, too trapped by his own discomfiture to say anything more. Sometimes he forgot that they were from very different worlds. She could not have known their ways. *Nu, if anyone is to blame it is I. I have too long neglected my role in teaching her about our people.* Again he was reminded of how little he knew his wife. *The fault is your own. If you merely took the time to know her, she would come readily to you.* A tempting thought indeed, but he dismissed it. There was still too much for him to do. He simply didn't have time to be a husband. *Maybe if there is peace,* he thought wistfully. Maybe.

CHAPTER 6

Katya looked up to catch the light that streamed in through the colored window panes. Each piece was an array of texture, and together they masterfully composed the portrait of the Lord and His disciples. Behind where the altar stood full of candles still lit from the Christmas service two days passed, stood a cross that held the stone image of their risen Lord. Kneeling down on the small cushioned stool that had been placed before her, she bowed her head. *Mine Lord, I thank Thee for the birth of thy son, and for the peace He has brought into the world through His sacrifice. May this day bring honor to Thy name, and may this nation continue to walk in Thine ways.*

As her prayers continued, coming as easily as the breath that pushed past her lips she thanked Him for all of her blessings, and for the wonderful holiday she had spent with her new family. Christmas at the castle had been a joyous treat, filled with the warmth of familial love. Together they had shared the traditional morning *gustare*, made of the most scrumptious Romanian dishes, caroled among the townspeople who congregated in the square, and exchanged gifts. She had been surprised to receive one from Gabriel, a beautifully carved comb with a silver engraved hand mirror, but even more astonishing was his reception of her gift.

It was a handcrafted dagger that her aunt had brought to her attention in the *marketplatz*. From Gabriel's reaction, one would have thought she had bought him the moon. Though she remained wary of his congenial treatment of her in public, the heartfelt embrace was one she would cherish.

She had even received a visit from her father during the holiday week. At first, she had feared his presence would somehow darken the occasion, but she was relieved to see him again. He had looked peaceful, if only for the season's cheer. Neither of them mentioned his relationship with Frau Schüller, and Katya was glad. She didn't think she was ready to hear about it. Overall the time with him had been welcome, even Gabriel had managed to be cordial, though she knew he was still leery of the man. Turning her thoughts back to the Lord, she finished her prayers.

And thank you Father, for the husband you have given me. May this New Year bring us closer together, and may we seek to honor you in our marriage. Amen.

Standing quietly, she made her way to the front, where she lit a candle and received communion from the friar who stood waiting. Once outside the chapel she sat on the stone bench only until she saw the Queen exit behind her.

"How were your prayers this morning, my dear?"

"Very peaceful, Your Majesty. This season has been a blessed one of the Lord."

"Indeed, it has."

"I was only sorry to not see Gabriel; does he attend at a latter hour?"

The Queen paused in her walking, withdrawing her hand from the folds of her winter cloak. When her gloved hand rested upon Katya's shoulder, she looked to see sad eyes returning her gaze.

"Though he dares not be absent for the holy day services, it pains me to say that Gabriel no longer makes a habit of attending the chapel otherwise."

How like him to be there only when others would note his presence, so as to keep up a good appearance. *You must not be so hard on him*, she chided herself. *Perhaps he has fair reason for staying away.*

"Then I will continue to pray for him. In this, God Himself is the only answer."

"You are wise beyond your years, my *fiică*."

To hear the Queen call her daughter, did wonders to Katya's disposition. She felt so accepted here among the royal family. By everyone but her husband. *But that too may change*, she added encouragingly, *I must only believe.*

"Thank you, Queen Melita."

The Queen lifted her hand gently. "Please you must call me Mamă, at least when we are alone."

"Yes Mamă." Katya smiled, her heart expanding tenfold. "In truth, I have not always felt I was able to rely upon the Lord for the seemingly hopeless matters in my life, but I am learning that He hears me when I call, and that He is a good Father."

"To me even more so, since I have laid my own father to rest. Though my husband, the King, has become my right arm in many things, it is the Lord alone who gives drink to my thirsty soul."

They resumed walking, their even breaths filling the air before them with a vapor that could be seen in the morning chill. Seeing as how the chapel was on the south side of the castle, they were awarded a few minutes to themselves before they were met by the large oak doors of the main entrance. Katya couldn't have imagined being so surrounded by such loving and caring people.

Was it only months ago that she sat alone in her father's home, wishing for all the world that she had a friend?

"Blessed indeed." She whispered to herself, now that she had parted ways with the Queen at the main staircase. Having returned herself to the small sitting room that joined her bedchamber with Gabriel's, Katya decided to continue her time with the Lord. Pulling out her Bible from the small chest at the foot of the settee, she opened its cover slowly, her fingers grazing over the inscription written in her mother's hand.

To my darling Katya,

May the Lord be your lamp in both hard times and good; His grace shining before you to keep your feet steady. Know that I love you with all my heart, and that I pray for you each and every day. Be strong, mine tochter.

Love always,

Your, Mutter.

Though she had read it a dozen times, the words never failed to pierce her heart. *Oh Mutter, if you could see me now, you would be so pleased to know I am loved.* Instantly her thoughts went to Gabriel, and the impersonal marriage they shared. Would her mother be disappointed in her? *Nein, she would only say that God worked in mysterious ways, and perhaps this too was a part of His plan.* She smiled at that, and then turned to the book of John, picking up where the ribbon mark had last been left.

When she swept into the study, her eyes determined, and her chin set, Gabriel knew he would have to yield to whatever she had on her mind.

"Mamă, what brings you here this morn?"

Queen Melita continued forward, until only his desk separated them, and looked him full in the face. His mother could be a fearsome woman when she had it in mind to be.

"Gabriel, I demand to know why you go on neglecting your bride."

"What do you mean?"

Neglect was such a strong word. Why, she made it seem as though he were no better than her father who had left her alone to be raised by a governess.

"Need I remind you that you are newly wed, my son?"

"Of course you do not." He didn't like where this was headed, and though he longed to rub his temples from the growing ache, he kept himself still.

"Why then do I see your bride wandering the halls of our *castelle* alone, with no husband on her arm?"

"I have been busy, as you know. That is not to say I am excusing myself from what you deem as neglect, but nor have I had the privilege to act the part of bridegroom as others may."

"War or no war, she is your responsibility too."

He sighed deeply, shifting uncomfortably at how right his mother was. What did he think? That he could go on pretending as if she were no more than a chess piece upon the board of war strategy? *Nu, she is more than that*, he reckoned, *if only it wasn't all happening at the same time.*

"Yes mother, you are gracious to remind me of my duties." He suddenly felt so overwhelmed by it all. "Country, kingdom, crown, and now wife, I bear each of these upon my shoulders, but I am only one man. How will I go on?"

When he saw the forming tears in his mother's eyes he knew he had spoken the words aloud. He stood and lifted a hand to ward off her sympathy.

"No, do not worry over me Mamă. I will do as you say. I will go now and find my lady wife."

He turned quickly and exited the room, not wanting to give in to the silent urge to be wrapped in the warm embrace of his mother, like he had so many times when he was a boy. *But I am a boy no longer. I am soon to be king, and therefore must learn to shoulder the obligations of my position. What's more, I am a husband.* With each step he took in pursuit of his bride, he determined to make things right between them. No longer would it be said that he neglected his wife. From now on, yes even in this, he would do what was required of him. He would be the better man.

Of course, he hadn't thought finding her would be so difficult. It only piqued him further to be reminded that he knew so little of his wife. Where did she go to avoid the morning's chill? What did she do to pass the afternoon? When she hadn't turned up at the stables, and couldn't be found in the solar, Gabriel decided to retrace his steps to her bedchamber, hoping that her lady's maid would have an inkling as to where her mistress spent her time.

He knocked once, and then entered. Clearing his throat loudly in hopes that someone would be in attendance.

An older woman peeked her head around the door of the wardrobe, unused to seeing the prince.

"What is your name?"

"Florin, Your Highness." She bobbed quickly, her head not coming up until he spoke.

"And where might I find your lady this day, Florin?"

"She was only just here, my lord. But 'as gone to the library saying she wanted to find a book she once read."

The library. It was the very place he would have been this morning had he not been called away.

"Thank you, Florin."

"Yes, Your Highness."

Wasting no time, he made his way down the staircase and unto the library. The door was left open, beckoning him in further. It took him no more than a few seconds to place his wife, for she was seated in the chair nearest the fireplace. The very one he often took when he was afforded the leisure of reading.

"Lady Katya."

Her head lifted above the pages of the book in response to hearing her name, but she was very clearly surprised to see that it was he who had called out to her.

"Your Highness, I did not know you were looking for me."

He stepped nearer, and crouched down before her.

"Am I to be Your Highness forever, dear Katya?"

Her eyes went wide at the sound of his lowered voice, and he couldn't help but smile when she inched away from him.

"Of course not. My pardon, Gabriel."

Perhaps his mother was right, perhaps he had been neglecting her. If this scene were played out by Lucian and his wife, Adelina would have thrown her arms about Lucian's neck, drawing him close enough for a kiss. He knew, for he had seen it a dozen times, but of course he was not like his brother. *And she is certainly nothing like Adelina;* he waited for a sense of resentment to come, but none did. In fact, he found that it mattered little that her eyes were blue, not green, and her hair was golden rather than amber.

"What book have you chosen from these shelves?"

She looked hesitant, and very unsure of herself, but then she lifted the novel from her lap.

"I was only rereading the words of St. Augustine. His collection of studies on the book of John fascinate me."

Seeing her here in the library, a place that had often been a solace to him over the years, brought him quiet joy. Even more so, when he learned she was an avid reader. Mayhap even a blooming scholar. This tiny bit of her character revealed fascinated him, making his next question so much easier to offer.

"I find I know so little about you, Katya. Could I persuade you to go for a ride?"

Being this close to her he was able to watch the change in her irises as she contemplated an answer, the quiver in her lower lip that she bit down on, in what he presumed was an unintentional habit, and the stilted breath that exposed how affected she was by his nearness.

"I would enjoy an outing very much. I haven't been to the stables since my arrival."

Her honesty was refreshing. Other ladies would have played coy, trying to exact a persistence from him. Gabriel stood, backing away a couple of steps so that he could see her in full view.

"Then it is a fitting first outing for us. Shall I meet you there in say, twenty minutes? Will that give you enough time to change?"

"Yes, that will be time enough. I'm glad to have brought my better riding habit with me. I had so much trouble choosing what to pack. Vater only allowed me two trunks so that we would travel lightly."

He paused in his retreat. "Do you mean you are operating from a partial wardrobe?"

She too seemed to hesitate, and he wondered if she was gauging his mood.

"I have yet to run out of things to wear, Gabriel. But yes, most of my things stayed behind in Germana, where I would have returned had plans not…changed."

He thought about this for a moment. Plans certainly had changed, but they need not exist as though it was a temporary arrangement. At the present moment, he was not sure when she would be returning, if, she would be returning to Germana at all.

"That will not do at all. We will send for the remainder of your things, and I will speak with Mamă about having a seamstress come and fill in what is missing from your wardrobe."

"It is not necessary…"

He cut her off, more than a little disturbed at the severity to which she had been overlooked.

"Nonsense, madam. Every bride has a trousseau, do they not? And as the future queen, you are more than deserving."

Before she could speak further, he left the library. After giving word to his mother about the need for a proper dressmaker, and seeing to it that a missive was sent to Herr Nuremburg about having his daughter's things fetched from their estate, Gabriel went to make himself ready. Though her articles would not reach them for some time, he would see to it that she was wanting of nothing while they waited. As always, Rogen was waiting for him with his riding pants, and a fresh tunic. He must have caught wind of the prince's change of plans from Florin, who was sure to be dressing his wife.

"Your efficiency is very appreciated, Rogen. I do wonder how you manage to keep one step ahead of me."

"I have my ways, Your Highness. Besides, I find you have enough on your plate these days without havin' to bother with keeping me straight."

"You are right. At times I find myself wearing so many different faces, that I fear I don't rightly know which is the real me."

Gabriel looked up to see Rogen peering at him sideways. The man seemed as startled as he was. Indeed he didn't even know where such a thought had come from, for he hadn't felt that way before. *It must be the threat of war. That is all.* Waving Rogen away, Gabriel finished dressing on his own, anxious to be away from the window of transparency he had opened.

"That will be all for now."

"Yes, my lord."

Rogen bowed his way out, and just like that, they were back to master and servant. *Just as it should be.* Meeting Katya down by the stables, Gabriel showed her to the horse he had picked out.

"I was unsure how well you ride, so if you find her not to your liking, you may request another for next time."

He hoped he didn't sound too hesitant when he said next time. *Surely, if all goes well, we will spend more time together.*

"Vater has a couple of horses on his estate, but I was rarely ever allowed to ride them. In troth, most of my experience with these creatures comes from the summers I spent here when I was just a girl."

"That does not surprise me. I know how fond Elisabeta is of riding, and as much of your time was spent with her, you probably had your summer's worth of the outdoors. I am only sorry today is overcast. The view will not be anywhere near as grandiose."

"Oh, you mustn't say that. Romania is a beautiful country, no matter its season."

"As you say. I always thought winter had an appeal. With all covered in snow, as if it were all being washed white like a blank canvas for the coming spring."

She smiled brightly, and he moved to help her atop her horse, before mounting his own. Together they rode across the back pasture that stretched along the Gorganu River. As they moved south the land slowly climbed upwards, leaving the river behind them in the bed of the valley.

"So tell me, how are you adjusting to life within the citadel?"

He patted the neck of his dapple gray gelding. The horse sat him two hands higher than Katya's mare, giving him a perfect view of her profile.

"Being here has given me a renewed sense of purpose. That isn't to say that it has been easy, for challenges are to be expected, but I feel up to the task. When I think of how empty my life was back home compared to how full it is now…well I'm thankful that the Lord has blessed me so."

Not wanting to begin a religious debate, he neatly steered them away from anything to do with the Lord. He knew she attended Mass as often as his mother did, but he certainly didn't feel the need to share about his own faith, or lack thereof. He felt taxed enough as it was, having opened up a bit to Rogen. *Not that much was revealed anyhow, and besides the man isn't one to prattle on to others. No indeed, your secrets are still your own.*

"I'm pleased to hear it. Might I ask what fills your days?"

She seemed pleased to share with him, filling him in on her daily tasks, and weekly gatherings with his mother. He mentally took note of each thing she said, determined to know her better. Soon his mother would see that he was no longer shirking his duty, in this too he would prove excellence. Her conversation carried them all the way to the neat meadow that was tucked between two clusters of trees.

"We can rest for a bit just up here. I had the *bucătar* put together some lunch. From the way it smells, I would say she packed us a feast. Are you hungry?"

He could tell she was about to answer him when her stomach rumbled. Though she seemed embarrassed, he could only laugh.

"Come, let us feed you before you scare away the animals with your thunder."

She smiled herself, and seemed to relax at his jest, though they both knew no animals would be found in the middle of winter. After helping her to the ground, he retrieved the simple basket and rug from his horse's saddle bag, handing the basket to her as he laid out the mat. Once seated, she pulled from the sack cabbage rolls, smoked jumari, fresh grapes, and a warm biscuit for them each.

"Mmmm. This is a feast indeed. I will have to thank your cook when we return. I don't believe I've had the chance to meet her as of yet, and I would so love to become better acquainted with all who help the castle to run."

"Why do you say that?"

"I believe it is important to know those I will be working with. One day I will be their mistress, and not only will they be my staff, they will be my people. I truly want to be a good queen."

He knew she would. Though he was still learning about her as a person, he knew this was true. Aside from the minor lapse with the pastries for the children, Katya had performed famously at his mother's banquet. More than a few people had made comment to him about her elegance that night. He hoped that they had also shared it with her. But what if they hadn't? *You could always tell her. She would probably receive it well if it came from you.* Before he could analyze that thought, he jumped in.

"You already make a *prinţesă magnifica*. Being queen will suit you."

She blushed and ducked her head. Glad to have complimented her, Gabriel reached down for something to eat. He took a bite out of the cabbage roll she had set before him, his mouth warming at the taste of bitter herb and jelly. When he looked up, it was to find her gazing at him, a grape left forgotten in her hand.

"Gabriel, I want to thank you for inviting me to come with you."

"I'm sorry it took me so long to do so. Am I suitable company then? Perhaps not as fun as Elisabeta, but..."

She laughed with him, and he settled further onto the blanket, eager to hear how she would respond.

"You are more charming than you give yourself credit for, my lord. I'm sure not even Elisabeta could have wrangled such fineries

She beamed at him. “I am glad. It will help if my aunt sees that we are not adverse to one another.”

“Your aunt? Will she be coming for a visit again?”

He had bent to sweep up the mat, and now wrapped it into a ball so that it would better fit in his horse’s saddle bag.

“Do you not recall? We are expected at her residence tomorrow evening in fact.”

Katya watched as his brows furrowed, his mind trying to recall his earlier agreement to attend the family gathering with her.

“Ah, you are right. Forgive me, I do intend to escort you. Tomorrow you say? When are we to return?”

“I believe it is just for the week’s end. We are to celebrate the New Year with them. If needed we can return on *Montag*.”

He only nodded. Seeing the conversation over, she moved toward her mount, accepting his gentle hand up. Neither one spoke much on the return ride, Gabriel only pointing out a pair of red stags trotting across the meadow below them. When the stables crept into view, Katya had the distinct urge to turn her horse around and retreat back to their spot, as she would now remember it. Would he too retreat? Returning to his former, frosty self? *Only time will tell,* she thought to herself glumly.

“It would seem as though they have started without me after all.”

She looked to where the men had gathered in the far field just beyond them. Unhooking her leg from its sidesaddle, she dropped to the ground and handed her horse to a nearby stable boy.

“I hope you are not overly disappointed.”

“Not at all. But I must be off. We wouldn’t want any of them to suppose I wasn’t taking the training as seriously as they, would we?”

She smiled at his jest. “Certainly not.”

“Until tomorrow then.”

"Yes, tomorrow."

She watched him until he disappeared around the wooden stall. Turning back to gather their things, she noticed that in his rush he had forgotten his jacket. Rather than run after him, she decided to simply return it to his room. *'Tis unlikely he will be needing it for training*, she justified. In any event, it seemed a rather wifely thing to do. Directly after she returned the basket to Tusta with much praise over their generous meal, she made her way to her own quarters with the intention to do just that.

"How was your ride, my lady?" The ever-vigilant Florin had met her at the door. Having anticipated her need for a warm bath after her time in the winter's air, her lady's maid helped her out of her soiled habit and into the ready tub.

"It was wonderful, Florin, and I thank you for this. You are such a dear blessing to me."

Sinking down into the pool of steam that rose from the water's surface, she let out a contended sigh.

"No trouble at all. 'Tis my pleasure to serve you, Your Highness. Shall I put these away for you?"

Katya glanced to where she had deposited Gabriel's jacket. "*Nein*. I will see to it when I'm finished here."

"Yes, my lady."

With the room all to herself, she retraced her steps until she was back in the *lea* with Gabriel. Playing the scene over and over again, she committed each word, each look to memory. The way his eyes crinkled when he laughed, the smile that was so rarely seen, she had wanted to steal it from his lips and tuck it into the folds of her heart.

"Oh, but I love him…" Her whole body stilled beneath the blanket of liquid affection that poured over her.

How could this be? Love doesn't happen as fast as that. Indeed it takes time, years even, to grow from shared affection to something akin to what my parents had shared. Some couples don't ever find love in their marriage, especially marriages of mutual interest like ours, she reminded herself firmly. Isn't that what this was after all? Gabriel had sought her hand to confirm his claim on the throne, to bear a son who would one day take his place. Besides Gabriel hadn't married her for love, this she knew well. Men wanted girls like Adelina, not like Katya. *Wasn't she the one he had picked in the first place? It wasn't his fault that his younger brother had stolen her away. Now he is stuck with me, for the sake of his kingdom...*

While her thoughts had run astray, the water had grown stale, leaving a chill to settle on her skin, much like the one that settled around her heart. Withdrawing from her morose thoughts, she wrapped her robe around her and stepped from the metal barrel. Absentmindedly she picked up his jacket from the duvet and headed towards the door that connected their bedchambers.

Though the lock on its hinge was unturned, Katya had never before sought entrance to his room through this portal. She paused for only a moment before grasping the knob and giving herself access to his quarters. Her eyes peeked around the space, as though she were an intruder, and perhaps she was intruding. When it was confirmed that she was alone, she allowed herself a moment to take in the room's contents.

Just as she might have imagined, everything was in perfect condition. The furnishings were of the best quality, the drapings grandiose, and the wallpaper golden. A room befitting the most austere of royals. Strange that a part of her wished it had been plain, and simple.

Rather than linger and get caught, for now she very much felt a stranger in this foreign place, she hastened forward to lay his coat on the edge of the massive bed. When she pulled back she noticed a yellowed parchment lying on the floor. Had it slipped from his jacket?

Bending down she retrieved it, and opened it up. An image looked back at her, one that seemed vaguely familiar. She couldn't recall its pertinence to her memory, only that she had been a child when she had first seen it. *I will have to ask Gabriel about it later, perhaps he can reveal where I would have seen such a carving.* With a promise to do just that, she returned to her own chamber and made ready for the afternoon's activities.

Her downcast mood tagged along behind her, dragging her spirits well into the evening and even into the next day. When finally she could take it no more, she shut herself in her room, hoping that the silence would help her escape, or at least help her sort through her encroaching feelings. It did neither. Rather, the confined space suffocated her. She knew what she needed to do. She needed to visit *her*.

Before her mind fully registered a plan, her feet were already taking her there. To the frozen plot of ground where her mother had been buried long ago. Ever since returning to Brasov she hadn't dared visit, in fact she hadn't been here since the day they had lowered the casket, and Katya had kissed her mother goodbye with a bushel of wildflowers she had picked from their yard. Today there was no such flowers to be picked. Katya tucked her hands deeper into the folds of her woolen shawl and moved to stand before the lonely gravestone. Upon it was scribed the name of Katerina Murta Nuremburg.

With dry eyes, Katya stared at the imposing rock. She didn't know what to say. The cold had begun to seep in through her layers, and she knew she shouldn't stay out here for very long.

"*Oh mutter*. I am so overwhelmed by all this change. How can I be in love with a man who does not want me?"

Feeling more than a little foolish, she looked around. When she spotted a small log she moved toward it and brushed away the thin layer of snow before sitting upon its damp surface. She tried to draw strength from the knowledge that her mother was in heaven right now listening to her daughter's pitiful plea, but it was to no avail.

"I wish you were here with me. You would know just what to do. Why did you leave me so soon? Why couldn't you be here when I need you most?"

Tucking her legs beneath her gown, she rested her chin on a propped arm, and began to count her breaths. It was what she had done since she was a small child, a trick her nursemaid had taught her to keep her from getting upset. There was something peaceful about the steadiness that came from inhaling and exhaling slowly.

"Lord, I know You are here with me, and I am thankful that You are taking good care of my dear mother. 'Tis only that I feel lost without her gentle guidance. Please Lord, steady my heart in all this, and direct my steps unto Thine path before me."

And may I not be misguided in my love for Gabriel, she added silently. Looking again to the headstone she made her final address.

"*Mutter*, you mustn't worry about me. *Vater* and I are doing well. Please know that we love you very much. And…and I will keep my promise to you. I will have faith, and follow the Lord just as you did…"

Finishing her words, she sat silently. She hadn't heard him approach behind her, and his sudden presence gave her such a fright that she nearly jumped out of her skin.

"Katya?"

She stood up so fast that her booted feet caught the hem of her garment, and had Gabriel not reached out his arm, she would have fallen on her face.

"I was just finishing. I didn't know anyone was out here."

"My pardon. I have come to collect you. The carriage has been made ready for us. Do you need more time?"

"*Nein*, I am ready. *Danke*."

Moving away from the hand that still held her upright, she bent to press a kiss to her fingers before smoothing them over the letters inscribed there. *Auf wiedersehen, Mutter.* She breathed out a sigh of relief. Perhaps now that she had braved coming out here, the next time would be less painful. Resuming her stance, Katya looked to where Gabriel still stood waiting for her. Now if only she could muster up the same courage to face him with her newfound feelings.

CHAPTER 7

Gabriel sat watching her from across the carriage. After he had returned her to the castle, it hadn't taken them long to depart. Unlike the other women in his life who often slowed him down or created an unnecessary fuss, Katya had been already packed, collecting her few final things and even beating him to the carriage. *The woman is an enigma*, he reflected.

Dressed as she was in her cream colored traveling coat with her white wheat hair wrapped up in a blue headscarf, the sunlight catching her just right, she looked as though she was glowing. He often felt that way whenever he was near her, as if there were a tangible warmth emanating from her peaceful posture. As if she carried a piece of the sun within her, shinning wherever she went.

Instantly he was reminded of a story his father once told him, about a young prince who traveled across the land to find the answer to his aging father's ailment, and save the kingdom. After defeating a giant and outsmarting a troll, the young prince had come to the place where he met the Fairy of the Dawn. Upon seeing her the prince had fallen deeply in love, and pressed thrice kisses upon the maiden's lips, whose radiance then made the sun beam more brightly, the flowers bloom more beautifully, and the stream's waters taste more sweetly.

Katya must have felt his stare, for she turned her own head to meet his gaze. Their eyes locked and held. *And you, Katya, do you glow more radiant when you are kissed?* The thought brought his gaze to her lips, and his mind to the kiss they had shared. Gabriel hadn't known lips could taste so sweet. He had only ever kissed one other, the Lady Serbana, and only because his younger brother had goaded him into it. That one had been chaste, no more than a quick peck, but this…this was all new for him.

He didn't enjoy being so unsure of himself, the way that he had begun to feel whenever he was around her. Looking back up at her, he saw that she was blushing again, a faded pink that made her cheeks look like rose petals. To distract himself he sat back further on his seat.

"What does a weekend with your family hold for us?"

"Well, I suspect tonight will be a quaint dinner with just the six of us. Then tomorrow is bound to be bursting with activity. My aunt is well known for her ability to host the most splendid outings."

"I will take your word on the matter. Forsooth, I cannot recall the last time I visited the *limba germana*. Has much changed there?"

"I cannot imagine it ever changing. Indeed, it looks exactly as it did in my youth. 'Tis why I love it so."

"I see now that our alliance will do more than strengthen our military forces, indeed it will work to further unite the diverse peoples of our nation. The *Germana* have considered Brasov their home for almost as long as the Romani people."

He noticed that she had flinched at the callous description of their marriage, but neither did she comment, instead she asked, "What people lived here before you?"

"It is said that our ancestors descended from a people known as the Dacians. They came to this land from the north. Before us, there were only smaller nomadic tribes that I presume either intermarried with our people, or moved elsewhere."

"Then it is as my father has said: Brasov is a country of babes."

Folding his arms over his chest, Gabriel leaned back and looked out the window. Her comment rankled him. A country of babes? *Ha! We may not be as large as other nations, but we are nobler and mightier.*

"Your father is a fool. His opinion carries no such weight with me."

"My father may be many things, but he is no fool. I am sorry that my comment offended you, Gabriel. I did not mean it as such."

He offered her a single nod, but remained silent. Perhaps the remainder of their ride was best carried out as such. Without quite ignoring her, he filled the following hour with observing his country. He had meant no falsehood when he said that it had been a long while since he had traveled outside the citadel. The faces that met his gaze as he looked out the small window were no more than strangers to him.

Not for the first time he wondered what kind of king he would make. *I am glad to have accepted this invitation. From what Katya has told me, Herr Ranald is a most influential man in these parts.* Having only met the man once before at his wedding, and only briefly then, he made a note to know the gentleman better. *A wise ruler takes counsel from few, but advises many,* he heard his father's voice in the back of his mind, reminding him to be cautious when meeting men of position.

When at last they pulled up to the house, he was sorely glad of it. His long legs had begun to ache from being crowded for so long, and he hadn't dared to rub at them. Moving for the door he noticed that his companion had succumbed to slumber. She looked so very uncomfortable with her neck craned as it was that he was pleased when his movement forward caused her to stir.

"Are we there, my lord?"

My lord again, eh? He would have to correct that, and quickly before she spoke as such in front of her family. He reached out to smooth back the wisps of hair that had gotten free.

"I thought we had agreed on Gabriel from now on?"

Her eyes widened when he drew closer, but he only pressed a small kiss to her cheek. When he pulled back, he saw that she still hadn't moved, and he wondered if she were even breathing. The thought that he could affect her so made him smile.

"If we do not go in soon, they will wonder what is amiss. Surely the servants have already seen our carriage pull up. Shall we?"

Her chin dropped ever so slowly, but it was sign enough that she was with him. Drawing her from the carriage he made quick work to see their things taken within, before leading them up the front steps.

"It is just as Elisabeta described it to me. She wanted me to be well prepared, you know. I'm sure she wishes you had asked her to join us. It seems she is equally fond of your family."

"Yes. The past three times I have visited, she has come along. She even sent me with a gift for young Britta. Some fabric, I think. My cousin is very gifted with embroidery."

"And my sister does so love to be fashionable."

The two of them were shown to a sitting room with the sound of her laughter making them known. No sooner had they been seated, then their host and hostess rounded the corner.

"*Wilkommen*, our esteemed guests! You have come just in time for dinner."

"But first you will want to freshen up in your rooms, will you not?"

"Of course, how thoughtless of me. This is why I oft leave the more important details to my gracious wife. She is a precious gift of the Lord to me."

"Only because you are so deserving, my dear husband, has the Lord blessed you so."

Gabriel watched the interchange between husband and wife. While Herr Ranald was tall, lanky, and simply dressed, his wife was a woman of small stature, whose motherly figure was tastefully arrayed with the finest of silks. The mutual affection between them was clear from their light-hearted banter. Indeed, he could see that they not only loved each other, but they respected one another, an admirable trait in his mind.

"Shall I show you to your rooms?"

The look he got from Katya as they followed the flighty creature who flew down the hall before them, made his stomach drop. He had given little thought to their rooming situation, his mind having been otherwise preoccupied. *Perhaps this is God's way of playing matchmaker after all.* He couldn't say he hadn't entertained the idea of them becoming more intimate, especially after the day they had shared, but he just wasn't yet willing. Trying to keep up with both his runaway thoughts, and the Frau Rina, who spoke equally as fast as she walked, Gabriel was surprised when she stopped suddenly before an empty corridor.

"Though our dwelling is no *burg*, Prince Gabriel, I wanted you both to have plenty of room. As we have no other guests staying with us presently, I've had the staff prepare the east wing…"

Still catching up, Gabriel took his cue from Katya, whose expression of relief caused him a mix of emotions. On the one hand he was overjoyed that he didn't have to ask about two rooms, for his pride would never have allowed him to acknowledge their situation, and yet he had almost, if only for a moment, wanted to have no other option.

"This will be more than adequate, Aunté. We are pleased to be here, and will join you shortly, *ja*?"

"Ja." Katya's aunt stopped long enough to kiss Katya's forehead, before she headed back down the hallway.

Gabriel would have liked to say that the chattering had acquitted now that the older lady had left them, but he could have sworn he heard her voice carry her on with her round the bend. It would seem she had so much to say, that she even spoke to herself.

"Your aunt is certainly a woman of words."

"She is indeed, but my uncle is a man of action, and so she says they are a perfect match."

"Indeed, it seems they are very close."

"Oh yes, they are childhood sweethearts. Herr Ranald claims he loved her at first sight, but I have to laugh because he is older than she by at least seven years, so she was just a babe when first they met."

She turned away from him then, leading him further down the walkway before she stopped at the second door. With a shy glance she pushed the portal open and stepped over the threshold. The trail of her skirts teased him as she disappeared inside, leaving him in the now empty hall. *You are the fool, my friend.*

Freshly changed and clean shaven, Gabriel sat himself at the bountiful table. Rather than have servants carry out the courses one by one, it would seem they were to have a buffet style feast. He did not recognize all that was laid out before him, but if the smell were any indication it was bound to be a satisfactory meal.

"Let us say grace, shall we?"

Gabriel bowed his head as a perfunctory notion.

"Our Heavenly Father, we thank Thee for these vitals that have been prepared for us..."

Though he was not unused to the blessing of the meal, the exchange seemed more personal somehow. Herr Ranald spoke as though to a friend, making Gabriel itch to open his eyes and peek about the room to see if the One to whom he spoke were actually present. For reasons unknown to him, the man's prayer made him uncomfortable, and he was glad to have it soon come to it's end.

"So tell me, Prince Gabriel, what is the kingdom doing to keep us out of war?"

The comment ambushed him, and he turned abruptly. Seated as he was directly to the right of him, Gabriel could see that the man was earnest in his interest in the country's proceedings. The clear concern in Herr Ranald's eyes eased him.

"War is not on our horizon, not when I will do all that is in my power to prevent it."

"A bit boastful, do you not think?"

"Not at all. We are a nation who prides itself on the peace we have enjoyed these last hundred years. With our allies' combined resources, and the diligence of our war council, we have extended a treaty to our opposition."

"And you have heard back from them?"

"Not as of yet, but we did not expect an expedient reply."

"Uncle, must we speak politics? We have only just come."

Gabriel hadn't realized that all were engaged in their conversation. Looking around he saw several pairs of eyes on him and his host, though the only ones remotely interested were that of the younger fellow, Georg was his name?

"You are right my dear. Forgive me, Prince Gabriel, for putting you on the spot."

"Nothing to forgive, sir."

The table talk then turned to include the others. Politics may not be his favored subject, but at least it was one he was well conversed in. Not wanting to be at a loss, he plated his trencher with the contents of the dishes nearest him. Mayhap if he was meticulous about his consumption, he would be spared the petty pleasantries.

"Tell me Aunté, what have you planned for us on the morrow?"

"Oh, now that would be telling."

Gabriel saw the sparkle in the lady's eyes, one akin to the look Elisabeta had whenever she was mischievous.

"Surely you will not keep them in suspicion, lady wife. Shall you not share with them but one detail?"

"*Sehr gut*, I will tell you something. On the morrow we will arise early, eat a hearty breakfast and follow the south trail until we reach the Glenstine Lake. It has nearly frozen solid this time of year."

"But why should we go there, *Mutter*?"

This was from Britta, Gabriel noted, wondering himself why they would want to see a frozen lake. Brasov had them all over, and one was just as sightly as another.

"Why, to go *eislaufen*, you goose!"

"I am not a goose, Georg!"

"Kinder, please have your manners at the table with you."

"Are we really to go ice skating Aunté? Why, that would be splendid!"

His wife's face was alit with a childish awe, reflecting the delighted expression of the two seated across from them. Gabriel, though, did not share their excitement.

"I thought so too. Herr Ranald has even procured a couple of sleds for us, as our carriages will not defeat the hilly terrain."

"Herr Ranald, how good of you."

"I helped too!"

"Indeed you did my son, and I thank you for it."

Gabriel only half listened to the family, his brain was trying to contrive ways to see himself out of the expected trip. He didn't know how to skate. Indeed, none had ever showed him. Thinking back to the winters of his childhood while his siblings were having daily excursions, probably ones similar to the one they would be on tomorrow, he was in his father's study. Training to become a king.

"If this is only one of our day's activities, I can only imagine what else you might have up your sleeve."

"No more will you get from me; on this I shall be tight lipped."

"Only on this my dear?"

Frau Rina tossed her husband a look, but he just beamed at her unmoved even when her lips turned to a pout.

"How are your lessons coming Katya?"

"Very well. The Queen is such a kind tutor; she has so much patience with me. Britta, you would be pleased to know I am coming along in my stitching. Oh that reminds me! Elisabeta gave me fabric for you, dear cousin."

"She did? Did you hear that Mutter? I am to embroider for the *Prinzessin*!"

The girl practically bounced out of her chair in bliss. It would seem, his sister had yet another adorer. Of the king's three children, Elisabeta had always been the most favored. Her bubbly personality worked well for her, as he had yet to meet a person she could not charm. With Gabriel, it was not so. Indeed, he knew many who only preferred him for his position. But what if he were not the eldest son? Who would stand beside him then? He looked to Katya. *What does she know of the man Gabriel, all I have shown her is the prince.*

"Yes, *mine tochter*, I heard." Frau Rina then looked to Katya, "Does this mean your new dresses have come in as well?"

"The last batch arrive a week hence, the rest have come already. It seems the royal dressmaker is used to clients of a varied taste.

I am not so picky as all that, so she was able to fill the order in a short time."

This caught his attention, and before he could remember his plan to keep silent, he addressed her.

"You were pleased with Madame Blouson, then?"

She turned toward him, her smile genuine.

"Yes, she was a delight to work with, and her suggestions were most appreciated."

"Very good. I am pleased to know you will have what you need to replenish your wardrobe for the winter months."

"What else must you learn to become a princess, Katya?"

"Well, Britta, apart from the roles I will have as mistress of the keep, I also must learn my duties at court."

"Really? Like what?" This, from Georg, but Gabriel leaned in to hear her as well.

"For one thing, the Queen is instructing me on how to make welcome the wives and daughters of foreign nobles, as the King and Queen often host families from other nations."

"What about the people who live here? Do they get to come to court?"

"Yes, them too. The Queen has invited many different people; some not even of rank. She also sees to their needs in lesser court, where people will come if they have a concern or a disagreement. I admit, I am still nervous around large crowds, but the people have been very gracious when I've attended alongside the Queen."

Interesting. He hadn't known she was mob shy. He was not one to share the personal details of his life like that. In fact, he couldn't think of a single person with whom he would openly share the innermost thoughts of his mind or the dreams of his heart. Even with his family, he only shared certain pieces of himself. What were the dreams of his heart? *To be king,* his mind asserted firmly.

*But what else...*Was he no more than the future crown? Truly, who was Gabriel Romalo? The question daunted him.

"Everything is so wonderful. Oh, how I have missed such meals."

"Have you tried the Spätzle? If I remember correctly, it is your favorite."

"You are right. Which one is it?"

She must have pointed to something nearest him, because Katya was scooting closer with her plate in hand.

"Let me," he grabbed her plate, and for the first time in his life, he served someone other than himself something to eat.

"Thank you."

"You are welcome."

After he made for himself another full plate of the vitals before him, the meal was thus concluded. Unlike at the castle, they adjourned together to one room, the children begging their father to play a game with them. The evening concluded thus, and though initially Gabriel had been reluctant to participate, he found he quite liked the German card game they had chosen. Out of the three hands, Katya had won two, and Herr Ranald the third. It would seem his wife had a keen knack for such games. On their way back to their rooms for the night, Gabriel couldn't help but tease her about it.

"Why did you not tell me you were such an astute gamer? I would have sharpened my own card skills."

"I have always loved to play games. It was what kept me from utter boredom when I was younger. Having no siblings, there were no other children for me to play with."

"Did you not live in town?"

"*Nein*, we lived in the country. Though we had neighbors not but a mile from us, my father was not one for entertaining. I am sad to say my poor nursemaid must have played hundreds of games with me."

Soon they were standing before her door. Having escorted her from the family's solar, Katya had walked with her hand loped through his arm. When she moved to pull away, he held fast to her, not wanting to put space between them.

"What happened to her?"

He watched her glance down at the hand that was holding hers. She whispered her response, her breath catching on her words. "My nursemaid?"

"Mhhmm."

He waited for her to look up, and then stared deeply into her eyes. He tried to imagine that young girl she described, with no one but a nursemaid to care for her. Something in his chest squeezed almost painfully. *Have all the ones who were meant to love you, left?*

"She was only a young woman when she looked after me. She longed for children of her own, and so when the butcher man from the market offered her a home, she married him. By then I was of age to look after myself."

The way she said it, her words showing a profound sense of strength, no doubt brought on by the years she had spent as her own defender, made him soften towards her. His father's words came to him yet again. *A good king uses his sword to protect, not to kill.* He thought with equal fervor…*I will defend you, dear Katya.* Though he didn't dare speak the words aloud, he made them a vow to his own heart.

"I am sorry she left you."

"It was time for her to go. What life would she have had with me? After all, my father would have never accepted her as more than nursemaid."

"Certainly you saw her again after she left, *da*?"

"Once or twice. She was with her third child the last time I had a chance to visit with her. She looked well. Happy."

"I am only sorry it was at the cost of your happiness for her to be so."

"Nein, you mustn't think that. The Lord has been with me always. I am never alone."

"How can you be so sure?"

"I have faith, Gabriel. And faith is the assurance of things we do not see, of things we *cannot* see."

"Let it be as you say then."

He dismissively waved away her words, not wanting them to spoil the moment. Releasing her hand from his grasp, he reached up to tenderly cup her cheek. With the way she was looking at him, one might have thought he'd kissed her already. As he leaned in, he felt more than saw her rise to her tippy toes, making her lips a much easier conquest. When at last he stepped backwards, he bowed gracefully before her hand. Pressing a gentle kiss to its soft form, he then bid her goodnight.

Just as Frau Rina had declared, the whole house was up early having broken their fast as the sun was coming up. Gabriel still had not found a way to excuse himself from the skating trip, not politely anyway. The last thing he wanted to do was give great offense to his hosts, and his bride's family, so with all the gusto that he could muster up, he donned his thick winter coat, and laced his leather boots.

"Gabriel, are you coming? The family is surely waiting for us."

"Skating does not appeal to me."

Someone may as well know my secret, he thought candidly.

"What did you say?" Her voice was muffled by the door that was still unopened.

Moving from his chair, he grabbed his fur hat, plopped it atop his head and pulled the handle.

"I said, I would have you know, that I have never been ice skating."

Her eyes laughed and her nose crinkled, as if she awaited his jest. When she saw there was none forthcoming, she gasped.

"You are serious, are you not?"

"I am in earnest. I suppose, most would have had the leisure to know such jollies when they were young, but I did not."

"Oh Gabriel, you needn't be afraid. I will help you. Besides you are a quick learner, I am sure. Why, I'll bet you'll best us in no time at all."

He stopped in his steps, and she bumped in to the side of him.

"I am *not* afraid."

His tone was darker than usual, but he wanted to be clear with her.

"Of course not."

Ignoring her fallen face, he continued forward.

"Good. Then let us be on our way."

Katya wasn't sure quite what she had done to earn his rebuke, but the silence between them irked her. *Men and their pride,* she thought with a huff. *And to think I awoke this morn eager to spend the day with him!* She needn't deny it. Her eyes had drank in the sight of his long muscular form, shod in a crisp linen tunic and dark hose. Gone was his royal getup, and smug jewels. With a fur lined hat and coarse winter coat, almost similar to the one her uncle now sported, he seemed normal, plain even. *Plain? Nein, Gabriel could never be plain, he was far too handsome for that.*

"*Prosit Neujahr*!" Her aunt called to them.

"A very happy new year indeed, Aunté."

The family then exchanged the customary greeting. When she moved to offer Gabriel a similar exchange, she noticed that he was at a loss.

"It is a blessing of good health, a kiss to each cheek from a loved one, and then you turn in a circle to represent the new year."

Ignoring his reluctance, she moved toward him. Holding to his shoulders, she reached up on tip toe to bestow a kiss on each of his cheeks, feeling the stubble of his unshaved jaw. When she stepped back, his eyes were glued to her face. To keep herself from blushing, she looked away.

"Now you turn around."

The family clapped their approval when he turned himself around.

"An interesting custom to be sure."

"We will make a German of you yet, my boy!"

Uncle Ranald clapped him on the back, and then motioned them all towards the back side of the stables, where they were met by the attendants who held ready their horses and sleds.

"I wish to ride with cousin Katya! Can I *Vater*?"

"No, my dear. Prince Gabriel and Princess Katya will share a sled of their own. Their sled is smaller and will be much more comfortable with only two passengers. Come now."

Britta's face quickly turned to a pout, and Katya offered her an encouraging smile.

"Never you mind Britta, we will have plenty of time to spend with one another this day."

When she turned to the sled that awaited her, she was met by the extended hand of her husband. Without looking at him, she accepted his offered arm and climbed in to the wooden vessel. Once he was seated beside her, a bit more snugly than she would have cared for at the moment, the stable boy handed over the reins.

"The lake is just over that ridge, and around the bend. We should be there in half an hour." Herr Ranald spoke to them from his seat in the sleigh before them, motioning to Gabriel.

"We will follow your lead."

Together they set out for the wooded trail, the bare arms of the trees arching up to cover their heads. Still, the sun peaked through, sending toward them shafts of light to make their path more visible.

"I am glad Aunté Rina thought to bring blankets. I had not expected it to be so chilly."

She opened up the covering to encompass them both. Without meaning to, she inched closer to his side, seeking his warmth against the brisk gusts. She felt him shift beside her and thought he would pull away, but instead she was surprised when he collected the reins in one hand and moved his other arm around her back.

"It is still early yet. Once the sun has reached its peak, it should be a beautiful day."

Tucked into him the way she was, she immediately felt warmer. His body acted like a shield, blocking much of the wind. Peeking out from her enclosure, she saw the identical bright red sleigh, along with the four hooded heads that trailed in front of them. Not having had the chance to ride in such a vehicle, Katya found herself enjoying the smooth motion of the sled against the packed snow. Most carriages made her queasy, but this was an altogether different sensation.

"Gabriel, why did you not learn to skate?"

When he did not answer, she thought perhaps that he had ignored her daring question, but then she heard him clear his throat.

"My father began to train me for the throne when I was but five years of age. Though I still had the summer's time to enjoy my friends and the company the castle kept, the winter has always found me indoors."

She pondered this, trying to imagine in her mind what he must have been like in his youth. From what she had been told, he had always been more of the serious sort. Now she wondered whether his unyielding nature had anything to do with the way he had been kept from a normal childhood. When most were just boys, he had been shaped into an early manhood with great weights of responsibility placed upon his shoulders, and the duties of the crown upon his head.

My poor Gabriel, how long you have borne this burden. Perhaps today she could awaken his childlike heart, or at least aid him in having some much needed fun. The carefree kind that would tickle him to laughter, and lighten his heavy spirit. *Dear Lord, may it be such a day for us all.*

"Tell me Katya, how often did you come with your parents to Brasov as a child? I can't recall but only two of your trips."

"We came every summer since I can remember, and then the last just before my Mutter passed when I was but ten and two years. This is the first winter I have seen in Romania."

"And how does it compare to your legendary Germana?"

"Brasov bears the season much more graciously than my homeland. In that I am certain. But each land carries its own splendor. Have you ever traveled outside your country?"

She turned to him then, wanting to see his answer, but when she did, she found that their faces were no more than a hands-breadth apart, making the reach to his lips all too irresistible.

He tasted as sweet as the spring water from her favorite creek back home. *Good heavens*, was all she could manage to think, as he deepened their kiss. It wasn't until she felt a jerk from the pull of the horses that she returned to her full senses.

"My apologies," she gasped, leaning back. Her face burned with astonishment. "I don't know what came over me."

Slinking back into the chasm of her coat, she all but wished that she could disappear. *You are supposed to be helping him to have fun, not enticing him with your foolishness!* Katya didn't even notice how he regained his grip on the reigns, righting the animals to a steady gait. She was too busy peering ahead to see if her discretion had been seen by the others. Gabriel must have picked up on her intentions.

"You needn't apologize. It is to be expected that we are affectionate with one another. We are newlyweds after all."

Did she detect a hint of laughter in his tone? Peeking up at him, she saw that though his eyes were on the road before them, his lips were indeed turned upwards. She didn't know whether to feel angry or relieved that he thought her sense of decorum amusing.

"And to answer your question, I have not traveled outside the boundaries of our Kingdom."

Forgetting her embarrassment, she sat up straighter. "Not ever?"

"*Nu.*"

"But why?"

He paused. She noticed he did that often; stopped to think before he spoke. It was yet another attribute that distinguished him as royalty.

"I'm not quite sure. Perhaps because many of our dignitaries and allied ambassadors have always come to court, my father never felt a particular need to send me to other lands on his behalf. Lucian, on the other hand, has been all over the world and back." He paused again, his brows drawing together. "It is strange to think that he has seen so much, and I have never even left my own backyard."

"When you are king, will you not be able to go far and wide?"

He shook his head. "There will be no need for me to travel then. No, if I am to see anything of the world, it must be before I take the crown."

"Then you have plenty of time, do you not?"

"My coronation is set for my twenty-sixth birthday, as it is tradition for such ordinances to fall on an even year."

"This summer then."

Before them the copse of trees had opened its mouth releasing them to a field of white. She knew their trail was meeting its end, as they could now see the crystalline lake not but a hundred yards ahead. They had fallen into such a pleasant comradery, that she fought to keep him talking.

"Where would you go? If you could travel beyond these borders, I mean."

"I should not even think of lands beyond my country. I am not going to be a king of other lands."

"*Gafellen,* Gabriel…?" She pleaded with him.

"As you wish." Drawing them to a halt just past where her uncle was helping her aunt down, he turned and looked at her. "If I were to go, I would travel to the coast of Africa. It is the furthest place my brother has ever gone. In that place, there are great oceans of sand, pointed towers that reach to the sky and shine like gold, and large beats like you couldn't even imagine. It is a picture not easily erased from my mind."

He climbed out, and reached back to give her a hand.

"It sounds very exotic."

"Hmmm. Yes, I suppose that is a good way to describe it."

"Thank you for telling me."

He nodded once before turning to lead them towards the frozen pool of water. Katya saw that her cousins were already unlacing their boots, trading them for the hard-cased skates with a thin blade brandishing the soles.

"Here are yours Katya, and yours Prince Gabriel. I do hope they fit. You seem of similar size to my Ranald."

They thanked her and went to try them on. Hers were a little tight, but she preferred them that way, as she knew they would help her keep a better balance once out on the ice. With the horses tied up and their coats buttoned, the crew tromped their way through the snow and out onto the lake. Not having skated in quite some time, Katya decided to hang back ushering her family on without her.

"We will catch up to you soon enough. But first let me get my bearings."

"You will remember it in no time my dear." Her uncle smiled at her as he whisked away to catch up with Georg.

"Never to fear, you have your charming prince to keep you from falling." Aunté Rina, ever the graceful lady, carefully glided her way to the open ice.

Reluctantly she turned to her partner. He had only just taken his first step, and she could tell from his clenched hands and tightened jaw that he was unsure of himself; that he hated it was so.

"Perhaps if you allow me to take your arm, we can lean on one another?"

Still he didn't move.

"Gabriel, are you alright?"

He looked to her then, his face a blank mask. "Yes, I am fine."

"Do you need help? I can show you. It really is simple, once you learn the trick of it."

"No, I can do it on my own. You should go on ahead. I'll be right behind you."

"But wouldn't it be easier if..."

"I haven't need of your help." His words were muttered, making him sound more annoyed than angry.

She decided to leave him well alone. "Alright, if that is what you wish."

He muttered something else, but she was already moving away. Her legs felt stiff, and she knew she was much out of practice. Keeping herself balanced she pushed forward with her right leg, then her left. Right. Left. Right. Left. With the steady rhythm of her gliding feet, she was able to pick up speed. Before long, Katya was taking longer strides. Her blades bite the ice, making a grinding sound that was music to her ears.

"Well, hallo!" Britta called out to her as she drew near them. The younger girl was skating in small circles, her hands poised like the wings of a bird, or more appropriately an angel.

"Where is your man, Katya?" Aunté Rina asked, Herr Ranald adding his own two cents to hers. "I hope you haven't left him already?"

She loved the way her family teased her. It made her feel like she belonged.

"Nein, I haven't left him. He noticed his laces felt a little loose, so he went to adjust them." Though she was loath to do so, she knew he would be upset if she brought attention to his inability. And that was something she didn't want, for she was quickly learning that her husband was a man of profound vanities. "He'll be along shortly."

They accepted her explanation easily enough. And she was thankful for it. Together they circled the far side of the lake, rounding back to the middle where the ice was the thickest. When ice hissed behind her, she froze. In fact, they all came to a halt. Spinning around she caught sight of Gabriel propelling towards them, his skates skidding slightly. Though his form wobbled, he remained upright.

"It seems I still haven't found my groove!" Gabriel called out to them in a jovial fashion. She regarded him closely. He seemed sincere enough, but the smile was stretched proving that he was only half coping.

"Brava, Prince Gabriel. Come skate with me. I'll race you to the edge and back!"

Having been studying him as she was, she watched the blood drain from his features. Looking to the others she knew she alone had picked up on his angst. Not being able to bear his silent agony, she stepped in to save him.

"Perhaps later Georg," she said as she looped her arm through his. His whole body was tense, and she wondered how he kept himself so still. "You do not mind terribly if he stays with me for now, do you?"

Georg rolled his eyes, his words the grumblings of a young man. "He *is* your husband..." Just as quickly he turned to his father, his eyes relighting with a ready challenge. "What about you Vater? Care to face me?"

"I'll wager I can still out pace you, but let us have a go, shall we?"

"Mutter, will you count us off?"

"It will be my pleasure. Are both racers ready?"

The older woman glanced at both parties, their nods giving her a clear signal.

"Alright, racers ready...*Eins, zwei, drei...los*!"

While the two of them sped off, an icy mist in their wake, Gabriel nudged her gently.

"*Mulțumesc*."

"You are welcome, my dear. Besides, it works in my favor, for now you must remain by my side." When he raised an eyebrow, she quickly added, "Lest you wish to be entangled in another of Georg's sprints?"

He barked a laugh at her impudence, startling her aunt, who looked at them suspiciously before grinning and turning back to the race.

"Go Vater, go! Georg is right behind you!" Britta's commentary continued until both skaters were nearly upon them. Though they were neck and neck, it was Herr Ranald who met them first. His blade scraped in a perfect curve, spraying them with tiny ice crystals. When Georg skidded up next to him, he hunched over with his hands to his knees.

Georg let out a belated breath, half collapsing on the frozen pond. Clearly winded, he only managed an, "I was so close."

Herr Ranald patted the boy's back brusquely, "You did well, my boy. Another year and you'll out lap me for sure."

The rest of the morning passed quickly enough. Gabriel had been right about the rising sun bringing an increase in temperature. By the time it had climbed the steps of the sky to sit itself upon its clouded throne, their small bunch was red cheeked. Even Gabriel appeared to have been enjoying himself. Katya was impressed by how quickly he had picked up the skill. The way he breezed past her, she imagined he was now nearly as steady on his feet as she was.

"I'm glad to see you've caught on." She said for his ears alone.

"Indeed, I am a fast learner." He winked at her, his infectious energy pulling a grin from her cheek.

As the others moved back to where they had left their boots, Gabriel took her hand and pulled her around the ice in a final loop. This side of him was rarely seen, she knew well. *What would it take to keep him as such?*

She wished she were an artist, so that she could capture this instant. Each stroke of her brush would portray his flushed cheeks and bright eyes. Their hands, two puzzle pieces that interlocked. She would even display her family in the background, their departing figures in the snow leaving an illusion of a stolen moment. Two lovers who were in another world altogether.

"Tell me, what you are thinking when you look at me in such a way?"

Katya blinked, and as she did her water colored thoughts blurred behind her eyes.

"I was only thinking how pleasant this morning has been."

"Only that? No, I think not." His whispered words tickled her face, for he had bent close to speak.

She saw that he understood her in a way she had not thought him able. Indeed, he was proving to be more perceptive than she had given him credit for. *What could it hurt?*

"In truth, I was painting our picture. Remembering every detail of this moment, so that I can have it as a treasure forever."

He heard the intake of his own breath, but nothing more. He felt as if he were in a tunnel of sorts, or walking against the wind. Her words pierced his heart. How is it she left him feeling so defenseless? He was disarmed by her honesty. She spoke to him of what was in her heart without reserve.

He could think of nothing else to say but, "Do you paint, then?"

She stepped back, breaking whatever spell her words had cast over him.

"I've dabbled in it, but never enough to be proficient. Had I a proper tutor, I think I would have enjoyed learning."

Together they stepped from the ice, switched their shoes, and returned themselves to their sled. The ride back to the main house was relatively faster. It wasn't until they had pulled up to the stable, that Gabriel recalled their conversation.

"My mother could teach you."

"Hmm?"

"To paint. She excels in most of the arts."

"Indeed? I will have to ask her about it then. Perhaps it can be added to the list of accomplishments I am to have."

"Are you overwhelmed with all that you must learn?"

He didn't know why he hadn't asked her such things before. Perhaps because he hadn't thought of it, or hadn't cared enough to think of it. But after spending the day together, he felt them drawing closer. A sort of intimacy was growing between them.

"Not really. In truth, I enjoy learning all these new things. I've discovered so much in this last month and a half."

He could see her excitement, and was pleased. He had never given it much consideration, but now he realized that he had always silently hoped his future wife would fall in love with the kingdom, just as she fell in love with him. It seemed that Katya was indeed a fit for her role as future queen. She would do him justice. A dazzling jewel to his crown.

"Come, *kinder*. The refreshments are ready."

Following their hosts beckon, they all made their way indoors, and were met by the delicious smell of warm chocolate. Each of them were given a cup of the steaming substance that stole away the remainder of the chill in their bones.

"*Danke*, Aunté. This is just what was needed."

"Isn't Bertel's hot chocolate the best you have ever tasted?"

The young girl beside him smiled, her upper lip mustached with the cream topping.

"It is very delicious." He smiled at her graciously.

"Time to run along now, children. We will leave our guests to their drink and *pfannkuchen*."

"But do not disappear too long," Frau Rina added to her husband, looking each of them in the eye. "Much more is planned for this evening. We will sup at vespers."

The two children quickly dispersed, their emptied cups clattering on the counter behind them. Herr Ranald and Frau Rina soon followed, leaving Gabriel and his bride to themselves.

"Glad I am to see that we will have a break before our next activity. I fear I might be in need of some rest after this morn."

"You aren't sore are you, my dear?"

She caught on to his teasing tone easily enough, scrunching her nose at him before finishing off the last of her cupper.

"Did your aunt say there were treats? Dare I ask what *pfannkuchen* is?" He searched around the small hall, looking for a tray.

"They are jelly-filled donuts. Another of our New Year traditions."

"Oh good! I am quite famished."

When he found them, he offered her one. Her dainty fingers plucked up a powdered ball of dough. She bit into it, her mouth filling with the berry custard. Katya then watched as Gabriel bit into his.

"Do you like it?"

He popped the remainder of the doughnut into his mouth, licking his lips with a teasing gleam.

"Delicious. Perhaps we shall have to get Tusta to adopt some of these customs you have thus shared."

Katya smiled and finished her drink, while Gabriel put away another two pastries, before looking to her.

"Have you anything in mind for us to do?"

He found that he didn't want to wander off by himself, any more than he wanted to be found by Georg and forced to play any odd number of games. Hopefully, Katya would have something better in mind.

CHAPTER 8

They day had passed more pleasantly than he could have hoped. It seemed Katya was a wealth of ideas when it came to her aunt's abode. She had showed him her favorite spaces from when she was a child. The library that housed a massive collection of poetry, one that rivaled what the castle kept. The south garden where they had ambushed an unsuspecting Georg with balls of snow. The poor fellow didn't know what had hit him, but his recovery was speedy and his response was expert. A short repast had been waiting for them directly after with a brazen hearth to dry their damp clothes.

Gabriel looked over to Katya. If this is how the New Year was to be spent, he would enjoy himself very much. They were now tucked into a wide alcove somewhere in the south wing. The afternoon sun poured in through the bay window, each panel shimmering with a different color of light. When she had suggested they use the servant's stairs to make their way to this place, he had balked at the idea. Never in all his life had he used the passages meant for workers and the like. But how could he have refused the large blue eyes that had looked up at him so?

"Gabriel, is it true what they say of the Dark Lord?"

She drew her feet in and tucked them further beneath her skirt. The room that held them was odd shaped, a sort of triangular outline. Perhaps it had been a child's play room at one time, or even a nursery. Now it held only a small chaise and rug. With no other furniture, the two of them had taken up seats on the floor beneath the window. He rested his back against the wall opposite her, and stretched out his long legs.

"What do you mean?"

"I've heard things; rumors I am sure. But they unsettle me."

"What sort of rumors?"

He hated to think of what she had been told, for he knew stories of the man had already been circulating about the land.

"Is it true that he is a powerful man? That he is an evil man? Some people say that he is not even a man at all. But how can that be?"

Her voice had gone to a whisper, and her gaze had moved far away. He wondered what images were playing about in her mind. His were always the same. Though he had yet to make the man's acquaintance, he saw him as this large lurking figure. He was cloaked in shadows, his torso hidden beneath a dark cape. The face was disfigured with a long scar that stretched from brow to chin. It was a face that haunted him in his sleep.

"I assure you he is a man, as real as you and I. And he is no more powerful than the army we are amassing." He hesitated, wondering how much he should share with her. It was one thing to put her fears to rest, but an entirely different matter to divulge their war plans. Still he ought to be honest. "You are correct in thinking he is a foe. Lucian recovered certain information about the man. It is said that he is practiced in the Dark Arts."

She shuddered, her shoulders trembling slightly.

"You will have to face such a man."

It wasn't a question. The both knew that if the treaty was left unsigned, Gabriel would indeed have to face this man on the battlefield. But he had a plan. In fact, he had made a deal with

God. Just this morning as he was lying abed, he and the Lord had come to terms. If the Lord would see to it that war was evaded and their country continued in it's reign of peace, then Gabriel would make good on his marriage vows and take Katya to wife. He scooted closer to her until they shared the same wall as a cushion for their backs. He then turned to look into her eyes, wanting her to see his sincerity.

"You needn't be afraid. I am confident that the Dark Lord, whoever he be, will agree with our proposal."

"I pray it is so."

His face was now much closer to hers. She must have realized it also. He watched with uninhibited interest as her gaze moved from his eyes to his lips and back again. He wondered then if she had guessed his thoughts, for she leaned in just as he did, and their lips met in the middle. Her kiss was just as he remembered it. Sweet. Supple. Indulgent. It seemed like the most natural thing to embrace her in this way, to share with her an intimate piece of himself, meant for no one else. When she pulled back, he pressed a gentle kiss to her forehead. His words no more than a whisper.

"Shall we go and make ready for dinner, then?"

She simply nodded, her face full of color once more.

He stood then, reaching out his hand to assist her to her feet. Together they made their way back to their rooms, where they would ready for dinner. He said nothing more, for his thoughts were too full of what was to come this evening. *How did one go about seducing his own wife?* His first thought was Lucian. His brother had more experience with woman than any man had the right to. *He's not here, nor would I seek his counsel in this.* Gabriel knew the man had since mended his ways. *He is not the man he was once. Indeed, I hardly know the brother who has come home to us.* He couldn't doubt the change he had seen in his brother. Even if he did question his newfound faith.

Making quick work of his evening attire with the manservant that had come to assist him, Gabriel silenced his thoughts, saving them for a more opportune moment. Checking his cravat in the glass piece held out before him, he stilled himself. *Come now Gabriel, you are the next king of Brasov. You have been prepared to lead a nation and trained for battle. What is one tiny woman?* Yet still his heart tremored at the thought of her.

"Will there be anything else, Your Highness?"

"No, that is all."

"If you will excuse me then, my lord."

The man bowed out, leaving Gabriel to face his reflection on his own. With a draw of breath, he squared his shoulders and marched from the room. It was time to claim his wife.

"Katya?" He knocked once. The door opened immediately.

She stood in the doorway smiling up at him, and he wondered if she could sense the effect she had on him; the way her nearness heightened his awareness of her.

"Are you ready then?"

"Yes." His eyes were still taking in the sight of her. "Is that one of your new dresses?"

An elegant blush crept up her jawline, blossoming her cheeks into ripened rosebuds.

"It is. One of my favorites actually." Her hands smoothed down the length of her evening gown, each fold of shimmering velvet bending beneath the weight of her touch.

"I can see why. You look enchanting, my lady."

He bowed slightly, before turning to extend to her his arm. She returned his grin, and placed her hand upon his bicep. His eyes followed her motions, and he noticed how well she fit him. How proud it made him to have her on his arm. She may be no match for Lady Serbana, but he found that Katya was lovely in her own right.

"Do you per chance know what your aunt has in mind for us this eve?"

"I haven't an inkling."

"Well then I suppose we shall be left to her mercy."

"She is harmless, Gabriel. I couldn't imagine her…."

Her cut of words stopped them both in their tracks.

"A soiree, oh how marvelous! It would seem my aunt has been busy indeed."

Before them stood the open doors of the dining space, each wooden panel a straight back servant welcoming them into the room. Only the room was nothing as it had looked last night. The long table that had been in the center was replaced with smaller, rounder tables upon which trays of finger foods were being eaten. Several maids circled the room, their arms laden with silver platters carrying fine goblets of what he hoped was proper wine.

"And it seems she has invited the whole family."

"The family?"

"The ones who remain here anyway. Even some of my mother's family is here."

She motioned excitedly toward a tan skinned lady and her dark haired husband.

"Come, I wish for you to meet them."

He led her forward, trying not to gawk at the total transformation that had occurred in such a short time. Even the windows and entry ways were covered in different fabrics. His sister would be equally awed by their hostess's abilities to put on such a charming, yet sophisticated party. Katya called out to her cousin and the lady turned toward them.

"Katya? *Surpriză plăcută!*"

"A pleasant surprise indeed. May I introduce you to my husband? Prince Gabriel, this is my cousin Alecia, and her husband Petrov."

They exchanged greetings just as a collective group of fine musicians took up their instruments. Their first piece was a classical Romanian song, one he favored immensely. They talked for a time, and Gabriel found he enjoyed the other couple's company. Once the first song ended, a much faster tune was picked, making it hard for conversation to continue. To be heard over the voice of the violin and the din of the flute, their group moved further from the ensemble.

"How are you, dear cousin?"

"We are well, are we not Petrov?"

"More than well! We are again expecting a babe. Another son to carry on my grandfather's shop." The robust man beamed with pride, making Gabriel wonder what it would be like to be a father himself. He peeked over at Katya. *She would make a fine mother.*

"Or a daughter. I shall be pleased with either." The tall lady smiled largely, her unabashed joy turning her brown eyes three shades darker.

"*Felicitări* to you both!"

"Thank you, Your Highness. And felicities to you as well on your marriage. You have found a good match in my sweet cousin, if I may say so. Though her skin is pale, and she has the coloring of the wild mountains, her blood is that of her mother's, may she rest in peace."

Gabriel saw Katya smile at the woman's tease. He wondered if her family saw her as a sort of black sheep. Though there were many families of interbred lineage, few of them ranked among the noble classes. Herr Nuremburg must have truly been a man in love to go against such norms.

"I thank you, and I couldn't agree more." He slid his arm around Katya's waist, drawing her a bit closer to his side. "My wife is a perfect picture of our nation, a beautiful blend of the peoples who share this land."

"Wonderfully said, Your Grace." He noted how her eyes had followed his gesture. She seemed pleased that they shared an affection between them.

When their conversation lulled, he motioned to a nearby server. Handing a glass to each of his companions before he took a drink of his own. The honeyed liquid slid down his throat. It was smooth and rich. Just the way he liked it. *Herr Ranald must have had a good harvest*, he thought as he quickly downed the contents in his cup before exchanging it for another. Soon they were being ushered out on to a large veranda of sorts that was enclosed effectively keeping out the winter's chill.

Unsure of how to navigate this sort of gathering, he allowed Katya to take the lead, following suit when she moved to join another couple at a bench far to the left. Once seated he noticed that platters of food were being distributed to each table, and much the same as the meal last night, the families were sharing the platters. Feeling slightly out of his element, he chose instead to take the time to observe his wife. How much he had missed about her these last few months, being so preoccupied with the war council. He found it unnerving that he was a man so prepared to serve his country, to lay aside his own desires and meet the needs of those under his power, but to woo a wife? He shook his head. In this he was both ill-equipped and unsuited.

By the time the meal had been partaken of, and the great company of guests had returned indoors for the final entertainment, Gabriel had her all but figured out. Though in large social settings such as the banquet they had for his mother, or their own wedding reception, Katya's character was of a reserved nature. In the same way when he saw her surrounded by people she knew only fairly well, she spoke little. Though her face was animated enough, making the other party pour out their very souls' to her, she only offered enough to be polite. But when she stepped into a circle of dear friends, or close relatives that is when she came alive.

It was as if he were seeing two different people, so changed was she by the people she felt most comfortable around. Begrudgingly, it caused him to consider how she acted around him. Did he too fall into the category of those she trusted enough to reveal her true self? More importantly, did it matter to him that he was counted among those she held dear? He knew it did.

"There you are. The play is about to start. I had thought you were behind me, but when I turned around you weren't there. Don't you like plays?"

He looked up to see Katya waiting for him in the doorway, her small figure dwarfed by the massive arch. Glancing to the right and left he saw that all had gone in, but him. Here he sat, lost in his thoughts, until the object of his musings came to him. It seemed she had asked him something, what was it? Oh yes.

"I do enjoy plays. I've been to so few that I'm sure I haven't seen this one. My apologies, I didn't mean to lose you in the crowd."

She paused, eyeing him more closely. He noted the depth to her blue gaze, mentally adding a keen intelligence to the list of traits he admired about her.

"Are you well, Gabriel?"

"Yes, of course." He stood to his feet, not knowing what was making him act so queer. Perhaps it was because he knew what he hoped this day to be for them, how he wished to conclude his evening. Or perhaps it was his fifth goblet of wine, the one he had only just finished. Standing to his feet, he followed her back inside, and together they took their seats next to Herr Ranald and Frau Rina.

The candlelit room cast a glow on the makeshift stage before them. He marveled again at how quickly the room was rearranged to host a small theater. Though there were only two half curtains at either side, the performers were able to enter and exit the stage with little hassle. The story that unfolded before them was one of woe, with a gargantuan amount of comedy dispersed throughout.

At one moment the character Revenge was scolding the knight who had been duped by his father's steward, when in walks his best friend disguised as the knight's fair lady. The entire assembly erupted into fits of laughter, but Gabriel only had ears for the sound of hers. His eyes couldn't help themselves. They sought out the ready smile that stretched to her high cheek bones. He was amazed at how she felt so deeply, her joy becoming his own. Without thought he reached out to her and took her hand. Her startled eyes ran into his. He returned his gaze to the stage in time to see that the knight had found his friend out and was shouting for a duel. Their hands remained intertwined upon his knee.

Halfway through the second act, Gabriel's heart began to pound more abruptly in his chest. His hands began to sweat, and he hoped that she didn't notice. He glanced to the grandfather clock positioned near the door. It seemed the needles upon its golden face were moving faster than usual. Two matching beacons, heralding the hour that was ever approaching. He tried to calm himself. He tried to distract himself, but the skin touching his own was distraction enough. Had she not worn gloves?

Gabriel followed the length of her arm until his eyes were met by slender fingers, and neatly manicured fingernails. Her hand was so small in his. He absentmindedly drew circles into her palm, enjoying the feel of her delicate skin. *If only you knew...*He thought to himself, wondering all the while if he should tell her. *There will be time enough for that.*

CHAPTER 9

Katya wore his scent like her own perfume, it's lingering clove a reminder of the night they had shared. She breathed deeply, savoring the smell. Her love for him was now in full bloom. She didn't keep it, or prune it. And she certainly didn't try to hide it. Though he hadn't said anything to give her hope that he might return her deep affections, she knew what he felt for her. Desire, yes, but more than that. He had held her so tenderly through the night, falling asleep upon her pillowed breast.

Katya glanced over to where he now dozed. It saddened her to have to return to the castle so soon, but she knew he didn't want to be kept away from the war council for more than a week's end. Silently she thanked the Lord for the beautiful gift that slept before her, his curled black hair crowding around his eyes. Never in all her life could she have imagined anyone so perfect being meant for her. His face was well sculpted, and his physique…why he reminded her of the Davidic statues displayed about the royal gardens. A lock fell over his eyes. She reached to smooth it away, and a hand shot up, capturing hers in its grasp.

"Oh!"

Warm brown eyes held her in place. Slowly, playfully, he brought her wrist to his lips, pressing a lingering kiss to the skin exposed beneath her short black gloves. She shivered. And when he grinned, her heart began to beat in time to the rhythm of the carriage wheels. *Thud thud thud. Thud thud thud.*

"Have we returned?"

She didn't dare move her eyes. Nor would her head give him his answer, so she whispered to him.

"Not yet."

His grin grew, unveiling the dimple that she was coming to love so well.

"Good."

He pulled her to him with one tug. Wrapping her in his arms, he kissed her soundly. She was only too pleased to return his kisses. It wasn't until the carriage began to slow, that she drew back, hoping she could right herself before they stopped completely. With one hand to her hair, she replaced the pins that had gone askew, and then began to clasp her coat buttons. A chuckle paused her hands in their work. She looked up to see Gabriel, his face amused, his eyes stalking her every move.

"You sir, are incorrigible."

"Do not worry, my dear. You look most pleasant."

"No thanks to you." She muttered to herself as she returned to her coat and scarf.

His laughter only deepened.

"It's glad I am, to see you so amused at my expense."

"'Tis only that you are ever so lovely when you aren't all tucked, pinned, and buttoned. When your hair is all askew…"

Before she read his intention, he reached out and stole a pin from her hair, loosening a piece so that it fell into her eyes. She shoved it behind her ear.

"Gabriel! Give that back."

He moved the small metal pin out of her reach, knowing she wouldn't leave her seat to retrieve it.

"I think not. Let but one strand be free, Katya. It becomes you."

His hand untucked the piece she had put away. Her whole body stilled as his fingers caressed the lock of her hair.

"It's so thick and soft."

She couldn't hide the smile that came from hearing him sound so enraptured.

"You should have seen my mother's. Her lady's maid was a miracle worker."

"Hmmm."

No more could be said as the carriage pulled up to the gate of the castelle, for the footman was now coming to unload their stopped carriage. Gabriel helped her down, and led her inside. As they made their way up the grand staircase and toward the west wing apartments, she felt her steps growing heavy. Her feet became like lead, until they stopped moving altogether. Gabriel turned to look at her, his brow puzzled.

"Katya?"

"Yes?"

He returned to her side where she was frozen in the hallway, lifting her chin so that she had to look into his eyes.

"Why have you stopped?"

"Oh 'tis nothing."

"Come now, you can tell me."

His voice was gentle, but still she hesitated.

"Are you unwell?"

"*Nein.*"

He didn't press her, only waited. His genuine patience worked to loosen her tongue.

"It's only that I do not wish for things to go back to how they were. Before last night."

Her words were choked, but she knew he heard them clear enough.

"Oh, *mein schatz*," His German brogue sounded rough to her ears, but the endearment was not lost on her, "allow me to put your fears to rest. Though your things will remain in your chamber, the door between us will no longer stay closed."

She only nodded, but followed him when he resumed walking. True to his word, the first thing Gabriel did when they entered through his chamber was prop open the separating door with a large stone from the fireplace. He then left her to change, with a promise that he would return after he met with his father.

The majority of the day had been eaten up by their travel, and so Katya rang for some food to be sent up to them. She hoped it was okay to do so, but she needn't worry, for Gabriel didn't return until well after dark.

"I hadn't noticed I'd missed the supper hour until I saw your tray. I'm famished."

She handed him the other half of the repast, having gotten more than enough food for two. He sat with her in her solar, and told her about his time with the King.

"It seems we still haven't had a reply. Father grows more worried every day, but I know they will sign the treaty. The Lord will not abandon us."

"I only wish the kingdom shared your faith in this."

Katya was pleased that he had hope. For she too believed that God would see them through this. He may work in mysterious ways, but He was a faithful Lord, one that could be trusted in.

"They will see. I only need a little more time."

She wasn't sure what he meant by that. Perhaps he was referring to something his father had charged him with. When he had finished his meal, she cleared away the tray and utensils. Having already made herself ready for bed, she slipped down the hall to use the necessary, before returning and joining him in his room.

In the morning, Katya awoke to an empty bed. Sitting up she peered around the space, taking in all the fixtures that made it so uniquely his until her eyes had returned to where they had slept. She smoothed out the indentation left behind from where he had lay only a short while ago, her fingers tingling from the memory of having him so close. As a child she had often woken up to the terror of nightmares, and wished that someone had been there to comfort her. When she was especially young, her mother had stayed with her. But now she wouldn't have to be alone. Gabriel would be beside her, his arms encompassing her in their cocoon.

Not wanting to lay abed, and waste the day, she arose. It was a weird feeling, to have to return to her own room, but she liked that the door remained open. She prayed it was a hopeful symbol of what was to become of their marriage. Pulling her nightdress over her head she wrapped herself in her robe and rang for her lady's maid. From the little bit of light that came in through her curtains, she could surmise that it was still early yet. But she needn't fret, for Florin was ever efficient.

"Which dress will it be today, Your Highness?"

"The blush one, with the white lace cuffs, please Florin."

"Did you sleep well my lady?" A smile played about the older woman's mouth, drawing attention to the tiny wrinkles that proved she smiled often.

Katya wondered what the woman might have thought about the open portal, or if she had even noticed it. Clearly she had.

"I slept very well, thank you. And you, dear Florin, did you find your rest last eve?"

Katya could not see the woman's expression, turned backward as she was, but she felt the woman's hands still for just a moment on her clasps.

"You needn't worry 'bout me, my lady. But I thank you all the same."

"Still, it does my heart good to know you are also being taken care of. I couldn't imagine what I would do without you, Florin. You have been a gift from God these last months."

Having finished the ivory buttons that lined the length of her back, Florin returned to the front to straighten her hem, before ushering her over to the boudoir, where she began fixing her hair.

"It is my pleasure, Princess."

Holding the looking mirror up so that Florin could see, Katya wondered something.

"Did you grow up in Romania, Florin?"

"Yes, my lady. I have served the Romalo family for most of my life. My mother was also a lady's maid, you see."

"And in all that time, there was never conflict in the land?"

"Conflict? Well, there were skirmishes to be sure, and even fighting amongst our own people. But not war. The last battle our nation fought was said to be in the time of Prince Gabriel's great-grandfather. And that was rumored to have only lasted a year. There now, how does that look?"

Katya moved the mirror closer so she could peek at the woman's creation.

"It is very fine indeed. Thank you, Florin. But tell me, how can that be? That such a great nation would be so undisturbed? It seems the history of the Germana people has known nothing but war."

"Who's to say? Methinks it is the hand of the Almighty over us. Our King Andrei, has been a man of faithfulness. I believe the Lord has blessed this nation because of it."

She nodded in agreement. Hadn't she just been thinking that same thing?

"Yes, you are right. I pray now that His faithfulness will protect us once more. Especially as Gabriel prepares to take the throne."

Katya knew she shouldn't speak so in front of the servants, but she had never thought of them that way. She had been a lady all her life, but the people who cared for her had always been like family, and she chose to treat them as such, no matter the separation in their statuses.

"If you don't mind me sayin', my lady, I have known Prince Gabriel since he was a boy. Though he walks in his father's footsteps, he doesn't keep the faith the way King Andrei has. He will need you in the days to come."

Florin spoke to her like a grandmother, her words both wise and gentle. Though she was surprised by the woman's criticism of her prince, she soaked up every word, heeding the message well.

"You must be strong and stand firm. For there is great evil lurking in the shadows. The battle that is coming won't be fought outside these walls alone; the battle will need to be fought in here."

Florin rested a withered hand upon Katya's heart. Her eyes were urgent and cautious. They had talked about the Lord many times in the past months, and she knew this woman to be one of sound faith, but she didn't quite understand what the woman was telling her. So instead she held on to the words, closing them up in her heart for a later time.

Several hours later, Katya was still mulling over her exchange with Florin when Elisabeta burst through the doors of the Queen's solar. It was often a quiet place, where she would retire after her morning instruction with the queen to work on her stitching or read up on the nation's history, as she was doing now.

"There you are!"

"I take it you've been searching for me."

"Yes, of course. Where have you been?"

"I haven't exactly been hiding from you."

Elisabeta made a face at her, her embellished gray gown swishing as she moved closer. Katya noticed this particular gown had an abnormally long train to it, one that was lined with black lace, and sparkling with colored jewels.

"A new dress, I see. Where did you find the idea for this one?"

"This one is just in from Rome. What do you think?"

She gave it a twirl, before bending down to lift the hem, revealing a pair of matching gray boots that extended up to her mid-calf.

"I had the boots made to match."

"It's beautiful, Elisa. And you certainly have the shape for it."

Her friend beamed, her hands going to her tiny waist where the black lace from her ruffled collar came to a point, before she sat down in the chair next to the fireplace.

"Thank you. And how do you like your new gowns? Isn't Madame Blouson a miracle worker? Such wonderful creations made with such tiny hands." Her friend sighed wistfully.

"Yes, she was most kind. I am not as knowledgeable about modern fashions as you, but she gave me a handful of styles to choose from, and together we were able to create a whole new wardrobe. I am so glad Gabriel suggested it."

It must have been the way she said his name, or perhaps it was the look that came over her face when she spoke of him. She knew not what gave her away, but her friend all at once sat up straight in her chair and narrowed her eyes at her.

"Something has happened."

Rather than deny her friends assessment, Katya merely said, "It was a wonderful weekend."

"Indeed. Why, you are positively glowing!"

Katya tried to hide her growing blush by returning her attention to the papers in her lap.

"Hmm. It must be quite serious." Elisabeta said quietly.

Pretending to be engrossed in her findings, she took a few deep breaths to calm her nerves.

"I won't pry, so you needn't be flustered. I will simply say I am most pleased for you and my brother. Heaven knows, Gabriel is in need of a little cheering up. The man can be such a sour grape sometimes."

"He is not so very morose as you describe. But I have noticed the weight he wears, and hope that in time he will allow me to share his burdens."

Elisabeta grew serious for a moment, her hand moving to cover Katya's. "Give him time, my friend. If I know anything about my brother it is that he is set in his ways and slow to changes that involve the heart. That is why you are good for him."

"May it be so."

"It will. I just know it. Now, when do you go and see Mamă? I assume she still has much to teach you."

"I plan to meet with her after the lunch hour."

"Oh, how wonderful! Then we have the rest of the morning to ourselves."

The New Year had well past come and gone, with no word from the adversaries. Still Gabriel had not given up hope. Just this morning he had visited his private chapel, to remind God of the bargain he had made concerning his wife. Though the Almighty hadn't exactly reassured him, he remained confident.

As he stepped out onto the castle wall for his daily rounds he breathed in the crisp air. What a striking contrast he saw when he looked out. All around the land was experiencing its annual hibernation, the city was slumbering, the world looked as though it was barren and yet, he was coming alive. Falling in love. He had told himself not to. Had even reasoned with himself about why it would be unseemly to fall for her when their future was so uncertain. But he simply couldn't help himself.

"I think I am in love with her." He spoke the words aloud, as if daring himself to object to what was happening within his heart. Glancing behind him, he was relieved to see he was alone up here. Continuing his walk, he crossed over to the far side of the castle, where the southern wall faced the snowcapped mountains.

Though Katya didn't ask for much, she required all of him. It both terrified and intrigued him, making him want to give her everything he had, everything he was. *But what if I am not enough for her?* That thought alone gave Gabriel great pause. For he was not certain that he had what it took to be a proper husband for one such as Katya. Indeed, the more he learned about her, the more he knew that she was complete in and of herself. Perhaps it was her independence, or her solid faith in the Lord that she conveyed with every detail of her life. Whatever it was that she possessed, he knew one thing was for certain: Katya did not need him. But somehow she wanted him, and the truth of it left him feeling altogether vulnerable. And vulnerable was not something Gabriel did well.

"Prince Gabriel!"

He turned around to the sound of the voice calling after him.

"Franco, is anything amiss?"

"No, Your Majesty. All is well."

"You are not usually posted up here, have you been repositioned then?"

"Only for the remainder of the week. Cristo has been called back home. His missus is having their third child."

Gabriel observed him. He had only talked to either of them a handle of times, having run into the ever-talkative Franco down below where he was usually posted at the southern gate. Franco and Cristo were simple men, of plain dress and even simpler upbringing, but they always seemed to be happy. Content in their lot. In some ways Gabriel envied their modest lives.

"He is a close friend of yours, yes?"

"Yes sir, we have served together since we was boys. Neither of our Tata's stuck around long. Raised by only our mothers and being the youngest in our families, we both left home early and sought work. Course, that was time and a half ago."

The man had paused in his conversation long enough for Gabriel to see that there was no sign of gray in his beard or at his temples. He couldn't be too much older than Gabriel himself.

"I still remember when it was his first child. Right scared, he was."

"You will have to give him my compliments, to him and his wife."

"I'm certain he'll be right pleased to hear it. His oldest, Randt, is to turn five this summer. He is a grand fan of yours, Your Highness. Told his da he'd like to grow up to be one of your knights."

"He did, did he? I'm sure it will be just as he said. Many knights start their training around that age. Perhaps Cristo will have to bring him around to meet with my brother. Lucian would be eager to have a squire."

"Do you mean it, Your Majesty?"

"Indeed I do, Franco."

And he did. Lucian had mentioned to him once before about how busy he was becoming since taking over as the Vintenar, who organized the king's army. Mayhap, this was just the kind of young man he was hoping to train up. *Though he may not have time to train up one so young. Ah well, Lucian can decide what is best for the boy.*

"Well, I shall have to tell Cristo right away! He will be so pleased for his son. Though the boy's mother might not be as eager to see her son go off to learn fighting."

"It's a mother's duty to fuss over her children."

"And dear Mother, old as she is, is no exception. She's a constantly worried over me. I told her a hundred times all I do is keep watch over the castle. I haven't even been in a proper fight. Course that 'tis all to change…"

Franco realized his overstep, and shrugged helplessly. "My pardon, Your Majesty."

"Times *are* changing, Franco. But we cannot expect that the world will forever be the same."

"Of course not, Prince Gabriel. If it comes to a battle, we will see that our nation is not without protection."

"I have no doubt of it. You are a fine soldier, Franco. You and Cristo both."

"Thank you, Your Highness."

He nodded to the man, bidding him good day as he continued further along the wall. He passed several more guards at their posts. Each one a man with a family at home waiting for him. What would happen to them if they were forced to gather an army and meet the Dark Lord upon the open fields of Tala Hal come spring? He suppressed the images of wounded and dying men that had sprung to his mind. *The Lord will not let these men die*, he reminded himself. *I have kept my end of the bargain, and now He will keep His.*

He heard the commotion in the hallway long before the guard began banging on his door.

"Andrei?"

His wife's sleep induced voice tickled his ear.

"Never mind, my love. I will go and see."

Swinging his legs over the side of their large mattress, King Andrei shrugged on his robe and hastily made his way toward the door. *Whoever had it in mind to wake him at this hour better have a good reason*, he thought grimly. On the other side of the oak partition, he was met by the anxious face of his captain.

"Your Majesty, the southern wall has been compromised. There has been an attack on the castle."

His dulled senses sharpened immediately, bringing him to full attention.

"What is the damage?"

"It was all done in stealth, Your Highness. We have men tending to the fire that was started in the guard tower."

As the man spoke, Andrei moved toward his dressing closet, pulling on a waist shirt, and pair of hose. Once he had strapped his boots and donned his outer coat, he returned to the man.

"Have there been any casualties, Vidor?"

By this time Melita had come to stand beside him, her arm wrapping instinctively around his waist.

"Yes, my lord."

"How many?"

The man's face grew rigid, but he did not look away.

"Seventeen in combat. But the guard house was locked from the outside when it caught fire. I do not yet know the total, but I would surmise we lost anywhere from thirty to fifty men."

Andrei felt himself stagger at the thought of the men whose lives were taken, and he was glad for the support of his wife's strong arm.

"Thank you, Vidor. I will be along shortly."

Turning to Melita, Andrei placed his hands upon her shoulders. For many moments he said nothing, for he had not the words that could prepare either of them for what they were about to step into. He almost wished he could return them to the sanctity of their bed, pull the curtains closed, and lay himself in his wife's arms where they would be shielded from what was taking place. Looking into her eyes, he knew she shared his sentiment.

"It would seem our peace treaty has been denied."

"But Andrei, how would they have known the layout out of our castle? It was no mistake they targeted the guard tower."

"How indeed?"

He didn't want to think it, but the answer was clear. Somehow his enemy had access to the inside of this fortress. Now all he needed to find out was how. Or better still, who. Placing a firm kiss upon his wife's head, he stepped toward the open door.

"Gather our guests in the solar on the second floor. No one is to go anywhere near the main floor, nor outside. Not until we can be certain they have all been dealt with."

"Very good. I shall also have cook prepare an early breakfast. And Andrei?"

He paused.

"Please be careful."

"Always, my love."

King Andrei's mind moved as quickly as his feet. There was so much to be done. When he stepped out into the inner bailey, he saw for himself the damage that had been done. The charred remains of the gate house, having once stood as one of the highest points, now amounted to a rubble heap that reached a hand's breath above his head.

"Father! Over here."

Trying to drown out the images of his men who had been trapped whilst they burned alive, King Andrei followed the sound of Gabriel's voice. He had hoped the cold weather would work in favor against the blaze, but it wasn't so. Instead the dry air had fed the hungry beast. The torch in his hand shook slightly as he rounded the sight where buckets of water were still being thrown upon the flames licking up the stones. Each hiss and crack sickened him.

"I have sent Lucian with a small regiment to pursue the perpetrators, but..."

His voice was hesitant, unsure. Indeed his face was pale, and Andrei wondered if his son was similarly haunted by what had happened in the very walls with which they had always found sanctuary.

"Tell all, Gabriel."

"It's as if they were never here. They swept in like a nightly fog, vanishing with the morning sun."

"Surely some of our men caught sight of them."

"*Nu*. All we have are bodies. And few at that."

"Even the dead still speak. Have them searched for any clue that will tell us from whence they came."

"But surely we know this is an act of war from none other than the Dark Lord!"

"We will not allow our judgment to be clouded in this matter. Not when so many lives have been lost." When the younger man hesitated, Andrei grew impatient. "See to it, Gabriel!"

He wasted no time in seeking out Vidor for an updated report. The man had little positive to say. It seemed the men had used hooks to scale the south wall, had taken out five of the lookouts posted along the parapet, and snuck their way past the soldiers on the night watch, all without having alerted the central guards.

"What manner of men are these, Your Highness?"

"That is what I aim to uncover. Good work, Vidor. Please alert me the moment Lucian returns."

As he made his way back inside the castle, he returned his torch to an empty sconce. He would no longer need the tool's light, for the dawn had finally caught up to them. The day would uncover what the night had kept concealed, and all would know of the attack against their nation before the bells rang midday. Looking up the main staircase, he pictured his guests, lords and their ladies combined, disgruntled over having been taken from their beds at so early an hour. Thankfully, he knew his beloved wife would have soothed their grumblings, her effortless compassion keeping their minds from dwelling overly long on what transpired outside.

Climbing the stairs two at a time, he returned to his room to hurriedly change his clothes, ridding himself of the smoky scent. When he entered, all eyes turned in his direction. It was a reaction he had grown so used to, indeed he expected it. But never before had his heart been so heavy as he faced the men who had for the past three months stood beside him in the war council meetings, putting in long hours to see that the nation was kept from war. *And all of it was for nothing.*

Rather than address their expectant faces, he avoided the crowd gathered around the attendants who were serving food, and steered himself toward his queen. When all else failed, she was his one constant. It had always been that way between them, even in the beginning when they hardly knew one another, she had been his sole confidant. Even now, he knew she would gladly share his burden. It was what he hoped each of his children would find in their companions. A friend.

"The news is not good."

"I surmised as much."

"And here? How are we faring?"

"Tusta has worked up a bounty yet again. Her feast is filling their bellies, and has silenced their questions. For now."

"Yes, for now."

"What of Gabriel and Lucian?"

"You needn't fear. Both are well. I am waiting on Lucian's return before taking further action, but a decision must be made."

She only nodded. Her eyes filled with silent tears that he knew would not be shed here, among so many.

"Come, let me get you something to eat."

He followed behind her, as she ushered him towards an empty table in the corner. No sooner had he finished the last bit of his hot potatoes, then he was looking up to see Vidor waiting for him in by the doorway. He pushed his plate away and walked toward the man, throwing a swift glance over his shoulder to Melita whose eyes then followed him out of the room.

"Lucian has returned, Your Majesty."

"Very good. Let us pray he has some news."

He did not. In fact, he had only been able to trail the men as far as the forest that brushed up against the mountains.

"Their path was well planned. They knew exactly what turns to take, what trails to pursue. We didn't stand a chance at keeping up with them."

He patted his son's shoulder. "You and your men did well, Lucian."

They both turned to see Gabriel heading their way. He cut an imposing figure, with men flanking either side of him.

"We've found something."

"Among the bodies of the perpetrators?"

"*Nu*, among one of our own. Do you recognize this, brother?"

"A feather from one of Count Denla Quóis' odious hats, I presume."

King Andrei eyed the plume. It was dyed two shades of green, and looked to have been plucked from a large bird. An innocent enough piece, and yet if his sons were correct, it's thin blades would seal the fate of their future.

"Exactly, so. A signature of sorts. Clearly he is not hiding his hand in this."

"Do you think he acted alone?"

"You mean apart from the Dark Lord?"

"He is certainly arrogant enough."

A small commotion echoed from the corridor behind them. Their commander was making his way toward them with a dispatch of knights. In their midst was a man unknown to them.

"Your Majesties." The man kneeled before them, his scrapping the ground where it touched the walkway.

"Rise, Balshazar. Who is this man?"

The men spread their rank, better revealing the offender.

"We found him trying to hide in the bushes just beyond the southern tower. It would seem he has suffered an injury, my lord. They left him behind."

In agreement with what the commander explained, King Andrei could see what was left of an arrow shaft lodged into the man's right shoulder. What had seemed to be the glimmer of the sun on the man's chest, he could now see was a growing stain that soaked the garment in red. It was a wonder the man was still conscious. They wouldn't have him for long, if they left the wound as it was.

"Take him to the holding cell beneath the West Wing, and send Domn Kurtz to tend him."

Better that the man be fed and bandaged, then die before they even had the chance to question him, he decided.

"Yes, my liege. *Vino acum!*"

The men left quickly, giving Andrei little time to think through his next steps.

"Vidor, relay to my wife that the fire has been put out, and our guests may return to their rooms. Increase the number of men guarding the castle, and see to it that the townspeople are alerted to the danger. I want men on patrol through the streets and at our borders. Post guards at each of the main gates. No one is to enter or exit the citadel unless it is by your say so."

"Let it be done as you have said, Your Highness."

He then turned to his sons. Both of them looked haggard from the morning's activities.

"Your mother has food ready. I'm sure she, along with your wives and sister, are eager to see you."

They both nodded, and followed him inside.

"Gabriel you will gather the war council directly after you have broken your fast. We will adjourn in the Great Hall. Lucian you will accompany Vidor to the dungeon to unearth what you can about the wounded man."

The three of them parted ways, before meeting again in the solar. Much changed from the hour before, the room that once held so many now only housed the members of his family.

"Tată!"

Elisabeta ran to him as soon as he entered the room, her flowing skirts hindering her little. She threw herself into his arms, and began to weep.

"I was frightened when Mother told me what had happened."

"*Fetița mea.*" He whispered comforting words to her, rubbing small circles into her back until her tears subsided.

When her brothers entered the room behind him, she rushed to give them hugs too. Seeing his family all together, Andrei wondered what the next few days would mean for them. *Is war our only option, Lord?* He prayed there was another way. It was his eldest son that worried him most. Perhaps they would have to push back his coronation. He would not step down from the throne in the midst of such turmoil.

Andrei's eyes followed Gabriel as he walked past his bride and straight to the table laden with dishes. He wondered if his son had even seen her waiting for him. Gabriel's hands were stiff, his motions methodical. He gathered himself a goodly portion and moved to sit in the nearest chair. The king watched as Katya moved to stand beside him, her concern apparent in the way she fiddled with her gown. But Gabriel only shooed her away, and then returned his attention to his plate.

Andrei's heart squeezed as the girl returned to the window she had been standing at, a look of dejection on her face. His mind was torn. Perhaps he ought to go and speak with his son, but what would he say? That he knew the reason behind the invasion. *But do I? If only I could just see the Dark Lord for myself, maybe then I would know the truth.* He sighed, and began to rub his jaw. *Nu, I will find another way.* So instead he kept silent, hoping that a clear path would be shown to him. Praying that his son's marriage would not be the cost of his own folly.

After spending hours in debate, with several of the lords trying to persuade him otherwise, his father still showed restraint! *Was the man daft?* He immediately regretted the thought. His father was one of the wisest men he had ever known. He was a noble king, whose people had long since put their trust in him. If he thought they should wait, then perhaps waiting was best.

Crossing his arms behind his back, Gabriel stepped out onto his balcony. It irked him that he disagreed so readily with his father. Was he truly so self-serving that he couldn't bear to see things the other man's way?

He lifted his eyes above the surrounding wall where he could see clouds forming in the skies above him. *How fitting*, he thought. Looking out beyond the walls, the surrounding burg drew his attention. All day there had been large amounts of activity. People closing up their shops, leaving their homes, and moving outside the city limits. Where it was safer. Gabriel felt like they were failing them. The castle was meant to be a place of refuge for their people. Not a battle zone.

Moving his gaze away from the pitiful sight of empty streets and hollow walkways, he took in the inner sanctum of the grounds. He immediately picked out the burnt edifice that had once been a noteworthy structure, its pointed peak having flown one of the Brasovian flags, with the Romalo insignia across its girth. The courtyard itself was filled with people, mostly soldiers going about their duties. His eyes nonchalantly searched the crowd below him. That's when he saw her. She was standing between his mother and sister. It looked as though they had just come back from the chapel, though he didn't know why he was surprised. Surely the church wouldn't let a war scare keep them from hosting their hourly prayers.

She was dressed in blue velvet, with black gloves. Kid leather boots peaked out from under her skirt as she walked. Her cheeks held a pink rogue from the afternoon sun, and a wimple covered her golden blonde hair. He remembered the way the strands felt like silk between his fingers. He remembered that, and so much more. Leaning further over the balcony, he shielded his eyes from the glare hoping to catch a better sight of her. Hoping to see how she fared. When she suddenly looked up in his direction, Gabriel shoved himself back from the edge of the stone rail.

How could he have been such a fool! His "pact" with God was doomed from the beginning. His marriage was supposed to have fixed everything. Wasn't that why his father had pushed him to find a wife so soon? A queen would have secured his throne, given him heirs, stopped the war, and God *knew* all that. Doubt began to creep in, resentment its steady friend. *Of course, the All*

High and Mighty wouldn't have seen fit to grant me this one simple request. Before he could stop himself, Gabriel scoffed.

"I did what was right by her, didn't I? Then why haven't they signed the peace treaty?"

He knew better than to expect an answer, but still he waited. The wind had begun to pick up, and he felt himself being nudged backwards by it's long arm. His father had once told him to have faith. To believe in a God who reigned in love and grace, but he could not. Would not.

"Do You even hear me?" He tried again. Still, nothing. "People have died because of You!"

Something cold and wet hit his face, and he moved back inside. Shutting the door tightly against the wind, he watched as rain droplets pelted the window pane. Each tap was like a pierce to his heart. Each pellet, a tiny stab from the blade of rejection. *What does God have to do with a man like me? He has His kingdom, and I have mine.*

Gabriel closed his eyes, but couldn't keep them that way. He knew Katya would be coming inside also. His gaze sought out the door that connected their bedchambers. *I can't face her.* Not when he was so uncertain of what lay between them. Now that his pact with God was at an end, did he still want to be with her? It hurt him too much to find an answer. So, he moved forward and shut the offending egress. Three steps were all it had taken. Such a small distance for him to close out the woman he thought he had come to love.

Gabriel moved to sit on the bench at the foot of his bed. The wooden surface held him for many long moments. Not knowing how long he sat there, he was almost startled by the hesitant knock on his door. Deciding to ignore it, he neither looked up, nor made an effort to stand when the door then opened. He only hoped it wasn't *her.*

"Prince Gabriel? Are you well, Your Highness?"

It was only Rogen. Gabriel wondered if he should open up at all to the man who had served him well for so many years. Though he longed for a friend, he held back. It just wasn't the way between them.

"In the years you have known me, Rogen, have I ever been ill?"

"No, my lord." Rogen paused, as if sensing out his master's mood, before continuing. "Unless you count the time you had stomach pains from eating too many bristle berries."

He felt his lips lift slightly at the jest. Tearing his gaze away from the fixed spot that had, for no other reason than to distract his wandering mind, held his attention, he looked up at Rogen with a proper grimace.

"If I remember correctly you were also there. Except your ailment also produced a reddish rash around your lips."

"They were not called *bristle* berries for no cause."

"We were in bed for weeks."

"And our mothers were too distraught to tan our hides, like we sorely deserved."

They both chuckled over the memory of it, and for once Gabriel felt a sort of affinity with the man. Perhaps that was why his tongue felt loosened.

"Are you certain you are alright?"

"I am not, but then neither can I expect to be when all seems to have come crumbling down around my feet."

Rogen then came to stand in front of him. His face serious.

"You are doing the best you can, Your Highness. We all see that. And we will stand behind you no matter what comes."

"I thank you Rogen. Now, what word have you brought me?"

His manservant paused slightly, as if considering whether to speak more on the matter, but the moment had passed. Instead, he nodded and made known his reason for having sought Gabriel out.

"Your brother is waiting for you. He has finished with the prisoner, my lord."

Ah, yes. The prisoner.

"I will go to him straightaway."

Gabriel left then. He was eager to learn what they had found out about the man. If anyone could make him talk, it was Lucian. Thankful to have escaped catching sight of his wife again, Gabriel made his way to the West Wing where his brother stood waiting for him equally as desirous to know all.

"And what of the war council?"

Gabriel straightened his surcoat that had begun to slip during his brisk walk.

"Many are crying out for blood, but father has once again calmed the storm."

"And the counter attack?"

"No measures will be taken at this time."

Lucian made a face. One that adequately reflected some of Gabriel's earlier thoughts.

"That's why I hope you have something here that will prove the Dark Lord is indeed behind this."

"Father wants peace, and that is right, but to what end?" His brother's impassioned speech was highlighted by the use of his hands. "When even at this moment another group of mercenaries could be headed here, or if not here then to one of our villages. There are too many helpless people out there. Action needs to be taken. And soon, Gabriel."

Once again, Gabriel felt the weights of responsibility and duty take their place upon his shoulders. To better carry the burden, he fisted his hands, clenching them behind his back.

"You are right, we cannot keep all safe. But the council requires more than just words. What of the prisoner?"

"Come. See for yourself."

Lucian led Gabriel down a set of stairs that went directly to the dungeon. The stone passageway was cold, and dimly lit. The air grew staler the further they descended, until he was choked by the acrid stench of decay and waste. At the end of a tunnel the path opened up slightly, revealing a short row of four cells, two on one side, two on the other. Lucian led them to the farthest one on the right.

"Give us a moment, Captain."

"Yes, Your Highness."

The man used his key to unlock the cell, and then retreated to the far side. Most likely having stayed at the edge of the steps where he could be within calling distance, should they have need of him.

"*Vous allez parler avec nous, oui*?"

Gabriel watched as the man nodded to whatever Lucian had asked him.

"He is not from here?"

"No, he is from France."

Gabriel nodded, looking deeper into the cell, which was really no more than a small space containing only a straw mattress, an untouched bowl of broth, and a chair. The very one in which the prisoner sat now.

"Ask him why he is here? Who sent him?"

"I don't need to. I will have him tell you himself. His Romanian is a bit broken, but it understandable."

As Lucian started off again in the man's native tongue, Gabriel observed him. His arm had been bandaged, and his face had been cleaned of all the blood, but something was different than before. He looked…

"Scared." The word slipped from him in a whisper, having not meant to be spoken at all.

"Yes, he is. He even begged us to kill him rather than send him back."

His brother's words were telling enough, but it was the man's eyes that gave him away. They jutted back and forth around the room, never landing on any one object for too long. Almost as if he were seeing things around them. *But what?*

"Tell Prince Gabriel what you told me, Jean."

When the man finally spoke, Gabriel had to listen closely to catch all the words, for some were offered in Romanian and some French. Much of it he could not make any sense of. But it was clear that this man had been sent with the sole purpose of causing war. Now if only he could understand who had sent him.

"He hates them…anyone *qui suit*…The Way."

"What does he mean?"

Lucian translated the question, and waited for the man's reply. The man had begun to shift on his chair, unable to keep still. His eyes still wandered the room, looking for something, but he remained attentive to what Lucian said, and began to answer. His speech hurried.

"He's talking about Christians." Lucian paused, listening for more. "He says that his Master is against us because our nation upholds the faith. But there's something more. He keeps mentioning revenge. That *we* are to blame." Lucian turned back toward the man, "Blame for what, Jean? *Blâmer pour quoi*?"

"I cannot…He will *voir*…uh…see."

"Who, who will see?" Gabriel stepped towards the man. His words urgent. His presence demanding answers.

"The Dark Lord!" Jean's words were no more than a shrill cry, and no sooner had he spoken them aloud than a flush of real terror swept over the man's face. His eyes fixated on something behind them. Instinctively Gabriel swung around in an effort to counteract the attack, but no one was there.

"This man is half crazed!"

Jean had thrown himself to the floor and was curled into a ball, his hands cramming themselves against his ears in order to block out whatever he was hearing inside his head. Gabriel and Lucian exited the cell and shut the door, neither of them having been prepared for this kind of reaction.

"There is evil afoot."

"Let us be away from here. We have all we need to tell father and the others. Vidor!"

The captain had already begun coming toward them, having heard Gabriel and the Frenchman's cries.

"What shall we do with him, Your Highness?"

"Leave him here for now, but keep watch round the clock. Have two men posted if need be."

Gabriel marched himself down the hall and up the stairs, not looking back to see if Lucian had followed. He had his information, now he wanted to be as far from this place as was possible. Something about the look in that man's eyes did not sit well with him.

CHAPTER 10

Another week had passed since the initial attack. People were bustling about, everyone seeming to have purpose. Everyone but her. A group of men had begun reconstruction on the guard tower. Gabriel, Lucian, and the King were preparing to send men to aid the fighting that had broken out along the border. Even the castle servants were busy with the extra amount of people who were now being housed within the castle grounds. It made Katya feel useless.

And what of this morn? Were the blankets you sewed for the soldiers not a great aid? She thought back to this morning, when she had been with the Queen and her ladies. Together they had organized a group of twenty women to sew blankets and kerchiefs. Though the snow had melted away, a clear sign that spring was coming, the nights were still bitter cold. Especially for men with no roofs to house them.

Katya drew her legs up underneath her. Where she sat now, in the attic tower of the west wing, she had a clear view of the southern hills and the tall oak trees that were regaining their color. None were allowed to leave the castle walls and though she often enjoyed the indoors, even her favorite places like this one were slowly losing their charm. *There must be something else I can do.* She was in desperate need of a diversion. Anything to take her mind off of her husband.

He had pushed her away the morning of the attack. Had even closed the door between their rooms, something she had been shocked to find. But still she didn't know why. What had she done to make him turn away so suddenly? It was more than just the war, she knew. *Pray for him.* The words came to her from someplace deep inside. Scooting herself up to lean against the window's edge, she looked down to where the chapel's bell tower peeked back at her. The more she looked at it, the more it seemed to call out to her. Inviting her to come and find solace. *Alright, I will come.*

Standing to her feet, she was startled by the door opening abruptly behind her. Even more startling than that, was the man who had opened the door. *At least this time he has come himself.* Seeing him in person was much more preferable than the servants he had been sending to relay his messages.

"You mustn't wander off, Katya. People have been looking for you."

People? Did he mean that *he* had been looking for her?

"My apologies, Gabriel."

She bent to pick up her shawl, pausing to clip it around her shoulders, before fixing her gaze on his. His eyes twitched ever so slightly, and she wondered what it was he really wanted to say.

"Well." He shifted his stance. "If you are finished hiding yourself away, perhaps you could find something for Elisabeta to do. She is driving me to distraction with her questions."

He scolded her like a child, but she didn't mind. She'd rather him say anything at all. Even anger was better than the cold silence that had returned. The way they were standing now, in the same room but still not together, reminded her of when they were first married. But this time it was different. Very different.

Back then she had watched him struggle, had seen how he fought against the things raging on the inside. Had even felt him being torn between the crown and the man.

And now? She asked herself silently. Now, it was like they had become one whole, instead of two pieces. Now she carried his burdens within herself. She too was torn apart when he struggled, because now he was somehow a part of her, and she a part of him. Katya couldn't keep herself from moving towards him. But she did not say what was on her mind.

"I will go and find her, and Adelina too. Together we will make ourselves of use."

"Very good. I will leave you to it then." His words followed him out the door, taking him away from her.

Determined to go and visit the chapel before seeking out Elisabeta, Katya made her way down the long and narrow staircase. As her feet led her towards the outer courtyard along the rear of the castle mount, she thought of the priest who had befriended her as a child. Back in Germany, her nursemaid had often taken her to the old town cathedral. It was there she had first met Friar Hanz.

She smiled fondly at his memory. He had been an older man with gray hair at his temples. She had liked his deep voice, and the stories he told. More than that, he was the one person who had given her hope when she spoke of her mother, and had taught her more about the Lord. Friar Hanz had, in some ways, become a father figure for her.

Having reached the chapel, she looked around for one such minister, and immediately saw a robed figure lighting the candles at the altar. When the man turned toward her, she noticed he was younger than she had expected. *Why, he cannot be more than five and thirty!*

"Buna dimineata, Your Highness."

"Good day to you, Father."

"What brings you here, my child?"

"I confess I am worried about the fighting going on, the way it has taken a toll on my husband. He hasn't been…the same since it started."

The priest then showed her to a nearby bench where they both sat. His hair was tawny and cropped short, his face was all odd angles and long lines, but his eyes were kind.

"Yes, war is an evil affair, but oft times 'tis deemed a necessary one."

"It is not only the war that worries me, sir."

Katya hesitated, glancing around to be sure they had privacy.

"Go on my dear. Your words are safe here. What troubles your heart?"

"The prince and I…well, we seem to be at war ourselves." She shrugged a little, feeling helpless when she spoke the words aloud. Thankfully he did not probe her, for she herself did not know much more beyond that. The young priest was silent for a moment, his head bowed in thought, or perhaps prayerful contemplation. When he looked up his face seemed to shine a bit brighter, and he spoke with profound wisdom.

"You must fight for him."

"But how so?"

"Battles are not fought by human might alone, Your Highness, but by faith in an all-powerful God. The Lord our Christ told His disciples to fast and pray. To seek first the Kingdom of Heaven, and the path of righteousness."

Katya was instantly reminded of the words Florin had spoken to her about fighting the battle in her heart. Perhaps this is what she had meant.

"And if prayer does not work? Then what shall I do?"

The priest sighed in disappointment, though his voice remained tender.

"Ye of so little faith...You must *believe* Princess Katya. Believe and do not doubt."

In her mind she wrestled with this. From what she recalled of her mother, she knew the woman was of great faith, and so it seemed was the King and Queen. They each had founded their lives around the truth of Jesus Christ as the Son of God who loved them and cared for them. It was her belief too, but to what end?

"I will leave you now. If you seek Him here with all your heart, He will be found by you. But you must be ready to listen."

She thanked him, and watched as he disappeared down a narrow corridor. Looking about she knew there were several places she could choose from to pray, but because no one else was near she decided to stay where she was. Unfolding the cushioned pew she knelt down, her hands folding automatically on the bench before her.

"Heavenly Father, please hear my cry. I do not know how to fight this battle, but I wish to be strong. Aide me in my faith, and forgive my unbelief."

An unwelcome emotion tightened her throat, making her eyes burn from the threat of tears. She knew she had a choice. She could wallow in her own self-pity, crying over her situation, or she could turn to the Lord and let Him heal her. His arms had always been the ones to bring her comfort, and only His words had given her strength. He alone had seen her through her mother's death, her father's rejection, and only He could change Gabriel's heart. So when she felt Him draw near, she opened her heart to Him. In the stillness, in the quiet, a voice came to her.

Finally, my brethren, be strong in the Lord, and in the power of His might. Put on the whole armour of God, that ye may be able to withstand in the evil day, and having done all, to stand.

It was scripture, she knew, for somehow it was familiar to her. Had her mother read it to her once? Katya was not sure, but her heart filled with renewed resolution.

"Thank you, Lord. May I hold your word close to my heart. If there is any way I can help Gabriel and his men, please show me."

She spent the better part of the next half hour on her knees in the chapel, praying and pouring out her heart to the Father about all the cares she had been burdened with. Once at peace, and with her mind set to a new course, she stood. She waited only a moment to see if the priest would return so she could thank him, but he did not. So instead she began her walk back to the castle. When she rounded the corner to the garden gate, the one with the tall statues sporadically placed throughout, she thought she heard a dog barking.

One moment she was seeing the cobblestoned path that sloped up and into the keep, and the next she was seeing something else entirely. Laid out before her was the old east wing of the castle, the one now rarely used. In the vision, her and Elisabeta were playing hide and seek, as they often did when she was a girl spending the summer's there with her parents.

This time it had been her turn to hide. She crept down the hall to the open atrium where massive tapestries hung from the walls. Wanting to find the very best spot, she had scooted towards the back wall, to the tapestry that covered the furthest corner. Pushing the heavy fabric aside, she was intrigued to see a carving in the stone of the wall. It was faded and a little dusty, so she had wiped it as best she could until at last she was able to make out the face of a wolf.

"Katya?"

Someone was calling her name. She blinked a couple of times, in an effort to clear her vision.

"Katya, are you well?"

The image in her mind began to fade, bringing her back to the present where a concerned Lucian was clutching her by the upper arm.

"Was ist passiert?"

"I asked if you are well. Come, let me find you a place to sit." Without her consent, he lifted the latch to the gate beside them and drew her forward before showing her to a marble bench.

"I am fine, Lucian. Only, I've just had the most peculiar thing happen..."

"What is it?"

Suddenly it clicked. "The sketch from his coat, I remember where I've seen it before!" She shot up from the bench, her legs ready to take her straight to Gabriel. Surely it was a sign! *Oh, thank you Lord!*

"Woah there, do slow down. Perhaps you wouldn't mind telling me what it is you're speaking of?"

Katya didn't want to waste any more time, but then she wondered if it might be better for Lucian to relay the message to his brother.

"Yes, of course." She sat back down beside him, collecting her thoughts as she did. Next, she told him of the vision she'd had, and where it had taken place.

"In the old east wing you say? Why no one hardly goes there anymore, ever since the new one was constructed. I believe it has even been barricaded off."

"Perhaps the servant's stairs are still open. That is the way we took to keep from getting caught."

"Yes, I do recall the tomfooleries you two were often into." He grinned at her. "But this is news indeed. I must go and tell Gabriel. You will be alright if I leave you?"

He still looked as if she might faint or something, but she reassured him that she would do nothing of the sort.

"Gabriel! I must needs speak with you."

"I can't now, Lucian." He had told Vidor he would meet with him. That was over two hours passed, and he didn't like to keep people waiting. "We shall speak on the morrow."

His brother would not be so easily dismissed, and Gabriel found himself coming nose to nose with him.

"Nay. We must speak now. It is about the wolf engraving." Though Lucian's voice had lowered, Gabriel still took the precaution of looking about.

"What do you mean?"

"I was just speaking to your lady wife…"

"Katya?"

"…and she told me she had seen it before."

"How does she even know about it in the first place?"

"Now that, I did not ask. I merely thought you had discussed it with her."

Gabriel thought on that. How indeed had Katya known about the image of the wolf? He certainly had never spoken of it. He thought of going and finding out just that, only to recall why that would not be so good of a decision. His mind was still reeling from their encounter this morn. The way she had been all curled up in front of the window, looking terribly fetching with the day's sunshine gently caressing her figure. He called himself to attention.

"Never mind that. Where did she say she had seen it?"

"In the old east wing. She remembers it from when she was a child."

"But as children we were warned to stay out of that part of the castle."

Lucian merely shrugged. "Surely you did not always do what you were told dear brother?"

Gabriel grew irritated at his brother's sheepish smile. He hadn't the time for games, not when they finally had a clue to work with.

"Show me."

Without another word Lucian turned on his heel, and began his way through the mazelike halls of the fortress. They wove in and out of several connecting corridors until at last they had made it to the servant's quarters. The service floor was located beneath the main level, and stretched out to both ends of the east wing. It adequately housed more than fifty servants and staff who bunked two to a room. Gabriel hadn't been in this part of the building in ages. He didn't know what made him more uncomfortable, the confined hallways or the prevalent threat of being caught somewhere he had no place in being.

"If I remember correctly, the stairs leading up to that section are just over...here."

Lucian turned into an alcove that lead straight off the main walkway. Before them was a wooden door.

"Think it is unlocked?"

"Only one way to find out."

Gabriel stepped back while Lucian tried the knob. When it didn't budge, he began using his shoulder to give it a push.

"You are welcome to offer assistance at any time."

Noting his brother's out of breath comment that reeked with sarcasm, Gabriel turned himself to follow suit.

"Very good, on the count of three then? Ready, *unu, doi, trei!*"

The two of them ran forward and went crashing through the portal that suddenly opened it's arms to them. Tumbling into the bottom step, Gabriel caught himself by his hands. Lucian had done the same, before he burst into laughter.

"Well, that was refreshing!"

"Yes, yes. Let's not tarry, shall we?"

Picking himself back up, he stepped back out into the hallway and grabbed the nearest torch. Using the light he carefully shut the door behind them, not wanting to return only to find themselves trapped. The staircase was narrow and the ledges were thin, making their ascent no easy feat. With careful steps the brothers climbed past the main floors, going all the way up where the old east wing should have entrance.

"Another closed door." Gabriel noted grimly.

"Hopefully this one will open more easily."

Handing off the torch, Gabriel tried the handle. It succumbed graciously beneath the press of his hand, groaning like an old man as it opened. When his eyes adjusted fully, he was able to make out a large space, sectioned off by two walls. He moved toward the first room.

"Be careful of the floor, Gabriel!"

Held back by Lucian's hand, Gabriel looked at his feet to where Lucian was pointing. Large holes ate up the ground, where single wooden planks lay exposed with nothing beneath them.

"Perhaps this is why they closed it off."

"Yes, I remember Father saying this part of the castle was in dire straits." Taking the torch back from Lucian, he held it up.

"It seems we will have to navigate the more sturdy looking parts of the floor. From what you described, we need to somehow get over there."

He motioned toward the wall opposite them, the one that still had a few large but terribly faded tapestries hanging on it. Moving with caution they made their way over, having to go the long way round in order to avoid the particularly gaping depression that eyed them from the middle of the floor. When they got to the atrium that Katya had mentioned, Gabriel and Lucian spread out and began looking behind each of the tapestries that remained.

"Gabriel, over here!"

He followed the sound of the voice coming from behind the room one over. His heart sped up. *What if they really found the emblem? What then?*

"What is it?"

"I think I've found something. Bring the light over."

Gabriel stepped closer and held up the torch light once more, as Lucian began rubbing his hands over the surface. He then blew against the dirt that had accumulated, where the fabric had fallen away. When he did that, a familiar symbol rose to the surface.

"Well, would you look at that."

"It's the same one alright."

The wolf here looked different from the picture on his parchment. More animated somehow, as if the texture of the wooden paneling wizened it's features. The hooded eyes pierced him, daring him to unearth its secret. *What are you doing here?* He silently asked the animal.

"Surely, this must mean something?"

Gabriel noted the hope in his brother's tone, one he dared to share. He still didn't know what connection this figure had with the Dark Lord, but he knew that if he sought hard enough, he would find the answers.

"Gabriel? Have we seen this before? I mean, apart from the one you found in the library."

They stared even harder at the image before them. A memory tugged at the back of his mind, it was fuzzy and he didn't recall more than a single face.

"Rogen!" They said the man's name in unison. Lucian filling in what Gabriel had forgotten.

"He used to take us to his fishing spot, blindfolding us for half the trip so that we wouldn't know our way there."

"Yes, I remember now. He said he didn't want us to come back ourselves and take all his fish."

"And just up the one hill, was a huge boulder with the face of a wolf hidden behind its bushes."

Though he couldn't be sure, Gabriel wondered if Lucian's face reflected a bit of crimson over this particular memory. The only reason his brother knew about the stone was because he had once tried to follow Rogen, his curious nature getting the best of him. Lucian was only a boy at the time, so when he had hidden himself in the bushes on the hill and had come across the wolf, the symbol had frightened him, giving him away and leaving him in the hands of a very angry Rogen. Lucian must have been going over the memory in his mind as well, for he whispered indignantly.

"I thought he was going to feed me to his beloved fish…"

"You came home crying so hard I couldn't even be sure it wasn't a real wolf that scared you so."

"It felt like it was real."

His brother's weak defense made him chuckle. But the thought of getting Rogen involved sobered him quickly enough.

"Do you think we can find it on our own?"

"*Eu nici*, Gabriel! I haven't been there in years. In fact, I don't know that I ever went back after that day. We'd have more luck finding a hidden treasure than that man's fishing hole."

"Well then, I suppose we have to make Rogen take us there."

"He can be trusted. Besides he doesn't have to know why we're going. We'll just tell him about the parchment you found in the library and that we remembered the very same one from the stone mount."

"And if we find something? Then what?"

"*Ce va fi, va fi.*"

What will be, will be. He didn't like it, not one bit. But if it was the only way, then what choice did they have? And so that is exactly what they did. Another hour later, having found Rogen into the open enclosure, having to duck his head, but once he was fully inside he found that the tunnel was wide enough to hold an average male.

“It’s a passage way, I think.”

“But where does it lead?” This from Rogen, whose eyes had become saucers.

“Let us find out.” Lucian extended his arm, allowing the other man to go before him. Gabriel could tell his brother was just as eager. He was always one for an adventure. Using his hands on either side of him Gabriel then blindly led himself down the first section of the tunnel. When his hand bumped into a protruding object, he swiped the unwitting torch from its holder, searched for a piece of flint on the ground and struck it against the siding. The small flame illuminated the space around them to four paces in each direction.

“It looks as if it goes on forever.”

“Not so, do you feel that draft? I’ll bet there is a bend up ahead where the underpass will diverge two ways.”

Rogen was the only one who did not speak as he followed the two brothers further down the tunnel. Gabriel was thankful for the man’s silence, it helped him forget he was in on it.

“Well Gabriel, which way shall we explore?”

“We haven’t the time to pursue both. I expect our absence has already been accounted for. I will have to make it up to Vidor for abandoning him on such short notice.” He looked into black chasm before him, then to the identical one on the other side. Knowing they would have to come back another day, he decided to go with his gut. “This way.”

A peculiar thought crossed his mind as the abyss swallowed them completely within its depths. *If walls had ears, if walls had lips, would they speak of what they’ve heard?* Or would their secrets be kept sealed like the air tight space around him? Where they

easily enough in the servant’s wing, the three of them were on their way.

“You say you found the engraving in the library, Your Majesty?” Rogen asked, sitting atop his bay gelding as he led them further from the castle. The amount of turns they had taken made Gabriel realize he wouldn’t have been able to find his way back even if he hadn’t been blindfolded.

“That’s right.”

“How very strange. I had never thought it meant something. Just some ruin from past peoples who inhabited this land ‘afore us.”

Gabriel didn’t reply. He didn’t want to let on more than they already had. Going on horseback certainly saved them a great deal of time. When the forest opened back up again, the rest of the land laid down flat, making the two hills in the distance seem even more profound. When they came to the second hill, they tethered their horses to the low hanging branches of a nearby cypress tree.

“Should be right up this trail here.” They followed in Rogen’s footsteps as he led the way.

“Do you still fish here often Rogen?”

“Yes, Prince Lucian. Though winter has kept me away, I try to come at least once a week. This place helps me clear my mind. Gets me away from all the hubdrub of the castle.” He stumbled a bit. “Excuse my lord, I meant no offense.”

“Not at all. I too have a roaming spirit. ‘Tis why you’ll often find me running the hills with Kip.”

“He’s a fine piece of horseflesh, Your Majesty.”

“I know it. That beast is as faithful a companion as there ever was.”

It rankled Gabriel at how easily Lucian was able to converse with others. He didn’t ever seem to meet a stranger, nor did he seem at all put off by the gap in their station. *He is the second son after all. Not being the heir apparent allows him such leisure,* Gabriel thought with more than a little envy.

"Here we are."

They stood at the very top, looking out over a splendid valley basin bathed in golden sunshine. Down in the corner was a lake that was neatly tucked into a copse of large bushes. *O plasă de pește.* A fish's net, as Rogen always called it.

"It's all coming back to me now...," Lucian dramatically paused. His voice lowered as if he were sharing a secret. "That fateful day."

Neither he nor Rogen heeded his side remarks, but went straight to the stone mount whose head rose above the surface of the brush, its stature like that of a gigantic man. Crouching down, Gabriel began to search over its body, looking for any sign of the wolf. *There!*

He called out to them. "You told no tale, brother."

Lucian and Rogen circled round from the opposite side, stopping to see the image Gabriel had unearthed.

"Yes, just as I remembered."

"Except this one has no fur. Nor does it boast of the vicious fangs that wanted to claw your flesh."

In good nature, Gabriel jostled his brother's arm. They had found something at last, and this somehow in connection to the one within the castle.

"And what is this?"

He glanced to where Rogen was pointing, his eyes taking in something that hadn't seemed to be there before. Perhaps it was the way his body no longer blocked the sun from hitting the stone surface, illuminating a tiny scrawl beneath the carving.

"I cannot read it." He paused, and drew from his pocket the small scrap of parchment he had originally found in the library.

"But it seems to be the same writing as whatever is h
scroll."

Together the three men stared at the curved letters t
words none of them were familiar with. Though the c
was similar to Romanian, the letters did not spell out
they used.

"Perhaps it is Dacian writing, Your Highness."

"Why do you say that?"

Rogen returned his look, his role of humble serva
slightly under the context of the present situation.

"'Tis only that when I had asked my father abou
years ago, he said it must 'ave been engraved by the Dac
who dwelt in this land before us. A warning of sorts."

"A warning, or a marking?"

Gabriel knew that look, "Tell all, Lucian."

"When my men and I would hide the thing
transported, or even stolen, we would always leave a r
a nearby tree or on the face of a boulder. So that when
return we could find the very place the items were kep

"You think there is something buried here?"

"Nay, not buried per say, but hidden."

"Then let's look further. We shall spread out. There
this symbol is reoccurring. We must needs find what i

Lucian found it first. Not more than two hands
Wolf's right ear was a ridge in the face of the stone. To
any man it would seem like a typical crack often foun
as old as this one, but with enough pressure applied
the fissure deepened, until the entire symbol was push
reveal an opening in the stone.

"I didn't expect that." Lucian quipped, his humor wi

Gabriel's blood thrummed in his veins, excitemen
through him like liquid energy. Making the first move,

treaded shadows for over a mile, he wondered about the ones who had traversed this path last. Most of the tunnel remained on a somewhat even surface, until finally a slight incline drew them back to the surface. A wooden cutout stood out like a stranger among the stone surfaces. Gabriel stepped aside to allow Lucian in front of him.

"Will you do the honors?"

"With pleasure."

He rammed himself into the handleless frame, and with a loud crack the portal opened.

"Where are we now?" Rogen finally spoke up. Not having been with them earlier, he did not recognize the atrium.

"The old east wing." Gabriel stepped around them both, his feet warily avoiding the eroded floor boards. Lucian came to stand beside him, having closed the concealed door that bore the marking. Once sealed, the surface became camouflaged, even more so when it was hidden behind the tapestry that had once covered it completely.

"An escape route then?"

Gabriel glanced toward Rogen, not wanting to include the man in his conversation. But he needn't worry so, for the man was already standing off to the side, having resumed his servantly demeanor. It seemed the castle had that effect on people. Even Gabriel felt the camaraderie between them disbanding.

"But if so, then why did Father not say anything about the symbol? Surely he would have knowledge of this."

"We must find where the other leads."

"Yes, but not today."

They decided to keep what they had learned between the two of them for now. No telling what their father would say, or whether he would be entirely honest about his knowledge, for Gabriel still believed the man was withholding something.

We are close to something very real here, I can feel it, Gabriel thought as he readied himself for the evening meal. Rogen had found the time to lay out his clothes, but the man was not to be found. He grew wary over the man's unusual behavior. Gabriel only hoped he had not been mistaken in bringing the man along.

CHAPTER 11

He didn't have time to speak with Lucian alone again until some three days later, but by then his brother had moved on to other things.

"They are getting more daring, Gabriel."

He needn't ask what he was referring to. The attacks on the castle had steadily multiplied in the last week.

"We should have known they would never have consented to a peace treaty. Not their ilk. Indeed, we should not even expect them to go to war properly."

"We must act. An immediate response is pertinent."

"It isn't as simple as that."

"Isn't it though?" Lucian's words were as agitated as his stance. "Only today there have been twelve reports of incidents within our borders. Twelve, Gabriel! Shops have been burned down, people are being taken from their homes…our nation is in mayhem!"

"How are they getting in? We have already doubled the men posted at the western border."

Lucian's voice lowered, "Perhaps, they are not getting in, perhaps they are *staying* in."

"What do you know?"

"Rumors of men seen in the Leta forest."

"Rumors are hardly evidence. Our men are being trained and organized as steadily as we can manage. Reinforcements are due within the week, but I haven't the exact number."

Lucian stalked off, making Gabriel pursue him to the unoccupied corner of the training fields. All around them were bare chested men wielding swords or shooting bows. The sounds of fighting seemed to ease Lucian's tension. Gabriel watched as his brother tore off his own vest and bent to pick up a weapon.

"Care to spar with me."

It wasn't really a question, but neither was Gabriel dressed for the occasion. Carefully removing both his mantle and chest piece, he added his tunic to the neat pile and turned to receive the sword Lucian held out to him.

"*En guard*."

Their longswords met in the middle of their circular shaped mound, well worn by the booted feet of previous sparrers. The brandished edges tapped against one another, a metallic ringing meeting his ears.

"You have more than your share of doubts, I'd wager."

Clang, clang, side step, thrust.

"You don't know the half of it."

"I'm listening."

With learned concentration he met Lucian's forward step with his own defense measure, drawing their blade tips up before deflecting.

"Our defenses aren't strong enough to stay the advances. Pressure along the western border has increased, forcing our men to engage."

"That is expected."

Lucian advanced on him then, retaliating against Gabriel's unworried reply. With his skill set, he easily gained the upper hand. Gabriel had all he could do to parry his *molinetto*.

"Even with all our allies, and the necessary funds filling our coffers, I wonder at our nation's ability to sustain war."

Gabriel was out of breath now, his form waxing. Lucian's blade nicked his arm, drawing a hiss of breath between his teeth. He stepped back and out of the circle of engagement. Glancing at the offending mark upon his forearm, he watched the red liquid make a trail across his tan skin. A single droplet dripped to the ground staining the grass red.

"Blood will be spilt, brother, but I fear it will not be our enemy's. If Father doesn't move to gather the army soon, we will lose more than just our men…"

Gabriel bristled at the silent rebuke. "War takes time Lucian. A wise leader tips his sword in patience, and girds his loins with wisdom."

Lucian stepped back, a look of surprise crossing his face before it split into a grin.

"Now you sound just like him." Moving to his neglected tunic, Lucian tore a strip from it's sleeve, and handed it to Gabriel. "You will be a fine king someday."

"I do hope you are right. But first, we must see to it there is still a kingdom left for me to lead."

Her idea had worked wonderfully. She smiled to herself as she laid her bliaut across the back of her chaise; her happy feet turning themselves in a small twirl before she landed in a heap upon her bed. Stretching out her arms, Katya sighed blissfully her mind roaming back over the day's success.

After Lucian had left her in the garden, she had pulled together both Elisabeta and Adelina to share with them her plans for the soldiers. Having remembered her time with Friar Hanz, who was a Benedictine, devoting his life to caring for the sick with herbal remedies, she knew the wounded would need attention. So, with the Queen's permission the ladies spent the day cleaning out a space in the citadel for a *heilendes haus*, as Friar Hanz had called it.

It would be a sanctuary for wounded men to come, where they would find cots, and blankets, and the healers would have fresh water and bandages. Tomorrow they would go in search of the plants needed for the herbal medicines. Katya could still see the look on Adelina's face when she had mentioned this bit.

"Herbal tonics? I thought only the pagans condone such things."

Katya had smiled her very best smile. "I assure you, Adelina, I learned it all from my minister back home. As he said, 'Tis the good Lord who gave us such remedies at our disposal, to provide healing to the sick, just as Jesus did'."

Turning over on her bed she drew her feet from where they dangled. After they had finished with the space for the soldiers, Adelina had pulled her aside.

"I may not be able to join you so early in the morning." She had said. "You see, I've been having quite a bout of sickness when I awaken."

Katya had not understood her meaning straight away. "I hope you are not falling ill?"

Adelina had only smiled and reached out her hand to her. "No silly, I am trying to tell you I am with child!"

"Oh heavens, what wonderful news! Have you told Lucian?"

"Yes, just last night. He has been so restless lately. I was almost afraid all the fighting would dampen the news, but he is beyond delighted. We both are."

"It is the Lord's blessing indeed! God has a way of showing us His hand in all things."

Sitting up, Katya moved to finish changing into her night things, her hands going to her own belly. She knew she was not in the family way herself. Certainly she would have known by now if she had been. *What would it be like to carry Gabriel's babe?* When she returned to her bed, she wondered if she would ever have the chance. *If it is Your will Lord, let it be so.*

It was early when she woke; the sun had not yet risen and she felt for sure that the night still had hours left in it. What then had pulled her from sleep? She heard the noise again, and went to inspect. Crossing the space between her bed and her door, she gently tugged it open, peaking her head out into the hall. But no one was there. Closing the door behind her she stilled herself, listening. *Ah, there it is.* Moving toward the sound she went to stand before the portal that led into Gabriel's chamber. Coming from the other side was the sound of cries. *Gabriel?*

Without another thought she opened the wooden frame. Waiting till her eyes adjusted she then moved further into his room. When she saw her husband bare chested she felt somewhat sheepish at having entered uninvited, but when she took in his disconcerted form and the frantic cries coming from his lips she knew he was having a nightmare. Instantly, she recalled the terrible nightmares that had often plagued her as a child. Vivid horrors of her mother's death, or her father's unpredictable anger played about over and over in her mind. It was the reason her nursemaid had first begun taking her to the church.

"The devil is after your soul, child." Her nursemaid had told her, scaring her worse, "we must get you to Friar Hanz. He will know what to do."

And he had. The good Friar had silenced her fears by telling her of the Lord who was always with her, and as she grew old enough to understand, he had even explained her mother's death and the reason her father had grown cold.

Coming back to the present, Katya fixed her gaze once more on her beloved husband. Not wanting to wake him she went only close enough to reach out her arm and gently smooth his troubled brow.

"Shush now, *meine leibe*. 'Tis only a bad dream."

His cheek twitched beneath the pressure of her hand; his breath evening out. When he began to stir, she decided it best not to be found there and instead retreated to her own bed across the way. Whatever he was facing, he wouldn't have to face it alone. She would stand beside him through it all.

The next morning flew by. Katya and the other ladies they had assembled were able to collect more than enough herbs and plants for their stores. Thankful to be done early, she made haste to return to her room. Her heart was heavy over Gabriel. Since the night before, she couldn't stop worrying over his welfare. It wasn't until the dawning of the sun that she had finally drifted back to sleep, just in time to be awakened by Florin.

Now it was in her heart to pray, as the priest from the chapel had suggested. Kneeling beside her bed, she closed her eyes and lifted all her cares unto the Lord. She didn't know how long she stayed that way but soon she felt a shift; as though her burden had lifted and peace was bestowed in its place.

Hearing voices from the room beyond hers, she hoped at least one belonged to her husband. Katya suddenly had the distinct urge to go and see him.

"Gabriel?" She peaked her head shyly around the corner.

"Katya." He seemed startled to see her. His eyes went wide when she stepped fully into his bed chamber, having closed the door behind her.

Gabriel was there alone, making her wonder if he had been talking with anyone at all. Looking closer she could see that his hair was mused and his eyes were shadowed. An ache settled behind her rib cage. To see him like this, was to know pain.

"Did you need something, Katya?"

His firm voice didn't welcome her company, nor her compassion, but still she gave it.

"I have come to see that you are well, husband."

Her eyes betrayed her as they swept across the floor to his bed. The very one they had shared many nights ago. Chiding herself, she pulled her eyes away hoping to meet his gaze. He didn't look up. If only he *would* look at her. If only his gaze would hold her again. Maybe in that moment their eyes could at least have been lovers. *And I would know that he cared for me*, she finished the thought in her mind. But instead he turned away from her, his long form moving to stand before the window; his interlocked fists guarding his back.

"Husband? You are right to remind me of my role. Husband, prince, leader. It seems a great many things are expected of me this day. I wonder which will win out."

"Do you think that is what I care about?"

Gabriel scoffed. "It's what everyone cares about, madam. Wealth, title, position..." He pointed out toward the throng of people milling about in their daily tasks. "The whole lot of them. Every time I sit in a war council meeting, those men expect me to be their future king. The one who will lead them to victory on the battle field."

"But what of character, of heart?"

"Those are also important. A prince must be both discerning and compassionate, both firm and gracious."

He sounded like a performer rehearsing his script, each line offered up in rote memorization. It frustrated her that he thought only of himself as the heir to the throne. She went to stand beside him, looking out over the same landscape as he. But where he saw an expansive kingdom that would one day fall to him to toil over, a people who would become a burden in their own right, she saw a vast and wonderful nation that the Lord had brought forth a place filled with the blessing and favor of His providence.

"And the man behind the crown?"

"What of him?"

"Surely, you see more in yourself? I know I do."

She turned to study him then, watching as he stilled completely. His arms slowly unfurled from behind; a look of vulnerability crossing his features.

"It's all I have."

"Do you not see? All that we have is because the Lord has been good to give it."

She watched as he transformed before her. His muscles stiffened, and his frown deepened. Each word he spoke was cutting, like the point of a sword dipped in bitterness.

"What my family has is founded on the efforts of my father and his father before him. Our family line goes back centuries. The Lord does not have time to *trifle* with such matters as these. He may place a king on the throne, but it is the king who then rules his nation as he sees fit."

The way he spoke. The blackened look in his eyes. Suddenly, it all became very clear.

"When did you stop?"

His ranting ceased, and he turned to face her.

"Stop what?"

"Stop believing."

"I couldn't possibly know what you mean."

"When did your heart grow callused against Him? When did He become so small, so little, that you forgot it was He who called you in the first place?" She stepped toward him, hoping that he could see the love she had for him in her pleading eyes. "And when did you stop putting your faith in Him alone?"

Instead of acknowledgment, or even some sign of understanding, his face only darkened. It seemed she had struck an ominous chord. Something that ran deep and was rooted to the very core of his being. *This* is what she faced. A much greater enemy than the one at their border. Her fight was against the beast that had all but consumed her husband.

"You know not what you speak." His words were flat. Hollow. Empty. But she could sense the anger behind them.

"Gabriel, please. I can't live like this. I…I miss you."

Katya reached out her hand, but he jerked back, and she let it fall to her side. *How can I get through to him, Lord?*

"What of your family? Does not the Lord watch over them?"

"If so, then He is doing a poorly job of it. Lucian has been taken captive."

She sucked in a breath. Adelina had begged off this morning with a headache, but Katya had known it was more. Lucian had left yester eve with a small squadron to pursue the men hiding in the Leta forest. A dangerous gambit to be sure.

"Have any of his men returned?"

He moved to the other side of his bed, where he opened the chest of drawers and began rifling through it. Her question was left unanswered. Watching him withdraw from it a hooded coat, scabbard, and sword belt, she grew nervous.

"Where are you going?"

He ignored her and continued packing, so she switched tactics. She tried to argue, to make him see. But her words fell on deaf ears, until…

"Have you gone to your father? As king, he will know what to do."

"*I* am to be king! And I will hear no more of this. Leave me. Now!"

He didn't know what had possessed him. Never in his life had Gabriel raised his voice at a woman. Clenching the reigns in one hand he closed his eyes, and called forth the devastated look on her face when she had returned to her own room. It was an image that would forever be imprinted upon his mind. This time he had gone too far.

He had always known himself to have a great deal of supremacy. How could he not, when he was raised to be a prince after all. But his pride had become a silent sort of enemy. More akin to a thief that had stolen its way into his heart destroying any humility or tenderness that may have lingered there. Now, there was only left a steel plated apathy that neatly covered his own arrogance.

Blast it all! But she was right. He did not believe. Hadn't for quite some time. Even when he had made that foolish deal out of desperation for peace, he hadn't believed God would answer him, because he questioned whether God even existed. It wasn't that he didn't want to believe, for having a faith like that of his parents, or even his wife would bring him more good than the alternative, it was simply that God had never been made known to him. Not in a way that he could see or feel. Not in a way that was tangible. *No*, the only things that existed for him were his kingdom, his people, and his family. Those were what he knew to be real.

"Hiyah!"

Gabriel spurred his mount faster, hoping to outrun whatever storm was brewing. When he had received the report that Lucian had gone ahead with a group of his men to search the Leta forest, he had been angry, but hopeful. In more ways than one, Lucian was free to take the action that Gabriel could not. Even their father had seen the wisdom in what Lucian could recover should he find the men suspected for the crimes against the villagers.

But then his captain had returned with the news that they had been ambushed. The man himself had sustained a grievous injury, living only long enough to tell them that Lucian had been taken captive.

It was growing late, and darkness had already begun to set in. He had waited for the evening prayers to finish, so that the inner bailey would be empty before he departed. But now he could barely see the road before him. Above all, he hoped that stealth would work to be a far better tactic.

"Onward, Vixen. You know the way."

Following the path as far west as the next village, Gabriel slowed Vixen down to a trot. Coming upon the empty houses he knew that there were few families who remained. Most of them had fled once the attacks had begun seeking refuge in towns farther south. Sensing no danger he pulled back on the reigns, and brought his horse to a halt before he jumped down. He then walked them over to the well that was positioned in the center of the square, quenching the thirst of both him and his companion.

"Drink up, *cal*. You have done well."

Once they were both settled in an abandoned stable, Gabriel laid down in hopes of finding rest. Though his body was weary, his mind would not succumb fully to slumber. Instead it tossed and turned like waves in a storm. Reliving for the umpteenth time the conversation that played out between Katya and himself, Gabriel asked the same question that she had. *Do I still believe?*

He didn't know if he was ready to face such a demand, to know such a truth. But still he did not back down from its challenge. If he were to be the next king of Brasov, he would know this about himself. Shifting into a more comfortable position, if there was to be found one among the hay in which he had bedded down in, Gabriel turned his thoughts to his brother. How many was he up against? Were all his men dead? *Acht Lucian! What trouble you have found this time.*

He felt no fear for Lucian's welfare, only an acute outrage at the ones who would dare ransom a son of Romalo. Knowing he would need the rest, he silenced his wandering mind and closed his eyes. A few hours more and he would be back on the road, and then to the Leta forest.

Someone was in her room. She knew it the moment the door had opened, the movement releasing a cold chill and an interloping presence. The light from the hallway cast a long shadow over her bed. Sitting up very slowly she prepared her lungs to scream.

"My lady, it is only I, Rogen."

Sighing a breath of relief, Katya unclenched her fisted hands. "What is amiss?"

"My lord, the Prince…he is gone."

Katya shook the sleep from her head as she sat up straighter, trying to understand what the man was saying to her.

"What do you mean?"

"After the supper hour, he had me dress him for travel, and then gave me leave for the remainder of the night."

"But he did not say where he was headed?"

"*Nu.*" A moment of silence, and then, "I believe he has gone after his brother."

"How do you know?"

"It is my job to know, Your Highness."

It was what she had feared most. After they had argued, she had returned to her room to read her the few pages of scripture given to her by Friar Hanz, hoping the ancient text would calm her nerves. Somehow she had convinced herself that he was only planning to check on his men at the borders, or to seek information. But this was worse. What if it was a trap? What if the Dark Lord was even now lying in wait for her husband? Drawing up from her bed, she pulled on her robe.

"We must go after him. Find him before he himself comes to any harm."

Her eyes adjusted to the darkened room, and when they did she turned on her heel and headed straight for her closet. "Gabriel, what were you thinking?" Her words were muffled, but even if Rogen did hear her, he didn't respond. Not until she had reached for a weapon of her own did he seem to sense her sincerity.

"My lady, should we not alert the king first?"

She looked at the dagger in her hand. It was the last gift her father had ever given her, the spring before her mother had died. He had even shown her how to throw it properly, the two of them spending many a cool afternoon in the field behind their house. It was a skill she had kept up with even after her dear mother was gone, hoping that her achievements would bring back the sparkle in her Vater's eyes.

"I think not. 'Tis too late to wake the castle. If we catch up to him before he meets danger, we can persuade him to return with us."

"But how will you find him?"

He had her there, and well he knew it. Though he had not moved from his place by her door, his stance had shifted, making Katya wonder if he now stood with his arms crossed over his chest.

"I don't suppose you would have access to such information as that. As you say, it is your job to know these things, is it not?"

Hoping he would rise to the bait, for she sensed Rogen was as concerned for her husband as she was, she waited for his reply. It didn't take him long to capitulate.

"I know someone who could help, but I still do not advise you to go alone."

"I suppose you will just have to come with me then, won't you?"

She didn't give him a chance to respond. "Now I must change if we are to leave within the hour. That should also give you time to find out from your man where to go. Can you have horses ready for us?"

"Yes, Your Highness. I will be waiting for you at the northern gate, only do not go the way of the chapel. Instead, cross through the kitchens to the servant's entrance where they bring in the milk each day. Do you know the one of which I speak?"

"Yes, I think so."

"Very good then."

"And Rogen?"

"Yes, my lady?"

"Thank you."

Now that he was standing in the glow of the hallway she could see his simple nod, before he disappeared completely.

By the time they had saddled their horses a storm was raging. It was raining hard with sheets of water pelting her sideways.

"Thankful I am for this thick cloak and hood. How do you fair, Rogen?"

She peered out through the small opening, and did her best to make out his rain blurred features.

"I am well enough. My lady, are you sure about all this?"

"He is my husband, and he is in danger. I would not leave him out there all alone."

"Well then, we shall do our best to see him out of harm's way. If we take this road south, it will lead us to the Leta forest. That is where Prince Lucian is said to have been captured."

"Very good, I will follow your lead."

Riding as they were in the pouring rain hindered them from moving very fast, and with the wind blowing as aggressively as it was, she was having enough trouble keeping her horse steady. Together they traveled several miles before the storm finally let up. Though it was a warm night for spring, she felt a chill. Her cloak had kept most of the water out, but she still knew her clothes to be damp, especially her skirts.

"We shall stop just up here, Your Highness. There is a village around this bend where we can have a quick rest."

"*Nein*. I do not want to stop. If it is as close as you say, then we are almost there."

"As you wish."

Rogen kept pace with her the rest of the way, his eyes roaming back and forth to the growing brush on either side of them. They passed by several rows of empty houses, and for the first time Katya was able to see the impact of the growing unrest upon their nation. The road had begun to narrow a ways back, and now that they were moving beyond any remaining habitations, they were like sitting ducks. An easy target for whoever had captured Lucian.

"We will need to be cautious. Once we get to the edge of the forest, it will be better for us to travel on foot."

She had hoped they would find Gabriel before that point, but already the sun was unraveling itself over the horizon. Over the next mile her eyes grew heavy, so much so that she had to pinch herself to stay awake. When at last they met the road's end, she could feel a bruise setting in below her wrist.

"Come, my lady, let me help you down."

With great effort she untangled her hands from the reigns she had been gripping so tightly, afraid that if she fell asleep she would tumble to her death, and allowed Rogen to assist her off her horse.

"I ought to ride more often if I plan to endure any more such adventures." She said teasingly.

"It didn't help that half our journey was spent in the rain, Your Highness." He kept his hands gently at her shoulders until she was steady enough to stand on her own. "I am going to tie up our horses over there, so don't wander off too far."

Nodding to him she looked to the vast landscape before her. Tall cedar trees that stretched as high as the clouds dotted the forest. The pale pink dawn wove a breath of fog in and out of the massive foliage where it then swirled around her feet. If she hadn't needed to relieve herself so badly, she would be more concerned about what lay beyond the tenuous haze.

Not wanting to call out to Rogen with her intentions she simply walked a short ways, and found herself an enclosure that would hide her well. Her mind was so centered on how they would find Gabriel that she didn't even hear the men sneaking up on her.

"Come out lass, we know ye're in there."

Embarrassed and more than a little indignant over having been spied on, Katya quickly adjusted her skirts and stepped out of the shrubbery.

"Who are you, sir? Surely you do not make a habit of accosting unsuspecting women?"

Their faces were blank. Where she expected remorse, or at least the decency of chagrin, she found only empty stares. These were no ordinary men. One man, the one with the sword drawn, wore skin the color of leather. She surmised it's tint came from too many hours spent in the sun. The other man was fair haired and boyish looking. Neither of them belonged to this land.

"And what exactly are ye doing in this part of the forest, lass?" The fair one spoke again.

"I got lost." It wasn't a lie exactly, she told herself.

"I think naught. She looks of royal ilk to me Jas."

The tanned man used the tip of his sword to push back her cape, taking in the clean lines of her finely made riding gown. She stepped back from the man's unwanted touch.

"You'll have to be a commin' with us. Let's go."

Knowing better than to put up a premature fight when Rogen was only a number of paces away from them she went quietly. *Lord, please keep Rogen safe.* Forcing her to walk between them, Jas and the other man led her further into the folds of the forest's lair. It wasn't until they came fully out of the copse of bushes that she realized there was another man with them, one who looked as if he came from the Orient with his almond shaped eyes and long black hair. They hadn't gone very far when the men decided to split up.

"She wouldn't 'ave come alone. We'll go and find her escort, whilst you take her o'er to the camp."

Handing her off to the leather skinned man, whose grip was like an iron manacle around her arm, Katya was then led to a small clearing. Her heart was racing at the thought of being in the company of such brigands, but she trusted that her Lord had a plan. As he pulled her behind him, she saw a familiar face and relief flooded her.

"Gabriel!" The words left her mouth the moment she saw him. Not bothering to look around, her eyes remained glued to his figure. He seemed altogether unharmed except for the slight bruising beneath his left eye, and the blood spattering his shirt. *May it not be his.*

"*Liniște*!" The man's stern voice led her to where Gabriel was, a frown sitting heavily upon his lips. Her captor then made her sit upon the ground with her back to the tree, upon whence he bound her both hand and foot.

"I am glad you are well, Gabriel," she whispered when the dark-skinned man was out of range. Her voice did not have to carry far, for he sat on the other side of the tree with his back to her.

"Why have you come?"

"I did not come alone as you suppose, husband." Her own voice grew terse. It hurt that he didn't seem to care one wit for her own welfare. "I brought Rogen with me."

"Rogen? Where is he then?"

"Hopefully, he has gone back to the castle to get help."

"*Humph*." Gabriel grumbled, not looking the least bit happy to see her.

"Be quiet over there!"

A large man with a curved scar along his brow called out to them. *He must be the one in charge*, she thought keenly, for the dark-skinned fellow had gone to report directly to him, and now they looked as though they were discussing what they would do with their additional captives. Overall Katya had counted at least four of them, not counting the two others that had found her in the first place. Feeling Gabriel shift beside her she knew he was calculating as well. Though she could not detect his intentions it seemed he was also trying to free his hands.

"But you have no weapon on you. What will you do once you are free?" She whispered to him again moving her lips as little as possible.

"I will have to improvise."

Then she remembered. "I have a dagger hidden in the folds of my skirt. Perhaps, if I could get to it, I could cut us loose."

He only nodded, for Scar, as she was now referring to him, was coming their way. He had ordered two of his men out of their encampment, for what she could not tell. She only prayed it was not to alert the others. She didn't quite feel up to meeting the Dark Lord, or his malevolent army at present.

"I thought I'd told you to keep quiet. Are you asking for trouble then?"

"Your fight is not with her. Let her alone, I am the one you want."

"Let her alone, eh? Ha! Not when she will ensure us of your cooperation, *Prince*."

His voice was awfully high for a man so big. It made each of his words seem like shrills from an angry sandgrouse. When he moved toward her she knew the threat was real enough. That, combined with the menace clearly painted within his dark pupils, made her head feel fuzzy, but she tried not to cry out as he roughly loosened her bonds and dragged her to her feet.

Her wrists and feet had been bound so tightly that they were completely numb making her falter in her steps. As the pin pricks of returning blood flowed into her extremities she winced when the ogre of a man began pulling her away from Gabriel.

"No, please!"

She needn't fear, for help was soon coming. With a breath of relief she watched as Rogen stepped from the shadows of the trees, his body illuminated in the soft glow of the morning sun. The Lord had indeed heard the unspoken prayer of her heart, and sent an angel to rescue them.

"Release the princess!"

Scar whirled around to face Rogen. The moment his grip loosened upon her arm Katya jerked herself free and ran back to Gabriel. Their captor paid her little attention for Rogen had shoved the young man Jas in front of him. A fatal wound to his shoulder bringing him to his knees.

Turning her gaze away she withdrew the dagger from her skirt and began sawing at the thick ropes that still held her husband.

"Hurry, I must get to my sword before the others return and we are overtaken."

He felt the ropes slacken at his wrist and knew Katya was doing her best. Keeping his eyes on Rogen and the man called Gusta, he watched in shock as his seemingly ill-equipped valet effortlessly slayed the other man that had rushed at him from the side.

"Or perhaps not."

Once his hands were loose, he then freed his feet and stood. *Now where did they put my sword?* He didn't see it anywhere around them, and hated to waste time. So instead he scooped up the vacant sword from the man who had just fallen, and then turned to find Katya. She too was standing ready. The dagger in her hand made her look like the fabled *Gratea*, the women warriors his father had described to him as deceptively fierce. From what was written about them they had fought alongside their husbands in choice battles, winning the victory when their ranks were outnumbered.

His heart swelled. Even now she did not turn from him, and he knew he could count on her. But more importantly he wanted to protect *her*.

"Stay behind me."

As Rogen was already engaging the giant Gusta, Gabriel moved toward the last man among them. He was older and gristly; his face wrinkled by the sun. With little fear Gabriel took him on. The man only had a short blade with a rounded edge. One easily overcome by Gabriel's own borrowed weapon and prominent skill. Having dealt the death blow he caught the man's lifeless form and eased him to the ground. Rogen came to stand beside him.

"Where did you learn to fight like that, Rogen?"

They both looked to where the giant had fallen.

"All the young men of the castle are being prepared, Your Majesty. We train several times a week. Besides I have three younger sisters. I know how to look after my own."

"Yes, you have proven yourself more than capable with a blade. I see you have alerted my wife of my absence."

Gabriel's tone had grown hard. He wanted the man to know his displeasure in the matter.

"Yes, Your Majesty. She was adamant that we come aid you."

"You have put her and yourself in unnecessary danger...but, I am glad that you came upon us when you did. Else the King would have to send his army to rescue both his sons. A trial he would not thank me for."

"But Gabriel, where is Lucian?"

He turned back to his wife noting that her hair was a mess, and she looked as though she hadn't slept in ages. It only just occurred to him that they must have traveled straight through the night to have caught up with him. *But we haven't the time to rest now. I must get her to safety first.*

"I was overtaken before I could find out."

"I'll bet he could tell us." Rogen walked back over to the young man who was wounded. He seemed to have passed out.

"We will bring him with us, but we must move from here before the other two return. It is a small miracle that they have not heard the clamor and come already."

"*Dank dir, Jesus.*"

He overheard his wife's whispered thanks, and tried his best not to correct her. Any ground gained thus far was due to their skill, certainly not an invisible God whose hands were far away from them. It chafed him to think that she put so much faith into what could not be understood.

"Quickly, bind his wound so that we can help him walk."

Before anyone could move Katya was already bending to lift her outer skirt. She then ripped a long strip of fabric which she then handed to Rogen. When the bleeding was stopped by the white linen, Gabriel and Rogen pulled the man to his feet propping either of his arms over their shoulders, so that they could move swiftly through the forest.

"What is the plan, Your Highness?"

"We will head farther south rerouting ourselves to the village of Destol. I assume you still have your horses?"

"Yes, I was able to tether them well before pursuing Her Majesty."

"Good. They will be patrolling the main road, so we will have to make our way through the hills. Let us hope they haven't moved Lucian yet. This will be our only chance. If they take him across the border, he will be lost to us."

"Then let us make haste."

Her words gave him strength forcing him to admit he was glad for her company, albeit begrudgingly.

With little resistance they were able to carry the unconscious man from the furrows of the forest. Once Rogen was mounted on the gelding, Gabriel handed him up their prisoner, and then leapt atop the remaining horse. Looking down he met the expectant gaze of his wife who stood with her hands lifted towards him. Without a single hesitancy he reached down and pulled her into his arms, relishing the feel of having her near him once again. As they began the climb of the hill nearest them, having to slow their pace to traverse the treacherous terrain, he felt Katya nestle against his already tightening chest.

"Will this path not take us longer?" She had turned her head so that he could catch her words in spite of the whipping wind.

He moved his own head forward until their cheeks were touching. He could almost feel the warmth of her growing blush. "It will, but we cannot afford to ride out in the open. Besides the slower pace will make it easier on Rogen."

"What do you expect to gain from a wounded man? I pray you do not intend to kill him."

"He would do no less for us, I assure you." He felt her tense. "Still, should he tell us all he knows, and aid us in recovering Lucian, I would offer leniency."

Her shoulders relaxed then as if she was satisfied with his answer. With the sun at its highest point above them they entered Destol. Another barren burg, this one only recently unoccupied.

"Whoever left here was in a hurry. There are still canned apricots in their pantry, and salted meat in their larder." Katya had already begun looking around in the hovel they had taken shelter in.

"Help yourselves to whatever you find, and when he awakens be sure he gets some also."

While Rogen and Katya tended to the foreigner Gabriel scoped out the town looking for any signs of danger. It seemed all was quiet. *A good sign*. Heading for the town's well he gathered some water for the horses, and returned with another bucket for them.

"Is he awake yet?"

"Only just, Your Majesty."

Gabriel set the bucket down, searched the nearest cupboard for a mug, and filled it with some water. He walked beyond the thin hanging curtain to the bed that held the fair haired man.

"What is your name?"

"Jas."

Coughing as he tried to sit up to sip from the cup being held out to him, the man Jas drank deeply before falling back against the wall.

"You *will* tell us what we need to know."

"And if I don't?"

"It matters not to me. You'll most likely die either way." Gabriel's pointed words seemed to reach their mark as the man looked to his shoulder and the blood soaked bandage that had replaced his shirt.

"I'll be good as dead should I share with the likes o' you." His accent thickened with the pain. It seemed the effort to sit up had done him in, and Gabriel knew he wouldn't have much more time to get information.

"Where is my brother?"

"So ye are the prince? Gusta said as much, but I wasna' sure."

Gabriel jerked forward and pressed on the gaping wound causing a gritted yelp to come from the man's lips. His brow was covered with sweat, and his skin was paling rapidly.

"I'll not ask again."

"He's still…in the forest." The man's breathing was labored, his words coming out in chopped fragments.

"What else do you know?"

Jas barked a laughter. "That ye'll be accursed should you try to go up against the Count and 'is master. The one is half crazed; the other pure evil."

"Gabriel, please let me tend to him."

Katya appeared beside him from nowhere at all. He had hoped she wouldn't interfere. She didn't wait for his permission only moved around him to the man who was slowly fading before them. In her hands was a basket, from which she began to pull miscellaneous leaves, roots, and something that smelled like tree sap.

Jas put up no fight as she unwrapped the soiled linen and began applying the thick poultice she must have been making out in the kitchen. Once the wound was smothered in the dark liquid Gabriel watched as she then covered it with the leaves and thin flakes of bark. Halfway through her ministrations, Jas slipped back into unconsciousness. This allowed her to lift his shoulder and wrap the wound with fresh linen. Gabriel wondered at the state of her underdress, from where he knew she had taken the additional cloth.

"I will thank you not to interrupt me again."

She turned to face him her hands already crushing up the roots in a small dish. They had stopped their work.

"Had I not stepped in he would have died! Then what help would he be?"

Though she did not raise her voice, her chest was heaving. Her reaction fueled his own anger.

"Regardless, you will not do so again. Am I clear?"

"*Ja*. But know this, I *will* tend to him, even after you have collected all you need. He will not die until he's had a fair chance."

"Your mercy is unwarranted. He is the enemy."

"*Nein*, Gabriel. He is a mere man. 'For we wrestle not against flesh and blood, but against powers of darkness.'"

"I know not of what you speak."

The woman talked in riddles; her eyes begging him to understand her. But he could not. Instead, he left her to finish and went out to speak with Rogen. His valet was not in the living area as he assumed, but in the outbuilding where they had put the horses. The man was speaking softly with the gray dapple. The horse nickered in response to whatever he had said. He did not look up as Gabriel entered.

"What news?"

"Lucian is still being held somewhere in the forest." Gabriel propped his hip against the stall and crossed his arms over his chest. "Katya is tending to the man."

"She has a way with herbs. Seems she knows something of healing medicines."

"Yes."

What else could he say? He did not know this about her. It seemed there was still so much they had yet to learn about one another. Rogen finished combing out the horse's mane and set down the brush he had found.

"Do we know how many we are up against, Your Highness?"

"We do not. Without more information from Jas, we would be going in blind."

"Then we must wait for him to come to."

"I'm afraid that is our only option. Let us hope he is not out long."

Two hours later, Jas was sitting up in bed eating the small portion Katya had made for him from the food she had scrounged up. Gabriel noticed that his eyes held less pain, and his color was back. Whatever Katya had given him was working.

"What will it be then?"

"I'll tell ye what yer wanting to know, if ye give me your word that ye'll grant me my life."

Gabriel considered this. Out of the corner of his eye, from where he sat, he could see the skirts of his wife's dress peeking from behind the curtain. Fully aware of her eavesdropping her presence had its desired effect on him.

"You have it. Now, tell me what you know of my brother."

"He's being kept on the east side of the forest, in a cave that backs up against the mountains. 'Tis but five kilometers from 'ere."

"And the men guarding him?"

"We run in small groups. No more than twenty together at a time. The others are spread out between here and the Kilmore Woods beyond those hills." He pointed out the window to the peaks off in the distance.

"That is why our men have been unable to detect you."

It made sense. Small groups attracted less notice. *Little wonder the village people never saw them coming. They moved like ghosts in the night, just as they had when they attacked the castle.*

"And how do you know my brother is where you say? Have you seen him yourself?"

"No, I have not. But the guards are rotated each half day, and I 'ave spoken with a few of them meself."

From what little the man was describing to him Gabriel had to admit he was impressed by their tactics. It seems they had been well trained to conquer using stealth and subversion. It made him even more wary when he thought of the mastermind behind this operation. Gaining what he needed to pursue Lucian, he then returned to the kitchen where Rogen and Katya awaited him.

"You'll stay here with the man." He said firmly to his wife.

"Will that be safe, Your Highness?"

"Better than for her to come with us."

"You have some way to make him sleep, yes?"

She nodded.

"Good. We will be back before dark. Keep your dagger handy, and do not leave this house. Do not even go near the windows."

Not taking any chances Gabriel had Rogen tie the man securely to the bed, and saw that he drank all of the laudanum. He also made sure she had plenty of water.

"If he awakens, do not go too close to him. Be sure he already has water and such within reach."

"Gabriel, I will pray for you."

He knew she would say more, if not for the untimely presence of Rogen in the doorway with the horses. Not knowing what would happen in the next several hours, he reached for her hand and gave it a reassuring squeeze. It wasn't much he knew, but it was all he could think to do for the moment. Turning away, he took the reins that were held out to him, and centered his thoughts on regaining his brother.

With each passing hour her mission became more and more clear. She felt certain now that the Lord was calling her to bear up the shield of faith. To stand in the gap and see that a man, and his kingdom, return to the Lord. For if they did not, she feared they would lose everything. *Perfect love casts out fear,* the voice in her heart reminded her. She was determined to remain steadfast in that as well. No matter how many walls he put up between them.

"They haven't returned."

The man was right. They had been gone a long while. *Lord, help me to be strong in the faith you have given me.* Starting with this man.

"If your man does not succeed, they will find us and kill us."

"We will not die today."

Gabriel had warned her away from the man, and thus far she had kept her distance, but now the tonic was wearing off and he was wide awake. Keeping her back against the screen, she eyed him warily.

"How do ye know; how can you be so vary sure?"

"I feel it. In here." She placed her hand over her heart.

"Das crazy."

"As certain as the sun will set upon the horizon this day, I know that the Lord keeps watch over me and mine."

His eyes were shadowed with pain, but not from his injuries. Lifting his good arm, he reached out for the mug she had filled with water whilst he slept, and took a drink.

"Ye remind me of me mam. She was the same as you. Always going on about the Lord and Jesus."

"Did you listen to her?"

"Nah. I was a strong willed lad, with bigger dreams than me mam's one room shanty. The summer I grew strong enough to hunt on my own, I took off."

"And have you found all that you were looking for?"

Katya kept her voice gentle. For whatever reason, this man was opening up to her, a complete stranger, and she did not want to let the moment pass her by. She watched as his eyes closed, and he sighed deeply. A minute went by, and she thought perhaps he had fallen asleep, but then his voice filled the silence.

"No, your ladyship, I cannot say that I 'ave. Not like what my muther had, not like what you have."

"What we have is faith, Jas. Faith in the one true God. Faith that what He says about us is true. Do you know what He says about you?"

"Nothing good, least whys."

In that moment, all of her sessions with Friar Hanz, all the years of his reading scripture to her and telling her about the Lord, came rushing to the surface.

"The Holy Scripture says that 'Whilst we were yet sinners, Christ died for us'."

He answered her back, quoting a scripture of his own, "For God so loved the world that He gave His only begotten Son."

"So, you do remember?"

"I guess I must 'ave been listening after all."

A small smile tugged his cheeks, and Katya felt overwhelmed by the love of God for this man.

"Do you recall the rest of it Jas?"

His brow knotted for a moment, and then his eyes began to sparkle as he finished it.

"'That whosoever believeth in Him shall not perish, but have everlasting life."

"I believe that is true with all my heart, and because I have put my faith in Him, every empty place has been filled. It can be the same for you, Jas."

His head nodded once as if he was considering it, but then a cynicism crept into his eyes, and his gaze became hooded.

"I'll 'ave to be thinking on that, I will."

He said no more, only laid his head back against the wall and closed his eyes. She knew that was her cue to leave, and so she returned to the kitchen where she knelt near the single wooden chair and gave Jas over to the Lord.

CHAPTER 12

Katya's eyes opened slowly. She must have dozed off in her place beside the table. Looking around she tried to orient herself with her surroundings. *Oh yes, I'm in the village Destol. We have come to rescue Lucian.* Rubbing her eyes, she glanced toward the window. There was only a sliver of light still left in the day.

She hadn't meant to sleep, not while Gabriel was away, but she had not been to bed since the day before, and her whole body was still sore from the morning's ride. Outside she heard the whinny of a horse alerting her to what was coming. When suddenly the front door opened Katya jumped to her feet, her hand having easily found the handle of her dagger.

"Katya?"

It was only Gabriel, she told herself. Her hand trembled slightly as she lowered the weapon and looked into the face of her husband. *Thank you Lord, for keeping him safe.*

"Are you well?"

"Yes."

"Where is the foreigner?"

"He's asleep."

She watched as Gabriel took the three steps toward the back room where he drew aside the curtain.

"He's gone."

Her heart plummeted to her stomach. He had been tied to the bed. *So foolish, how could I have fallen asleep?* She looked at her husband's face. *He thinks I let him go.* When still Gabriel said nothing another voice sided with her.

"It wasn't your fault, he must have escaped."

She turned to thank him. That's when she noticed his own state.

"Oh, Lucian! What have they done to you?"

His arm hung over Rogen's shoulder. One of his eyes was swollen shut, and his whole face was covered in bruises. She wondered what other injuries he suffered that could not be seen.

"Do not fret, sister dear. I have suffered worse, and lived to tell the tale. These are but a few scrapes."

"Well, scrapes or not, I'll not have your poor wife seeing you thus. Rogen, set him down over here."

Pointing to the chair she had just vacated, she went to find the left over herbs, ignoring Gabriel's unmoving presence completely. Using the water in the bucket she mixed it with some of the Bora root to produce a thick, creamy substance.

"This may sting a little, but it will help with the swelling. And keep out infection."

With a gentle hand, she began applying the salve to the worst of his cuts. His breath whistled through his teeth, and his hands gripped the sides of the chair. Once it was done she felt him relax.

"We must keep moving. We are not out of danger yet."

"Nor will we be until we are securely within the walls of the castle. This man's reach knows no bounds. Not even our border defense has kept him out."

"Besides, if they find us, you are in no state to fight."

"I am not helpless, Gabriel."

Gabriel only nodded. They had managed to find another mount for Lucian, and so they readied themselves to leave.

"You will be able to ride?"

"I can manage it."

Katya could tell Gabriel seemed uncertain, but he didn't argue. Instead he mounted up himself, and reached for her. As they traveled along the dark road it wasn't long before Lucian's breathing became labored and he slumped forward in his saddle. They were only a few miles outside of the castle grounds at that point, so Gabriel called them to a halt. Rogen had to help Lucian down while Gabriel assisted her.

She was glad to have a break, for she had begun to fall asleep again. Her eye lids felt weighted like bricks. If only she could wash her face. *Perhaps there is a spring nearby.* Katya listened for the sound of running water. There seemed to be a stream not far from the road, though it wasn't visible to her in the dark. Seeing that the men were otherwise preoccupied, she left the roadside promising herself she would turn back if she couldn't find the stream in less than a hundred steps. As she counted along, she couldn't help but relish the idea of the cool water on her dry skin that felt grimy after so many hours on the road. *46...47.*

"Ah, here you are."

The brook wasn't nearly wide enough for her to stand in, so she knelt and scooped up some liquid with her hands. It was a full moon tonight, and without any trees to block it's glow she could see just enough to feel certain there were no other creatures coming to have a drink. Not wanting to be gone too long, she quickly scrubbed her face, using the cool water to wash off as much of the dust as she could see. The rest of her would have to wait until they were back, and she could have a nice bath.

He didn't even bother to make himself known.

"You shouldn't have gone off by yourself."

The sound of his voice so close to her, made her heart stop beating for a moment. *Why must he insist on sneaking up on me?*

Coming quickly to her feet, she faced him, her throat immediately choking up.

"I wasn't going to be gone long."

"Are you crying?"

She hadn't realized she was. A hand to her face confirmed that there were indeed tears on her cheeks. She swiped at them angrily, turning away from him.

"You scared me."

He could barely make out the words she offered him from over her shoulder. Facing her back as he was now he could see that her shoulders were shaking slightly.

"I didn't mean to."

After a couple deep breaths, she turned and he saw that she had done her best to remove any evidence. Only a single tear remained untouched. He marveled at the sight of it upon her cheek before it too was dashed away. His Katya, the fearless woman who would leave king and castle to see that he was unharmed. Whose unrivaled faith intimidated him, and whose humility left something to be desired in his own character, had broken. And the sight of it was almost more than he could bear.

"I shouldn't have wandered off. I will go back to the horses now."

She marched past him, but he caught her arm. "Katya wait…" She looked up at him in surprise and his words stuck in his throat.

When they had found Lucian and had cut him free from the netted trap he hung from, a fear had gripped his heart. He had been anxious to return to her, imaging all sorts of terrible things had happened. And though he had felt the threat of capture breathing down his neck the whole time, it was as if a strange presence had come down and covered them. Blinding their enemies long enough for them to escape unnoticed. He found it hard to believe, but somehow he knew God had intervened on their behalf.

"What is it Gabriel?"

"Your prayers. I think they worked."

Gabriel couldn't have imagined a longer road than the one they had taken to get back, and when he burst through the door to see her sitting in the rocking chair with sleep clouding her eyes, his chest had seized painfully.

"God is always with us, Gabriel. He wants to help."

"We understand God very differently, Katya."

Even when he found the man Jas to be missing, he hadn't blamed her. How could he? It was he alone who was at fault. *That man could have killed her!* He knew it well, so why had he left her so defenseless? That was the question that burdened him now.

"How can you understand One whom you do not know? He is not who you think He is. If only you'd give Him a chance."

Perhaps she is right. Perhaps I do not know the Lord. Not in the way she does. The eyes that looked into his glistened in the moonlight. Her fragile strength alerted him to his own weaknesses, but where he had feared to find shame or even rejection, he saw only acceptance.

"I already have, and He failed me." He still wasn't ready to have this conversation, especially here and now. "Come, we have tarried long enough. We need to get Lucian back."

She didn't say more, only nodded. His hand didn't leave her arm as he escorted her back. When they were saddled once again, some of the color having returned to Lucian's face, Gabriel lead them home.

Thankfully Vixen knew his way back to the castle well, even in the dim light of the moon above them. This way Gabriel could give himself over completely to the rampage of thoughts in his heart. He wavered between the evidence of faith presented to him by his loved ones, and the embittered vanity that was neatly coated in a practical logic he knew so well. One would lead him on a road less traveled, worn by difficult steps but would in the end bring him the greatest joy, and the other? The other would be all too easy to serve, asking nothing of him but requiring his very soul. When he met its end, he would be nothing of the man Katya believed him to be, nothing of the man he hoped to be.

A clear choice, it seemed. Yet why did he fight against it with all that was in him. What was this chain that had him bound so? Gabriel searched the darkness around him for answers, but all was quiet and still. He looked down to the head that was tucked beneath his chin. Katya's small frame was melded to his own, and he wondered if she had fallen asleep. Thrice she had dozed, her head bobbing in a painful manner, before he had pulled her firmly against him, allowing his arms to bracket either side of her lest she fall.

"The castle is just ahead, Your Highness."

His valet had ridden up beside him. His large frame in paradox with the lean horse beneath.

"Thank you, Rogen. For all your aid this day. It seems I would not have been successful in retrieving my brother as I had so boastfully thought."

"I serve at the pleasure, Your Majesty."

"And Lucian," he turned to look at his brother behind them, keeping his voice low. "do try not to get captured again. 'Tis such a bother to have to rescue you."

The younger man chuckle and then winced, his ribs have been clearly wounded also.

"I shall have to keep that in mind when next I discover something about our enemy."

"And did you discover something?"

"Indeed, I did. Though I cannot say how much truth it bears, it seems that Gusta, the giant of a man, worked closely with the Count. He was like a gabbing old maid who spouted on about the intentions of the Count to reign alongside the Dark Lord."

"He plans to take the throne then?"

"So it seems. Gusta was telling the other men that the Dark Lord's mother was the daughter of a Romanian nobleman."

"I do not know her, or her family."

"Neither do I, but if you ask me I would seek out our father once more. He must know something about the validity of these rumors."

They were approaching the castle gates now, and would soon be within the safety of their own walls. He knew Lucian would not be long in retiring.

"I have tried speaking with him on numerous occasions, and at every turn he has avoided it altogether."

"And mother? Have you spoken with her?"

"*Nu*, but what would she tell that father has not?"

"Who is to say if you do not ask, hm?"

The guards at the eastern gate house heralded their coming, and a handful of soldiers met them in the bailey.

"Your Majesties, we had no news of your return."

"We hope we did not worry you too greatly, Captain."

Lucian and his ever-present charm eased the concern on the men's faces though they all could see that he was unwell. When two of them helped his dismount and took him within, Gabriel ushered his own horse forward not wanting to wake his still sleeping wife. He knew this day had been overly long for her and in that moment, it would give him no greater pleasure than to see her to her bed himself.

At the front steps, he gently eased her down into the waiting arms of Rogen who remained at his side. Then he leapt down himself, and handed Vixen off to a waiting stable lad. With Katya returned to his arms, he carefully began climbing the steps to their chambers. Once he met the doors to his room he turned the brass knob and eased the portal open.

"Gabriel?" She murmured softly, her voice reaching up and into his ear.

"Yes, it is I. We are home."

"And Lucian?"

"He is being seen to by the medic, and of course Adelina is fretting over him."

"Mm."

He wondered if she were only half awake when she curled further into his chest.

"Sleep now, my dear."

Seeing as how it was dark and he knew his own room far better, he crossed the space effortlessly, shifting the covers aside before laying her upon the soft mattress. Next to his bed lay a candle that once lit bathed the room in a soft glow. If they had returned sooner, he would have ordered her a bath, but such commodities would have to wait until morning. So instead he removed her riding boots, cloak, and outer garments, leaving only her chemise.

He began to move away when his eyes caught on something. Upon her hand was his great-grandmother's ring. The one he had given her in the meadow. It was meant to be a symbol of his love and commitment. When she looked at it, did she feel loss? Or perhaps regret?

"God, if you are as real as she says you are, make yourself known to me that I may become the husband, the prince that would honor such a promise as that ring bequeaths."

He moved to blow out the candle, thus sending his prayer heavenward. Moving stealthily down the hall he maneuvered to where his mother oft spent her evenings: the southern drawing room.

"Mother?"

"Gabriel! We were so worried about you! Where is Lucian?"

She stood from her chair, her book forgotten on a side table.

"He is recovering in his bedchamber I would think. As he would tell you himself, you needn't worry, he has seen worse."

"And Katya? Elisabeta said she went after you. Whatever was she thinking?"

He knew his mother spoke from concern, but still it irked him to hear his wife being scolded. Though hadn't he done the very same?

"She thought only of stopping me from myself."

"Then perhaps I should thank her," Melita added with a smile at the way he had stood up for her.

"Yes, perhaps you should."

He moved to press a light kiss to his mother's forehead, thankful to be returned. A far better cry than where he *could* be this night. Still stranded somewhere in the Leta forest, left in the clutches of a foe.

"Mamă, what do you know of the Dark Lord? Lucian uncovered information that his own mother is the daughter of a Romanian noble."

He watched her closely noting how her eyes flickered before she moved to her seat. Probably in an effort to collect her thoughts, and choose her words.

"What has your father told you?"

"He has chosen to withhold a great deal. But I would know the truth from you now."

Her elongated silence stole the breath from the room. *It's true.*

"Then there *is* another heir to the throne."

"*Da*. But it is not a legitimate one. His claim would never stand up in court."

"How can this be?"

"Your great grandfather had a brother, Tristan. They had a falling out, and he left. But not before he had a son."

"I do not understand."

"Many years later, a young woman and child showed up to our door. She sought refuge here with us, and claimed to be the granddaughter of Tristan. Your father was wary of her, and fearful that she would try to usurp his throne for her son. So he turned her away. The whole affair was handled quietly, and she disappeared without another word."

He stared at her, the self-serving side of him refusing to believe his father would act thus. It was a blemish on their reign, an act of dishonesty that slandered everything their kingdom stood for.

"Why was this kept from me?"

"It was a long time ago. You were not yet born, and your father had only just taken the throne…" His mother must have seen the incredulity in his face, for she added softly, "Your father was a proud man back then, much like you are now. You do not know how heavily this has weighed on him."

But he didn't need to know. He could imagine it easily enough. If he were king now, he could see himself making that same decision, or one of its equivalence. Indeed, that is where his life would be headed soon enough, if he didn't do something to change it. Fear and pride were brothers of the same bosom; two millstones tied around his neck that would sooner bring him to the bottom of the Black Sea then give him the strength to lead his country.

A door opened behind them, the sound of heavy footfalls carrying a third party. He didn't even need look to know it was his father. Who else would enter his mother's private drawing room at this hour?

"A decision has been made. Come dawn we are moving the troops. Every able bodied man will be called to action. We have waited long enough."

"I couldn't agree more. Those men we found in the forest have acted on behalf of the Count, who grows more and more confident in our hesitance."

"I see that you are well. Why did you not tell us of your departure?"

"It seems neither of us have been entirely forthright."

The King glanced between the faces of his wife and his son. His own expression revealing nothing.

"I have told him about Tristan's granddaughter."

"Gabriel, I ... I should have been the one to tell you."

He had known this man all his life, had been raised up to become like him, and yet he wondered when he had stopped seeing him as a father and started seeing him as his king. Standing before him as he was now, still dressed in his night shirt and plain blue housecoat, he didn't look like a king.

"It may be nothing at all." His mother offered. "We do not even know that he is the same child."

His father sat down beside her on the chaise made for two. His movements tired and slow. "But if there was even the slightest chance, Melita."

"And the brother? Tristan was..."

He couldn't bring himself to finish the question, but he needn't for his father knew what he was implying.

"Tristan was your grandfather's older brother. Had he not left, he would have become the next king."

There was nothing more humbling than the truth. And the enlightenment that came with it. It mattered not that the Dark

Lord was not the rightful heir, for he *could* have been. And that meant Gabriel had allowed himself to feel pride and arrogance over a position that had not been intended for him. He came to it by chance. The reality of it all swallowed him.

"There are things you don't know about our people, about our Kingdom."

More mysteries. More hidden secrets. *Would it never cease?*

"Things? What things?"

"I had hoped to better prepare you, to shape you into the kind of man I had wished myself to be."

"You have. You taught me everything I know."

"But I failed to teach you the most important thing of all. Faith. Listen to me *now* son, heed my counsel in this above all the rest. Kings come and go, nations rise and nations fall, but the Lord is constant through it all."

There it was. That tiny bit of rope that stretched to the bottom of the chasm. He reached for it now, and allowed the peace of it to transcend his understanding. More than a prince, or the next king, he was a son. *A husband.* And if he so chose to be, he was a child of the living God.

She startled awake. Stirred by a movement close to her head. When she turned over she was surprised to see Gabriel there beside her. His long frame was illuminated by the glow of moonlight that carried itself through the window, a gentle intrusion that kissed his sleep softened features.

Katya smiled, her heart pleased to be near him. She took the opportunity to sneak herself in closer to his side, thinking this a scarce scene. One that might not be given her again, and then with eyes still full of sleep she lay her head upon the pillow near his and entered into a dreamless slumber.

When she woke fully the next morn, it was to a much emptier bed. One that still held his warmth telling her he had only just left. She arose quickly, and returned to her own chamber where she met Florin and began dressing for the day.

"Have you heard the news, Your Highness?"

"What news, Florin?"

"The king has declared war. The castle has been awake since the first sliver of light, and the men are already gathering in the courtyard. I expect you would have liked to join the Queen, but His Majesty asked that I not wake you."

Her mind went in a million directions, questions and cares fighting one another for precedence. Finally, a single thought emerged, *I hope I have not missed them!*

"Then I must hurry. Will you hand me my full wimple? We haven't the time to do my hair, so I shall cover it in this." Florin fixed up the remainder of her laces and went to retrieve the matching fabric long enough to hold her tresses.

"Do you know where I would meet the Queen?"

"She should be up on the parapet with the other princesses. It is custom for them to send the men off in a formal sort of procession."

"Very good. Thank you, Florin."

With as long of strides as her short legs could manage, Katya all but ran down the stairs and to the side stairs that would bring her out onto the castle wall. She stopped just before the open door to catch her breath before sailing out into the open. Thankfully the queen was still there, standing at the rail alongside Adelina and Elisabeta.

"Where have you been?" Elisabeta whispered to her once she took her place beside them.

"I fear I over slept, but thank heavens I made it in time."

"Only just! I am glad you are well though. You and my brothers had me overwhelmed with fear at your disappearance. And I thought *I* was the one prone to impulsive adventures."

"Truly, I did not think it was to be an adventure. My only thoughts were of Gabriel and his welfare."

"Oh, how romantic!"

Katya shook her head at her friend's fanciful notion. Just then a loud trumpet rent the air cutting off their conversation. She turned to the sound of it, and was met by a most wondrous sight. A sea of armor spread out before her, the early flickers of the sun glinting off the metallic waves. *There must be over a thousand men down there!* She couldn't have imagined anything more amazing, and yet her insides churned to think of where these brave men were soon headed.

"*Domnilor viteji, ca tine...*"

As the queen continued her address, a custom she noted that would be her role to fill one day, Katya's eyes searched the mass of soldiers. They were all donned in their battle gear with matching plumed helmets that made her task difficult. For a moment she thought perhaps he would not be found among them, and her heart soared. But then her gaze caught on one knight in particular whose vestiges were far more elegant that the men beside him.

He rode upon a large horse black as the night, Vixen she remembered was his name. The fearsome creature was also garbed in notable dress, from his muzzle to his flanks. When the gentleman in her sights lifted his head, she wanted to shout out his name. *Gabriel! How could you have left me without saying goodbye?*

It was a cruel thing for him to do. *What if he were wounded in the fighting, or worse?* She closed her mind to such thoughts. *The Lord* will *protect him. I will put my trust in Him alone.* With the queen's blessing presented to all the men gathered, the king, whose dress also separated him from the rest, offered his own exchange.

"It is for our queen that we fight. For the land she is mother to, and for the families we leave behind us. Be brave men, for today God is with us, and tomorrow we shall taste victory!"

The king then nodded to Vidor, the Captain of the guard who drew his horse forward and shouted, "Attention!"

Marching troops moved as one, drawing their feet together and placing their hands over their breast plates. In a single voice they called out, "*Sângele nostru pentru Brașov*!"

Our blood for Brasov. A powerful statement. She prayed the Lord heard their cry and honored their sacrifice. Bowing her head, she lifted up the cry of her own heart. *Precious Lord, be with our men as they go against the dark and powerful force that seeks to wreak havoc on our nation. We surrender ourselves to Thee, so may Thy will be done.*

"Amen." She turned to the voice in unison with hers.

"The Lord is faithful, dear Katya. He will see us through this."

Adelina's face was wet with the tears that streamed down it. She didn't even bother to wipe them, for she was unashamed of the zeal she felt. Katya's own heart stirred with a kindred faith.

"I believe it with all my heart."

Adelina reached forth and took her hand, their eyes returning to the men who were leaving them behind. The ground shook with the motion of all the horses' hooves stamping across the bridgeway. Following the equestrians, was another hundred squadrons of foot soldiers whose steps reminded her of the toy soldiers her cousin Georg had played with as children.

But the most prominent sound of all was the clinking of their swords brandished upon their hips. Swords yet unstained by bloodshed; yet untainted by woe and death. Katya couldn't seem to take her eyes from them. In her heart she knew the battle was already won, that the Lord had indeed bought for them the victory. But she also knew she had a role to play in the upcoming days and weeks. What, she did not know, but she would be ready when it came time for her to stand.

"Come ladies, let us adjourn to the solar. There are other preparations to be made."

The three of them followed Queen Melita back inside.

"How is Lucian faring, Adelina?"

"You know your brother, he is not one to stay abed. I am thankful for the laudanum they gave to help him sleep and to ease the pain. The physician was certain he has more than one broken bone. But he is confident of his recovery."

"I wouldn't be surprised if he joins the others before the week's end. Surely they will need his direction."

Katya thought for sure that Adelina would contradict her friend, but before she could it was the queen who spoke up.

"Lucian would do right to stand beside his father and brother, but only if he is recovered. It would do him no good to fight as a half-wounded man already."

"Yes, of course Mamă."

"Now, let us discuss the healing house. Has the sanctuary been made ready?"

All eyes turned on her. "Yes, Your Grace. We cleared out a goodly portion of the main hall and have set up several rows of cots for when wounded soldiers arrive."

"We also were able to improve upon the watering system, that fresh water can be brought directly from the southern entrance of the garden, for when we need clean water."

"And Tusta knows to have an abundance of vegetables ready within a moment's notice, should she need to feed more mouths.

Thankfully several of the plants in our gardens are nearing their season, and will soon be producing." Elisabeta added cheerfully.

"Very good. I am proud of each of you, for all of your efforts. Just because our men go off to fight does not mean we will become languid in their absence. Indeed, our hands will be kept busy, to care for the positions that have been abandoned, and the young families that will be without their husbands and fathers."

"Do you think families will begin to move back to their residences near the castle, now that the threat is confined strictly to our borders?"

"We are not without danger here, but we are well provided for. Not all the soldiers have left as we are in need of protection. I will send out a notice to all the young women and children, that our township will be a safe haven for all who have need of it."

Katya nodded, acknowledging the wisdom of Her Majesty to do that very thing. They would need one another in the days to come.

Having taken their morning meal in the solar, as the queen had thought it best for them to enjoy one another's company a little while longer, they ate what they could, though none had the stomach for much food. With warm tea in each of their cups, the conversation gently faded into lighter topics.

"How are you feeling this morning, Adelina?"

"I am well Mamă."

Katya watched as the lady absentmindedly placed a hand on her belly.

"I do admit this week has been a bit much for me, and I have taken to my bed on more than one occasion, but I know that each day she grows stronger still."

"You think it is a girl, then?"

Adelina smiled at her. "Yes."

"Well, *I* hope it is a boy!" Elisabeta sat forward so quickly she nearly spilled the contents of her cup. "Big brothers are such a delight you know."

They all laughed at her too cheerful tone. Soon they began discussing names for the babe, and Lucian's plans to transform the room adjacent to theirs into a nursery. The layout of their suite was very similar to hers and Gabriel's, but Adelina softly explained that they only used the one room. Katya's heart sighed at such a thought.

Mayhap one day, it would be the same for her. For a moment she thought she heard his voice in the hallway. Certainly it was nothing of the sort. *My mind must be playing tricks on me*, she grimaced at the conjecture. But then it grew louder, until he seemed to pass right outside their door, his stern timbre deepening as he moved away.

"If you will excuse me, ladies."

Katya did not even look their way as she set her cup down rather forcefully and hurried to the door. She didn't want to miss him again. If it were truly he.

When she stepped into the hallway, it was empty. Not a soul in sight. She chose to follow the direction she heard him go, and when she reached the corner she peaked around its edge. She had been right after all. There Gabriel stood, still covered in his battle regalia, as he dismissed the younger man he was speaking with.

Not even hesitating she ran to him, and threw her arms about his neck.

"*Umph!* Katya? Whatever is the matter?"

She felt his arms lock her into his embrace, not the least bit put off by the chain mail that bit into her sides.

"You didn't say goodbye. I thought you had left."

He pulled back from her, far enough that she could see the concern in his eyes.

"Forgive me, I didn't mean to cause you worry. I will stay long enough to gather the remaining troops that arrive within a fortnight, from our allies."

She smoothed his chest piece that had come unlatched before dropping her hands to her sides.

"It is good to hear that others will be with us. We are blessed of God to have so many who would stand by our sides."

"Yes. They have shown us greater favor than I would have imagined. It is only because of their combined efforts that we are able to fight straightaway. Otherwise I had feared we would not have the resources to go to war at all. And in that case we would have been forced to surrender."

She shuddered to think of such an option. But the Lord was with them, and they would not be overcome.

"And Lucian?"

"I was on my way to see him next. Would you care to join me?"

"I would like that. Shouldn't you take off your armor first?"

He attempted a shrug, but his shoulders did not move so easily beneath the restrictive material.

"I must get used to wearing it."

Taking her hand he wove it through his bent elbow.

"Did you sleep well last night?"

They moved to the stairs that took them up two flights where Lucian's room was.

"I did, thank you. I only wish I had not slept through so much of the ceremony."

She glanced at him from the corner of her eye. He looked straight ahead, unaware of her scrutiny.

"You needed your rest. I am glad to know Florin carried out my orders not to wake you."

"And if I had slept till noon day, and missed you in truth?"

He stopped then, making her steps cease as well. She wanted to avoid his gaze altogether, but he brought his face close to her own.

"I already told you I would not have left without your knowledge. You do believe me, don't you?"

"I would like to believe you, yes." Her voice was no more than a whisper, and he lowered his to match it.

"Truly Katya, I am not so cold that I would not bid you goodbye."

He stared into her eyes for a long moment, the brown depths of them warming her like the sun after a tender rain. When he seemed satisfied with whatever he was searching for, he leaned down and ever so gently pressed a soft kiss to her mouth.

"Now come, let us see how my brother fares."

They stepped across the threshold and into the darkened space where she assumed Lucian lay sleeping. Gabriel released her hand and moved toward the windows, pulling back one of the heavy drapes. Immediately light flooded the space, and her eyes had to adjust.

"I hope you are not to sleep the whole day, Lucian?"

The man in question opened his eyes slowly, a look of annoyance ran across his face, before he caught sight of his uninvited guests.

"Oh, 'tis only you. I had thought the doctor was come again. The man has been pumping me full of all sorts of tonics and medicines. All dreadful in taste and texture. Can you not tell Mamă that I abhor such treatments? Perhaps if she thought I grew worse from their effects, she would see fit to ban the man from ever entering my chambers again."

Gabriel laughed, and drew closer to the edge of the bed, where Lucian struggled to pull himself up.

"Here, allow me."

With fluid motions, he assisted his brother, while Katya took an extra pillow from the chair beside them and used it to prop him up.

"Thank you. I assume Father has departed then?"

"Only just. He did not take lightly to your mistreatment. I will be soon in following him, just as soon as the men from Herr Gustavo have come."

The brothers shared a look.

"Nu, you will not be joining me."

"You know you cannot keep me here. I will come, just as soon as I am able."

"You always were rebellious."

"Ha! Not so, I am merely as stubborn as you are brother. You may as well allow me to ride with you."

"I suppose that way I can at least keep an eye on you. But *only* if you are recovered. No sense in having you fall off your horse, or worse." Gabriel seemed ready to depart, his mind surely on many things, but then he turned back, "And Lucian, if you are to come, then you will most certainly continue under the doctor's orders. Every last one."

He moved towards the door then, sending her a wink and flashing a most victorious grin.

"*Shaa!*" Lucian tsked. "Bid him come then! Not even his cruel torture can keep me from joining my men."

CHAPTER 13

The day of his departure was soon in coming, but he was not yet ready to go. Something was burning in him. It sparked and fizzled like an unkempt fire. He knew what it was that burdened him so. *Have you asked God what* He *wants you to do?* Gabriel replayed the question in his mind for the hundredth time. It was the very one his brother had asked him only last eve as they made their final preparations for the men who had come from Germana.

Lucian had grown stronger every day, borne upon the will of a true fighter. He was glad to have the man at his side through all this. News from the front lines had come just as steadily. His father had written to them after the first day to tell that all was unfolding just as they had hoped. With the enemy unaware of their advancement, they had taken the men at the border by storm, pushing back their ranks and causing them to regroup. But then as the week wore on, the news had turned sour. It seemed his band of reinforcements couldn't be coming at a better time.

Gabriel peered into the enclosure of the King's private chapel. A doorway he hadn't darkened since that fateful day when he dared bargain with the Impossible. He reminded himself again why he was here. *I must find answers.*

He moved with laden steps towards the altar, where upon he then knelt on the cushioned stool, made soft for his luxury, but no comfort did he find. The question came to him again, and he dwelt on it. Not only had he not asked God what He wanted him to do concerning the kingdom, he hadn't asked God what He wanted for his life in years. He could not even recall the last time he had genuinely prayed, seeking the Lord's will rather than just demanding for his own. On the rare occasion he had graced their *biserică*, the only utterings that transgressed his lips had been the liturgical prayers repeated after the orthodox priests at Sabbath services.

"I have nothing to say it seems."

He spoke the words aloud, wondering if they were directed toward a supernatural being, or if he were truly just speaking to himself. He wondered what Lucian would have done. Hadn't he been at crossroads with the Almighty, a prodigal of all prodigals?

"I suppose that makes me more of the older brother, upon whom no homecoming was bestowed."

Gabriel began to fidget; his whole being made uneasy within these walls. In an effort to distract himself, he skimmed around at the interior of the place. The last time he had been here, he had hardly cared to take notice of the straw hewn rushes or the oiled linens with each one bearing a biblical scene. His eyes swung around to the wall before him. Up the steps and past the wooden table, holding both the prayer candles and the bowl of incense, was a sight that drew his attention. Had it been there before? *Of course it had*, he was certain every house of faith carried a crucifix chancel.

The image of the Lord Jesus hanging upon the wooden cross stared at him. He couldn't seem to take his eyes from it.

"If You are who You say You are, then show Yourself to me."

His heart cried out. It wasn't merely a demand he was making, it was a plea from the deepest place within him. He felt that if he left tomorrow for the war, and died in battle, he would be lost. The weight of his undetermined eternity was a black hole, a void so unending he knew he would be swept away in its trenches should he not find what he was looking for.

His gaze remained fixed upon the Christ, and so it was no imagined thing when the entire crucifix began to glow. Gabriel knew the windows to be shut and the drapes to be closed, as was the custom. An ethereal light slowly grew from the source of the figure, and he watched it grow until it extended forth encompassing the space before him. For a moment he stopped breathing altogether, so transfixed was he by what was occurring. Suddenly, he too was embraced in the radiant light. A feeling of pure and unexplainable love and joy poured through him. He felt his entire being made stronger by the pulsing presence that surrounded him.

I have called you by name, and you are Mine.

The voice that spoke was clear and firm, a sound that could not be denied by human ear, for it had not come from within. In holy fear, Gabriel bowed his head to the steps before him. Tears poured down his face, and in absolute humility he sobbed like a broken man before the Lord. Years' worth of purposelessness and apathy rolled down his cheeks. He stayed there on the stone floor for as long as it took for his heart to be reckoned with.

"I am not worthy to serve Your kingdom, but still You have shown me grace."

He whispered the words, knowing full well that God was near enough to hear them. If pride had been his prison, then the key that opened the cell of his soul was the grace freely given to him in that moment. Standing on shaky legs, he went to the basin to find a towel to wash his face with. His eyes glanced back at the crucifix. He would never look at it the same again.

As he then left the chapel, he pondered how quickly a life could change after one encounter. Feeling lighter, and more at peace with himself than he had ever been before, he hurried down the walkway. Right now Gabriel wanted nothing more than to find his sweet wife, and share with her all that had transpired. But it wasn't Katya who met him first.

"Your Highness, all has been made ready."

"Very good, Rogen. Have you made your decision then?"

"Yes, my lord. I thank you for thinking of my family in all this, but I would not forsake my country, nor my king."

"Rogen," He placed his hand on the man's shoulder, "you are an honorable man, and a good friend. I am pleased to know I will be fighting alongside you."

The look on his valet's face when he said friend made Gabriel feel a twinge of guilt over how he had treated him prior, but he reminded himself that everything had changed. He had changed.

"Now if you will excuse me, I must speak with my wife."

He entered the room slowly, hoping that her lady's maid was absent. Seeing that she was, he slipped through the door quietly and looked about for his wife. The space was not so large that he couldn't find her. She was sitting in a chair by the window, reading from what he knew were the Holy Scriptures.

Without word, he beheld her, seeing her with fresh eyes. She wasn't lavishly beautiful, not like the queen or even his younger sister, who already had more beaus than he cared to acknowledge, and yet he found her lovelier than any woman he had ever encountered. All of a sudden, he had a desire to know her deeper, to learn of her hopes and dreams, even her fears.

He must have shifted on the Parisian rug, for her head turned and her eyes flickered up at him. The look in her clear blue gaze spoke of love, as her face softened with a gentle smile. Without saying a word, he went to her and knelt at her knees.

"*Meine leibe*, what a dignified fool I have been. Will you ever forgive me?"

He then rested his head upon her lap, her hands finding their way to his hair as she stroked his thick curls.

"'Tis already forgiven, my love."

"I have so much to tell you…"

And so, he did. He told her everything, and together they wept over the kindness of the Lord to show them mercy.

"*Mein Gott, der niemals versagt!*"

"Indeed, He is faithful. And I have never felt more at peace with being the next king, if that be His will."

"And the war…Will I lose you so soon? After having just gotten you?"

"What would you have me do?"

He sat up and looked her in the eyes. As close as she was, he could see the different shades around her irises as her pupils changed in size. She placed her hand over his heart.

"I would have you go. Fight for your kingdom. Trust in your God."

He placed his own hand atop of hers, and promised to do just that.

"All we can do is have faith, and believe God for the rest."

That evening after dinner, the two of them retired early to their chambers, where they went out on the balcony to enjoy one another's company. Katya had pulled the blanket from her chaise for them to sit on as they gazed up at the stars. Each one a twinkling reminder of the Lord's wonder and might.

Gabriel too was overflowing with thankfulness. Pulling Katya against his chest, he stretched out his legs on either side of her, and pressed a soft kiss to her uncovered hair. To have her here within his arms felt right. He hated to think that tomorrow he would be leaving her behind.

"Lucian is himself again. When the doctor reported him recovered enough to fight, he thanked the man and all but threw him out of the room, so pleased was he to be done with the prescribed tonics."

"I wonder if Adelina is equally pleased."

Catching her tone, he hugged her close.

"She knows his duty is to his people, and besides she has seen him fight. Lucian can handle himself. As can I, so you needn't worry over me either."

"You are right. I should not fret so."

"It means you care, 'tis all. And a more pure heart I have yet to know."

In an effort to distract her, he pointed out his favorite constellation.

"The Great Bear. He prowls the sky each night, a hunter in his own right…."

They talked for what seemed like hours, laughing over the stories they had been told as children about the pictures in the heavens. Some of them were similar, and some were very much different. But that could be expected for two cultures such as theirs, one east and one west. One north and one south, and yet together they made a complete map. When finally they fell silent, the sounds of the night closed in on them.

"I love the night like this."

"Why are you whispering?"

She scooted forward and turned herself, so that she lay more on his thigh than against his chest, giving him a perfect view of her profile.

"I didn't realize I was. Perhaps, I don't want to wake up the world as it prepares for its bed."

“That is best; the sun can be an arduous day keeper.” He whispered back, encouraging her to continue.

“Everything is so soft and quiet…hidden, as if the night were a shield of unobtrusive darkness for any who should linger. As if it were a haven made for lovers.”

Her words were poetic. How had he ever thought her plain? Perhaps it was as Bunică would say, *there is nothing more wonderful than a man in love, and nothing more beautiful than a woman who is loved.* She sighed and looked up at him just then, sending his thoughts scattering. Her lips were close enough that he needn’t move very far to close the space between them. As softly as the night around them, he stood and swept her up into his arms and carried her indoors, his lips never leaving hers.

In the morning she dressed quickly, layering herself as Florin had shown her the day before. *Blessed Florin!* The woman had even been so bold as to borrow for her a plated breast piece, meant for a smaller man. It still managed to dwarf her chest.

“What are you doing?”

She turned to the disbelieving sound of her husband’s voice. Color instantly filling her cheeks.

“I am coming with you.”

“You most certainly are not.”

“I *have* prayed about this Gabriel. I too feel a call to action.”

“I couldn’t possibly allow you to be put in danger.”

Lifting her chin, she refused to back down.

“Katya…”

He drew towards her, his eyes going from the plate of armor that hung askew around her neck to her face. When he reached her, his hands went to her jaw, where he then leaned down and kissed her breathless. An attempt to deter her. And though she wrapped her arms around his firm waist in an effort to deepen the kiss, her resolve did not weaken. The castle was amuck with tales from the battle field. A scene of clashing blades, flaming arrows, and death scrolled across her vision. And then after last night… *Nein, I will not stand aside whilst he goes.* She had been left behind one too many times.

So, she pulled back and pressed him further. "Then at least allow me to go with you as far as the Doga Hill. Surely you will grant me this small request?"

His eyes narrowed, and she knew he saw past her game.

"Doga Hill then, but not a scarthing farther. And please," His eyes widened in mock horror, "leave the armor behind."

She laughed then. "It doesn't much suit me anyway. But poor Florin. It cost her a weeks' worth of Tusta's sweets for her to barter for this fine piece."

"Well, you will have to see that she is well reimbursed, for my wife will not be caught dressing as my men do."

She took the breastplate from around her neck and laid it on her bed.

"When do we depart?"

He grimaced openly. Katya hoped he wasn't going to change his mind. She needed to be with him. She didn't know why, but just an urgency to go.

"Within the hour. Do my mother and sister know you have planned to join us, or were you going to steal away with the masses?"

His words brought crimson to her face, though she didn't know why his implications should make her feel guilty.

"I wouldn't have lied as you suppose. In fac, I spoke with them all this morning."

Elisabeta had been shocked initially, then she thought it a grand idea. Adelina had only smirked, as if to say had she not been so far along, she too would have given life to such a notion. It was the Queen who had not warmed up to the idea of Katya anywhere near the battlefield. She would be pleased to see her returned on the morrow, unscathed.

"Very good, then. I had expected to come and bid you goodbye, but I suppose that will yet be delayed. As early as it is, I will see you safely home before dark."

The heated breath of the sun, warmed her face as she rode alongside somber statues. The silent ranks stretched before her on the road for what seemed like miles and miles. Gabriel had said the Germana people, her people, had been good to them rallying over two thousand soldiers to serve as reinforcements.

"Rogen?"

"Yes, Your Highness?"

"This is your first time to battle yes?"

He looked up at her from where he walked alongside the other men. She felt poorly that so many must walk on foot, while she was given the luxury of a horse.

"Other than the skirmish in the Leta Forest, yes."

Florin had told her about the valet who served her husband. She knew him to be a man of solid beliefs, whose character had earned him a position often reserved for men of a certain age. This made her believe him to be a kindred spirit.

"Do you sense something more behind this attack than just what it seems? Something sinister?"

"We are a peaceful nation, Your Highness. But the hearts of men are so quickly turned by pride and lust for power. It matters not who leads this army or that, from the very beginning the fight has always been between good and evil: the battle ground in the heart of man."

"You must have been talking with Florin. She said the very same to me not many weeks ago."

"A wise woman then, my lady. We speak no falsehood. It is our very faith that tells us it is so. Do the scriptures not deem it as such?"

She thought for a moment, remembering back to all that Friar Hanz had taught her, and even to what she had begun reading herself in the last months. A particular verse came to the forefront of her mind.

"For the creation was subjected to futility, not willingly, but because of Him who subjected it in hope; because the creation itself also will be delivered from the bondage of corruption into the glorious liberty of the children of God."

"Just so, Your Majesty."

Rogen's face lit with an inner joy that shone through his eyes. Even while all around him held the weight of foreboding, he was a beaming light of hope. The man was soon called away and she watched him sprint off, his heavy encasings making his gait seem awkward.

"Katya, look there." Gabriel called out to her as he maneuvered his horse closer to her own. He pointed to a ridge far enough in the distance to be visible over the tree tops.

"That is Doga Hill then?"

"Yes. We must travel over it to reach the western border. That is where the fighting is taking place. As we get closer, I wish for you to stay at my side. I trust not the shelter of these woods."

She did as he asked, watchful of how he commanded his men. Indeed, she was thankful that Lucian was there also. The two brothers were strong leaders keeping the ranks tight, and the men keenly aware of their surroundings. They made it to the far away hill in no time at all, their pace much swifter now that they were close to their destination.

Katya held tight to the spine of her saddle, as her horse lurched forward upon the steep incline. Once they made it to the very top the men then flanked outward, assuming their separate divisions under their commanders.

Approaching the edge of the hilltop carefully, she looked down over the valley that spilled around the footstool of the great peak. With great horror she took in the sight of war, a beast more horrible than she could ever have imagined.

"Your Highness, come away from there!"

She didn't know who had called to her, but it mattered not. The amount of red carelessly splattered upon the mud stained earth, was something she would never be able to unsee. *And for what*? She thought sorrowfully. *So that one man can sit upon another's throne? Lord Jesus, have mercy on our corrupt souls!*

"Katya?"

Gabriel was upon her in a second, pulling her from her horse and wrapping her in the shield of his embrace.

"They are killing each other, Gabriel."

A guttural sound came from his throat, but she didn't look up. Instead she pressed her face into the crevice of his neck, wanting to hide from the darkness she had beheld.

"My sweet, innocent wife. How I would have you protected from this. War is no place for women."

Something stirred in her heart, and she spoke with great conviction, feeling the insurmountable injustice of the bloodshed below.

"It is no place for man either. Gabriel, don't you see? This is not what God had in mind for His people."

"Often times, they know no other way."

"That is why we must show them."

The Dark Lord limped through the wooded demesne. His cloak was pulled well over the sides of his face, its black tail following behind him. Shrouding himself in darkness, he called curses down upon the man who dared betray him.

"Oh great Beelzebub, hear me now. May the head of Count Denla Quóis burn! May he writhe with the pain of a thousand needles! Send your legions to overthrow him, and take his soul to the fiery depths!"

His plan had been flawless. The voices had given him clear direction, but the Count had grown impatient, tactlessly seeking to go against his orders. Now that war was upon them, the insipid fool was missing. Just like a coward he had run away from the fight.

"Bahh! I curse his worthless soul, and his woman too!"

He should have taken her while he had the chance. The voices in his head had encouraged him to do that very thing, but he had been wary of the prospect. *No matter*, he thought to himself, *I will have my revenge.* Seeing a slight opening in the brush before him, he stepped far enough to the edge to look up towards the steeping mount. Upon it was the amassing militia of foreign aid his spies had told him of. He knew such support would overtake his own men, and in a matter of weeks, his losses would outweigh his gains on the battlefront. But he didn't care one whit for the lives that would be taken. His end was at hand, his revenge in sight.

"What now? Your servant lies in wait for your direction."

Turning back, he stumbled further into the forest. When he had meditated earlier the voices had led him here. For what, he was uncertain, but he knew the time had come. He sensed their dark presence, and waited. No response came. *Perhaps the spirits are unhappy.* Acting quickly, he found a large stone upon which to sharpen his blade. Moving through the undergrowth he caught a rabbit. The Dark Lord then took it back to his make shift altar, and slit its neck, spilling its blood. A sacrifice to please the gods.

"Ahh...They've come."

His eyes fluttered quickly, his mind filling with an electricity. *Farther east. A meadow with a short waterfall. There you will find the prince. Kill him, and send his body back as a sign.*

"I will do as you say."

A hesitation, and then the whispers grew softer. *But beware the woman, she will try to stop us.* Woman? Did they speak of the Count's mistress, or of another? Before he could ask, the presence lifted, and his eyes opened. He fell to the ground, his body weak from the vision. A fit of coughing overcame him, and he reached for the edge of his garment to wipe at his mouth. When it came away, it was soaked red.

With the help of the stone, he drew himself to his feet. His eyes couldn't help but gaze at the stains of blood that mirrored his own. Would *he* be the next sacrifice? Helel knew that his body was giving up. No matter how many elixirs he made, or how much strength he felt when the spirits filled him, afterwards he always noticed his illness growing worse, as if each encounter took away another small piece of him. Soon there would be nothing left.

Not wanting to waste any time, he found for himself a fallen branch and measured it off. Breaking the one end, he used the remaining stick as a staff that he could lean upon. His steps were uneven, his hunched frame making each footfall brought more painful than the one before it. The trickling sound of water told him he was getting closer. Swatting away the branches that dipped in his line of vision, the Dark Lord staggered through the last bit of foliage. Without the canopy of the trees, the sun's brilliance blinded him, and he cried out like a creature accustomed to darkness. That's when he heard horses approaching. Shrinking back, he moved to a small huddle of bushes that put him closer to the lake. Hidden in the camouflage of the shrubs, he listened carefully.

"Look there, a water fall! May we stop here to water the horses?"

"I suppose this will do, but then I am sending you the rest of the way with Franco. I need to get back the king will be expecting me."

Helel had thought he had stumbled upon an innocent couple, but then he saw them. The man was wearing the symbol of Brasov and was dressed like a prince. *At last! Upon this day, my mother's life will be avenged, and I will have the head of a Romanian prince.* He watched them with an unchecked rage licking up his spine. He wanted so badly to move now, to taste the blood of his enemy. *Be patient,* the voices reminded him. So, he bided his time.

First they watered their horses, dismounting and leading each of their animals to the pool of water. They seemed as if they were alone, for he caught no sight of the man named Franco. The prince was ever watchful, his eyes roaming across the meadow. For a moment the Dark Lord had felt he would be seen, but the man never once looked his way.

His whole body trembled as he prepared himself for what had only been a dream. *If only mother could see me now!* After their beasts had drank their fill, the prince dipped a flask into the lake, before giving it to the woman. He then repeated the motion for himself. When it seemed they were finished, he watched as the woman moved closer to the prince, before she stood on her tip toes and pressed her lips to his. His own lips drew back in a snarl.

Go now! Wasting not another second, the Dark Lord stepped from his hiding place.

CHAPTER 14

Arming himself with all the hatred he could muster, the Dark Lord drew his blade from his waist. It was still wet with the blood of his sacrifice.

"*Veniți... acum o mare.... sursă de... rău...*"

Reveling in their surprised faces, he continued his incantations, each word rising higher. Such a powerful force surrounded him that he felt almost immortal.

"Who are you?"

The prince called out to him. His whole composure had shifted into an unreadable mask, but the Dark Lord was undeterred.

"I am the Dark Lord, and you must be Prince Gabriel, son of King Andrei. Thief to my throne."

"I am not the thief!"

He saw the slight change in the man's stance, as if he was readying himself to go for his own weapon, having realized already that he had left it cinched to his saddle.

"I would not, if I were you."

He stared into the prince's eyes. They both knew that he was just far enough away from his horse, that if he went for the weapon, he would leave the woman unprotected. Long enough for her to come to harm.

"I thought you had come to fight? You will leave me defenseless then?"

"The same way your people left my mother! And she a child of your nation. No, a princess! You and your heartless King," he spat the word, picking up his arm to point the knife directly at the prince's heart, "would see us ruined and left for dead."

He had been so focused on the Prince, that he hadn't noticed the quiet murmurings of the woman until the voices in his head shrieked and hissed. A moment's glance told him that she was calling upon a higher power of her own. One that was a threat to all that had sustained him thus far. *The woman is dangerous. Kill her. Kill her now!*

When Katya had started to pray, Gabriel had felt a chill scrape down the back of his neck. His every nerve stiffened and he got the eerie feeling that something dark was controlling the hooded man. He could feel the evil emanating from him. His eyes having never left the man's face, he sensed his intentions before he had even moved. When the man lunged forward, Gabriel made his actions swift. He grabbed Katya and moved her behind him. The blade swiped downward, cutting only air.

The Dark Lord's voice was filled with a fury Gabriel had never witnessed. The blood curdling scream raising every hair on Gabriel's body. With a calm he knew could have only come from the Lord, Katya reached around him and gripped his arm.

"The Lord will fight for us, Gabriel. We need only be still."

He felt the powerful truth down in his bones, for ever since they had stepped into the clearing he had been overwhelmed by a strong sense of peace.

He covered her hand with his own. "I believe. Let the Lord prove Himself faithful."

Katya's words rang out clear and strong as she spoke forth, "Finally, my brethren, be strong in the Lord, and in the power of His might. Put on the whole armour of God that ye may be able to stand against the wiles of the devil...."

"No!"

Gabriel looked at the Dark Lord. He was nothing like he had been expecting. His visible features were of the plain sort, his eyes dark. Most of his squatted frame was concealed by a large black cloak that dragged on the ground as he had walked. Or more like limped, his one side having to lean heavily upon a staff. What made him stand apart was his face, and the way it was twisted up with a malicious sneer, as it was right now.

"Resist the devil, and he will flee from thee."

Katya hadn't even finished when the forbidding creature before them began to scream again, his hands smashing against his ears, his eyes rolling backwards. The forgotten blade fell from his fingers. Seizing the opportunity before him, Gabriel kicked it into the water, and grabbed the dagger from his boot cuff.

The man was then overcome by a fit of coughing. One that seemed to rack his whole body. Crimson blood appeared on his lips, making Gabriel wonder what kind of dark magic this man was a part of.

"He's dying, Gabriel."

Her whispered words reached his ears seconds before he watched the Dark Lord crumple, in them he heard her plea for grace, for mercy. Everything within told him that this man was the enemy. His pride screamed at him to offer the final blow, but a still small voice spoke above the rushing anger. *What was given freely to you, you must now freely give to another.*

His wife, his beautiful, sweet Katya, rushed to catch the falling man. She then knelt beside the Dark Lord's disfigured form, her head bowing in prayer.

"Lord Jesus, save this man."

"Nu! *Destul!* You mustn't say *that* name."

The creature's rasping breath bellowed the words with a sense of agony. When he began to thrash about, Gabriel moved closer, his dagger still gripped in his palm. He didn't know what the man was capable of, nor what strength he may still possess.

The hood had fallen away, revealing dark and painful looking sores spreading up his neck. The eyes that were now more visible, were sunken and hollow. He looked sickly, and Gabriel came to a very sudden conclusion. *He's just a man.*

Katya grasped firmly to the man's arm. "Be still now."

Her voice was low and calm, like a mother's. In her few words was more kindness than most possessed in their whole being. The man stilled immediately, his trembling body releasing all of its earlier tension. Gabriel knew the end was near. He had seen death before, and this time was no different. He must have known it too for with great effort he opened his eyes and fixed them on Katya.

"Who are you?"

"My name is Katya, and I am a servant of Jesus Christ. He is the only one who can save you now. If only you let Him."

He only nodded. "There is a light all around you." The man coughed, bringing more blood to his lips. "My name…is Helel."

"Helel, please forgive us for what was done to you and your mother."

Gabriel was surprised when tears came to the man's eyes. His whole face seemed to soften, but then he arched upward gasping for breath. His lungs filled with air, and then slowly, painfully, they emptied themselves out. And then it was all over. The Dark Lord who had haunted their nation for months now, was gone.

Katya, whose eyes had already begun to mist over, burst into tears then. Her shoulders shook as she wept over their enemy. The sound of her tears pierced the final pieces of his pride. How had he ever come to be deserving of such a compassionate woman? Right then, he knew that the grace of God, a favor he could never earn, had covered him in more ways than one.

"Your Highness!"

Gabriel turned. Franco, who was supposed to meet them to escort Katya back to the castle, appeared at the meadow's edge. He approached them, still mounted on his horse.

"What has kept you?"

"I'm afraid there is urgent news..." Franco stopped, having drawn close enough to see behind Gabriel. "Is that...?"

"The Dark Lord, yes, but he is a threat no more."

Franco then looked from Gabriel to Katya, who still wept over the man's deceased body. Several questions burned in the man's eyes but for once he had the good sense to hold his tongue.

"What news do you bring?"

Franco looked back at him, seeming to remember his assignment. The hairs on the back of Gabriel's neck stood up suddenly. Whatever Franco knew, he was hesitant to share. Never a good sign.

"Speak, Franco."

"It seems a battalion has breached the castle walls. The Count has been spotted among the men."

His heart bucked wildly against his chest.

"Have you notified the King? And my brother?"

"Prince Lucian is otherwise engaged, and it was the King himself who sent me to you. He has already taken some men back with him."

"Change of plans. I will be escorting Her Highness back. Franco, see that this man is taken care of."

"Yes, Your Majesty."

Katya was already moving to her own mount, where Gabriel helped her into the saddle. He then left Franco, and the remains of the Dark Lord in the meadow. His only thoughts now, as he spurred his horse into a gallop, was getting back to the castle as quickly as he could. For the duration of the ride, Gabriel prayed. He cried out to the Lord for the protection of his family. *Sovereign Lord, hear my pleas. Defend my family against evil. Deliver us from the hands of man. In you we put our trust.*

As they neared the portcullis, he saw that the castle had indeed been violated. A battering ram to the front gate had left it in pieces. Maneuvering his horse around the large wooden shards, and the fallen soldiers whose lives had been taken first, Gabriel gathered his courage, not knowing what he would find within.

They dismounted, not bothering to tether their horses in their haste.

"Katya, go and find my mother. She will have taken as many as she could and hidden in the space reserved for crisis. The passageway is found in the King's Room, behind the tallest bookshelf. Push the books on the middle shelf to the side. Behind them is a knob that if pulled will gain you entrance."

"And you?"

"I must find my father. You still have your dagger, yes?"

She nodded. "Good, keep it close, and avoid the main halls as best you can. I will come for you as soon as I am able."

He then pressed a quick kiss to her head before parting ways. When he next entered the side hall that would take him to the throne room, he listened for sound, but all seemed still. Too still. Turning towards the main stairs, he took them two at a time. The doors were already ajar and he peered in to see that the space was empty. *If not here, then where are they?* Holding himself still, he closed his eyes for a moment, seeking direction. *Lord, where do I go?*

He felt more than heard the tug to go left. Rounding the next corner, he found the space littered with the bodies of his knights, all dead except one.

"Saren, is that you?"

He dropped to one knee before his man.

"*Da*, what's left of me, Your Highness." His breathless words were choppy and slurred. The man was propped against the wall, his hand pressed to his side. A wound he would not recover from.

"What's happened here?"

"The Count Denla Quóis came upon us unexpectedly. We tried to stop him, my lord, but…"

"You did well. But tell me, where is my father?"

"The King?" Saren's eyes began to droop.

Gabriel grabbed the man's face. "Stay with me Saren. King Andrei, he is here?"

"He…he went after the Count. That scoundrel took your sister."

"Where, Saren? Where did he take her?"

Gabriel had to press his ear close to catch the mumbled words.

"To the catacombs."

The man's eyes shut completely, his body going limp. Gabriel pressed his forehead to the man's, his eyes clenching against the burn of tears.

"*Du-te cu, Dumnezeu.*"

He laid the man's head gently to the side, unsheathing his sword as he stood. The catacombs? *How did the Count know about the tunnels that led beyond the dungeon?* Saving the thought for another time, Gabriel wasted no time making his way to the stone underpasses. In order to move in stealth, he removed first his helmet, and then the outer plates from both his arms, along with the breast plate that clanked with each step.

Someone else was indeed down here, for each of the passages were lit. Shouts ricocheted throughout the enclosure, the sound of swordplay added to it, but he couldn't tell from how far ahead it came. He knew that soon the tunnels would converge into an opening before splitting off into three sections. With slowed footfalls he approached it, and stepped into chaos.

Narrowly dodging a sword that swooshed near him, he stepped to the right and rammed his shoulder into his attacker. The motion worked to put the man off balance, giving Gabriel enough reaction time to plunge his sword into the man's shoulder.

He then threw himself into the fray, where he was forced to duck sharply in an effort to escape being decapitated by the sword that flew overhead. Fisting his free hand, he drove it into the other man's solar plexus, a whoosh of breath expelling from the man's mouth before he fell to the ground with a thud.

Glancing around he saw several pairs of men engaged, but his father was not among them. Nor was the Count. In an effort to throw off the numbers, Gabriel pursued toward the nearest assailant.

"Your Majesty!"

"Need some back up, Geo?"

The man parried against his opponent's thrust, using his leaden foot to send a kick to his chest, knocking him backward into several others. He then grinned.

"I think we have it covered."

"I'll leave you to it then. Which way?"

"The east tunnel."

Gabriel nodded, and went in that direction. The echo of his own footsteps seemed endless, and for a moment he wondered if Geo had led him true. Sensing no immediate danger, he swiped his blade against his upper thigh and hooked it back to his hip. He would move faster, without the heavy silver in his hand. Suddenly, a scream traveled clear through the air, hitting him square in the chest. He knew that voice as surely as he knew the sound of his own heartbeat that drummed in his ears.

"Elisabeta!"

Forgoing stealth, he broke into a sprint. When he reached the end of the shallow channel, he heard the sound of gurgling water. The catacombs were an endless maze of tunnels that crossed over one another, but at some point a good number of them led back to this swirling body of water. Gabriel froze when he met the edge of the thin walkway, not wanting to be a victim of the deathly drop. Several things happened all at once, none of which he was able to influence.

First Gabriel watched as the Count thrust his sword into the king's unsuspecting abdomen. Then he saw Elisabeta leap up from where she had fallen and shove the Count backward, sending the man spiraling backward in a flail that then sent him to a watery grave. Lastly, he gazed helplessly as his father staggered once and then crumpled to the floor. *I'm too late.*

"Nuu!"

Elisabeta saw him from where she stood, but then she turned her back and sunk down beside their fallen leader. If it weren't for the narrow ledge that forced him to take careful steps, Gabriel would have shrunk down beside her, but instead he was left to watch from afar as his father pulled Elisabeta close. The man's words were drowned out by the noise of the splashing beast, but whatever he said caused her to move back and cover her mouth. When he had only a few steps left, he saw his father press something into Elisabeta's hand, and without looking at it she tucked it into her dress, nodding her head solemnly.

Had he been in another state of mind, Gabriel would have thought that odd, but a hazy numbness had come over him. Leaping the rest of the way, he hurried over to where he sister sat, her eyes filled with tears.

"Please don't go Tată. We will be lost without you."

The King placed his hand upon his youngest child's face, smoothing away the drops that ran down her cheeks.

"You will not be lost. Only remember what I said, and keep your promise, da?"

"Yes, I will."

"I love you, sweet child of mine. You must be brave now, for our people will need you. Your mother will need you."

Gabriel's own eyes filled when his father's voice cracked over that last part.

"Father?"

King Andrei looked to him then. He smiled, but his lips had already gone pale.

"I can carry you back, and get you help. You will recover from this."

Oh how he wanted the words to be said with more certainty, but they came out broken. His father grabbed his arm, his grip eluding to a strength he didn't have.

"Gabriel, this kingdom I now pass to you. You will be a fine king. Together, you and your brother will rid this land of the stench of our enemies. And when you have, you must be sure to honor the Lord. Be sure our people's hearts, your heart, never strays from Him. For we are His people, and He is our God."

"I vow I will do as you ask. I love you, my father and my king."

Gabriel then put a fisted hand over his heart and bowed his head, in honor of the man before him.

"You have all my love, son. Though this is not what I would have for you, I know you are ready."

His father's eyes closed then, and he laid his head back against the rock that held him upright. Elisabeta began to cry more openly.

"Is he gone?"

"No, but it will not be long. Come we must get him to his bed, and send word for Lucian."

An hour later, his father was returned to his bed, and Gabriel waited in the hall while his mother kept him company. Having prayed that Lucian would return to them in time, he was thankful to hear his brother's voice as he came up the stairs.

"Gabriel? How is he?"

He stepped forward and put his arm on his brother's shoulder, his actions saying what his words could not.

"May I see him?"

"He is waiting for you."

Together they stepped into their parent's bed chamber. Elisabeta was already there, having refused to leave her father's side. He let Lucian go ahead of him, and watched as the younger man knelt beside their father's bed looking more like a boy than a man.

His wife came to stand beside him then, her nearness bringing him comfort. Katya had found him as soon as the word rang out that their castle was no longer under siege, and now she entwined her arm with his, and leaned her head against his shoulder. As his brother said his final goodbyes, the family stood around and watched their beloved king depart from this world into the next.

Through it all it was Katya's steady presence that reminded him that God had not given up on them. That He was not to blame for this injustice. Only a month before, something like this would have only fueled Gabriel's unbelief and sent him even further down the road of selfish waste, but now? Now he knew that the Lord would be with them. Whatever their future held, he would put his faith in the Lord. *I give you my life, and my allegiance, Lord.*

As he turned to leave, the guards standing at either door knelt before him. "All hail, King Gabriel!"

CPSIA information can be obtained
at www.ICGtesting.com
Printed in the USA
BVHW031751190819
556236BV00001B/27/P

9 781973 670759